Mont Madness

Phillip Strang

BOOKS BY PHILLIP STRANG

DCI Isaac Cook Series

MURDER IS A TRICKY BUSINESS
MURDER HOUSE
MURDER IS ONLY A NUMBER
MURDER IN LITTLE VENICE
MURDER IS THE ONLY OPTION
MURDER IN NOTTING HILL
MURDER IN ROOM 346
MURDER OF A SILENT MAN
MURDER HAS NO GUILT
MURDER IN HYDE PARK
SIX YEARS TOO LATE
GRAVE PASSION
THE SLAYING OF JOE FOSTER
THE HERO'S FALL
THE VICAR'S CONFESSION
MURDER WITHOUT REASON

DI Keith Tremayne Series

DEATH UNHOLY
DEATH AND THE ASSASSIN'S BLADE
DEATH AND THE LUCKY MAN
DEATH AT COOMBE FARM
DEATH BY A DEAD MAN'S HAND
DEATH IN THE VILLAGE
BURIAL MOUND
THE BODY IN THE DITCH
THE HORSE'S MOUTH
MONTFIELD'S MADNESS

Steve Case Series

HOSTAGE OF ISLAM
THE HABERMAN VIRUS
PRELUDE TO WAR

Standalone Books

MALIKA'S REVENGE
VERRALL'S NIGHTMARE

Copyright Page

Cover Design by Phillip Strang

ISBN: 9798416501730

Dedication

For Elli and Tais, without whose support and perseverance to make me sit down and write, I would never have discovered the infinite joy of crafting stories.

Chapter 1

Jacob Montfield, his face hidden behind a thick greying beard and grime, and pushing a supermarket trolley laden with the rubbish he deemed collectable, was to the inhabitants of Salisbury, a market town to the south-west of London, a harmless eccentric. He was a polite man, pleasant to those he passed in the street, doffing his hat to whoever put money into his cup and always with a book in his hand. His taste in reading material was eclectic, dictated in part by choice and in part by what he could find thrown away.

Detective Inspector Tremayne, a man who rarely read apart from the racing guide and with five minutes to spare, had sat down alongside the man once, asked him about his life, only to receive the stock reply, 'Life is where I am now.'

In short, don't ask, and it was rare that anyone did.

At night, Montfield would push his trolley to a shop entrance or an alley, looking for somewhere quiet in summer, somewhere warm in winter, and on rare occasions to a shed in the garden of the house where he had once lived with his sister.

The man lived as he wanted, and although some shop owners had put spikes in front of their shops to repel him, others had attempted to deter him by offering to buy him food, which worked better than threats; a few, however, had threatened violence. Of those, one had followed through and put the man in hospital for a couple of days.

On leaving the hospital, Montfield's only comment, 'The food was great, but the place was too clean for me.'

The Poultry Cross, situated on the corner of Silver Street and Minster Street, had been in existence since the fourteenth century. It was a circular structure with a roof and buttress, built of stone, initially the site of a busy market, although now it was a Grade 1 listed structure, a prominent tourist attraction in a city that had more than its fair share. Montfield also favoured it in the summer months to get away from the heat. It was not where he should have been in winter, but there he was, sitting upright as he always did.

***

Apart from vehicular traffic navigating the narrow streets and people pouring out from the pubs, well-liquored on a Saturday night, there were always one or two tourists walking around late into the evening, taking in the ambience and the history, planning their next day's activities, maybe out to Stonehenge or travelling on down to Cornwall. Most would be holding the ubiquitous iPhone, recording the sights and themselves to send back to their family and friends, convinced they would be enthralled, not wanting to believe that the majority would not.

Tremayne, a man who did not care for ambience and history, was glad to have had a break after the last murder investigation and had taken the opportunity to take it easy and spend time with his wife, Jean. An uncomplicated man, fond of a beer, a cigarette and horse racing, but not concerned when a building had been built or for what purpose, nor about the people buried in the churchyards and their contribution to society.

Tremayne answered his phone.

'It's Jacob Montfield,' Clare Yarwood, his sergeant, said.

He hadn't expected to hear from her, although he was pleased she had phoned. After all, the two, inspector and sergeant, had been the stalwarts of Homicide for many years, and after a shaky start when she had been young and idealistic, and he had been a cynical, cantankerous man (he still was, he knew that), they had formed a great duo, each playing off the other's strengths, not afraid to express an opinion of the other, not above sarcasm.

'What about him?' Tremayne replied. It was after eleven in the evening, and he and Jean had returned from a night out at the cinema in Salisbury, a movie she had liked, but which he thought inane: boy meets girl, boy loses girl, girl dies. At least that's what he remembered of it, and Jean had not been pleased when after twenty-five minutes and the first mushy scene, his eyes had closed, and he had started to snore.

'You embarrass me,' she had said at the time, but afterwards, in the bonhomie of a pub – he, with a pint of beer, she, with a glass of wine – the two had laughed about him in the cinema. And besides, she knew how hard her husband worked, the hours he put in, the stress that came with his job as the senior investigating officer in Homicide.

'He's dead,' Clare said. 'In town.'

'Very well,' Tremayne replied as he raised himself from his chair. 'Where is he?'

'The corner of Silver Street and Minster Street, the Poultry Cross, just up from the Haunch of Venison.'

'Yarwood, just the address.'

'I thought the pub would have helped you. You're good at pubs.'

If he hadn't been tired and ready for bed, he would have come up with a suitable reply to his sergeant's sarcasm. However, he couldn't, but he'd remember, get her back in the future. Even so, he couldn't help but smile.

'No, you don't,' Jean said as he grabbed for his coat. 'Not until you've wrapped a scarf around your neck.'

'It's important. I've got to go.'

'Clare's more than capable of dealing with it until you're there. After all, you trained her.'

Tremayne knew that complaining wasn't going to help. With reluctance, although appreciative of the love of a good woman, he took a seat, waited for the hot drink she prepared for him, downing it in one go.

'Satisfied?' he said.

'Not really, but barring a guard outside the door, you intend going. Don't blame me if you come back with a cold.'

'I won't,' Tremayne said, but even if he did, Jean would be there with medicine and an electric blanket on the bed.

At the scene, a diminishing crowd of onlookers as some of them sobered up and wanted to get back home.

'What's the situation?' Tremayne asked.

'It looked as though he was just sitting here,' Clare said. She had been hoping for a quiet night as well; after all, it had not been long since she had found out she was pregnant, and her husband, Clive, had gone into the fussing and fretting mode, waiting on her hand and foot. She had to admit to enjoying the attention, but it wasn't necessary, not yet. And then, there was the issue of her mother, wanting to come to Salisbury, knowing full well that mother and daughter had a testy relationship, and that Clive, magnanimous, generous and courteous with everyone else, found her mother trying, always wanting to stick her nose in.

Clare looked forward to checking out the shops, buying a cot, organising the baby's bedroom, although she wasn't sure what décor to choose, not wanting to know the gender before the birth.

'You can't deny he's been murdered,' Clare said.

Tremayne had noticed the signs as soon as he had arrived, a handkerchief in the mouth, the bulging eyes, a wax-like appearance.

'Someone must have seen something.'

'He was frail, wouldn't have put up much of a fight.'

'Even so, the middle of Salisbury. There's always someone walking around or driving past.'

'Those walking could have been half-drunk, and for those driving by, what would they have seen? There's a light fog; their vision wouldn't have been that clear, probably focussing more on the road than a homeless man sitting on a stone seat.'

'Who found the body?' Tremayne said. Even with Jean's scarf and the hot drink, he was feeling the cold, pacing on the spot to keep the circulation going, to stop his feet from freezing. His sergeant had fur-lined boots; he didn't, just the usual black leather brogues. He wasn't a man for fashion or for dressing sensibly.

'I did,' a voice from behind said.

'And you are?'

'You know me, Inspector.'

'One of Salisbury's finest reprobates and a world-class jerk. That's two out of three, Maloney. What's number three?'

'Mr Maloney's a witness,' Clare said, surprised by Tremayne insulting the man.

'Take no notice, Sergeant,' the sixty-year-old, very drunk man said. 'That's Tremayne, always ready with a putdown.'

'Jerry used to be from here, but he moved away,' Tremayne said. 'How long ago, I can't remember.'

'Thirty-one years,' Maloney said. 'Moved north, up to Scotland, got ourselves a little hotel, rent out rooms to the tourists, not that it makes a lot of money and the weather's more miserable than down here. But we're happy, the wife and me.'

'Christine, how is she?' Tremayne asked.

'She'll be tickled pink when I tell her that I ran into you.'

'Could someone tell me what's going on,' Clare said.

'Sergeant, I used to be a police officer in the early days, friends with your inspector. We used to get up to mischief back then,' Maloney said. 'Jean? How is she?'

'She's fine. You'll have to come to the house, the two of you,' Tremayne said.

'I hate to be a party-pooper,' Clare said, 'but we've got a dead man.'

'Jerry had a bit of luck, won the football pools.'

'Your sergeant's right. I reckon you should focus on the murder, and we'll meet up later, get drunk.'

'Not possible, not these days,' Tremayne said. 'My health's not as good as yours.'

'Mine's not great, but once in a while, it doesn't do any harm. Otherwise, life would be boring.'

'Jerry, what did you see?' Tremayne became serious.

'I'd just come out of the Haunch of Venison. I was staggering over this way, heading to our hotel, and I came across him.' Maloney looked over at Montfield as he spoke.

'If you were drunk, Mr Maloney,' Clare said, 'how did you know he was dead?'

'Once a police officer, always a police officer. Instinctive, I suppose. And the name's Jerry, none of that Maloney nonsense, makes me sound as old as Tremayne looks.'

'Very well, Jerry, you saw Jacob Montfield sitting down. Then what?'

Clare looked at Tremayne and then Jerry Maloney. She had to agree with her inspector's friend. As drunk as he was, Maloney had a glow about him, a *joie de vivre*, a man who embraced life and dressed accordingly. By two years, Tremayne was the younger of the two men, but Maloney looked like he would live for another thirty years, whereas Tremayne looked tired and worn out.

'He was too upright, as though he had been propped up, which I didn't reckon he had. And it's a freezing night, and we're all wrapped up against the cold, but the dead man, his jacket was unzipped, and his footwear wasn't much use.'

'That was how he used to get about,' Tremayne said. 'He's well-known in the area, regarded as harmless.'

'On a night like this? No one, no matter if they're as mad as a hatter, chooses to freeze to death.'

'You're right. Montfield wasn't stupid.'

'Anyway, that's my story,' Maloney said. 'I gave your sergeant a statement. Now, if you'll excuse me, I better head off, get an ear-bashing from my wife, tell her about meeting you and your sergeant. If you need more from me, we're at the Red Lion Hotel; call in anytime, down here for five more days, plan to see the sights.'

As Maloney wandered off, a slight sway in his walk, Clare looked over at Tremayne. 'One of your drinking pals from the past, when men were men, and police constables got drunk too often and chased too many women?'

'He was with me the night I met Jean. A friend, not seen him for years, and then here. Another murder, another chance to prove your mettle.'

'I've done that enough times already. It's just you, Inspector Tremayne, can't take a hint and retire, let me have your office,' Clare said.

'If you two are finished,' Jim Hughes, the senior crime scene investigator, called out, 'I think you should see this.'

***

'What is it?' Tremayne said as he and Clare walked the short distance to where Hughes was down on his knees, carefully pulling the man's jacket to one side.

'It's this,' Hughes said.

'But why? It makes no sense,' Clare said.

'It did to Montfield. Not something you'd expect to find on a man who pushes a trolley around the city, sleeps out rough most nights.'

'It proves that his murder wasn't the random act of a drugged-out psychotic.'

Tremayne bent down to get a closer look, but he felt his back give, causing him to think twice about joining Hughes in front of the body. He looked over at his sergeant, although she pretended not to have seen his discomfort.

'Montfield knew he was in danger, although if that was the case, why was he still walking around in full sight? He could have always retreated to his sister's place.'

'Well, he's wearing a bulletproof vest so the man must have been important or a threat to someone.'

'Was he?' Clare said. 'To us, he was harmless, but what do we know about him?'

'Any more?' Tremayne asked Hughes.

'Not for now. We'll wrap up in the next few hours, get the body off to Pathology, let them cut him up, find out about underlying medical conditions, let them confirm the cause of death.'

'What do you reckon?'

'What you can see. A handkerchief in the mouth, a hand or cloth over the man's nose, and he would have suffocated. What's remarkable is that no one saw it.'

'Remarkable,' Tremayne agreed. 'And if the murderer managed to do it without being seen, it has to mean he was close by, choosing his moment, able to be out of sight for a few minutes, to blend back in soon enough.'

'A pub?' Clare said.

'It's as good a place as any. Easy enough to say you're popping out to make a phone call, have a cigarette, kill Montfield, and then be back in time to buy a round for everyone.'

'Which would mean someone highly visible, extrovert.'

'Jerry Maloney,' Tremayne said. 'The man fits the bill.'

'Too easy, too early,' Clare said.

'He was a friend when we were younger, and then he disappears, returns after an absence of over thirty years, and to top it off, he finds a body no more than fifty feet from where he was getting drunk. Coincidental, is that what you reckon?'

'If it was him, why find the body? Why report it to the police?'

'The best alibi there is.'

'I'd agree, only Jerry Maloney's no fool. He would have known you wouldn't fall for it.'

'Probably didn't know I was still here, wouldn't have figured me as someone who'd be in charge of Homicide. When we were younger, Maloney saw himself as a cut above the rest; thought I was a dullard.'

Clare wanted to smile; Hughes burst out laughing.

'He had you pegged,' Hughes said as he stood up.

'I've had enough from Yarwood tonight, don't you start. Montfield's dead, murdered in plain sight,' Tremayne said. 'And Maloney's the only person we have at this time. And as to why Montfield's wearing a bulletproof vest, considering that he's been pushing his trolley around Salisbury for the last twenty odd years, it makes no sense, no sense at all.'

'The vest, is it new?' Clare asked.

'It's not old,' Hughes said. 'We'll pass it over to Forensics, see what they can make of it.'

Tremayne and Clare left Hughes with Montfield's body. Due to the cold and the hour, a large crowd hadn't formed at the site, but tomorrow, when the shops opened, uniforms would secure the area with metal barriers instead of the usual tape.

So much for shopping for cots tomorrow, Clare thought.

Chapter 2

Deidre Montfield, Jacob Montfield's older sister, was not popular in the street where she lived: the epithets of strait-laced, prim, starchy and schoolmarmish applied to her at various times by her neighbours.

Tremayne had been forced to tell the woman at the doorway, instead of inside the house, of her brother's death. Even though it had been one in the morning before he and Clare arrived at the house, the woman wouldn't let them in until she had dressed. And then, on entry, both Tremayne and Clare had to remove their shoes and hang up their overcoats on an old-fashioned, standalone coat stand.

'I can't say I'm surprised,' Deidre Montfield reiterated once Tremayne and Clare were in the house.

To Tremayne, it seemed as if she was blaming her brother for getting himself murdered, instead of asking the usual questions, such as 'How did he die?', 'What are you doing about it?' and 'When can I see him?', interspersed with bouts of crying.

Clare had checked before arriving at the house and found out that Deidre Montfield had a history of complaints about her neighbours: the man two doors down a closet pervert, and as for her next door, a shameless hussy who ran around the back garden naked.

As Sergeant Hoxton, the person who invariably dealt with complaints about the woman, said later that day, 'Deidre Montfield's difficult. As for her next door, they have a hot tub on a wooden deck, and she wears a bikini. The pervert, he's eighty, if he's a day. If you're looking for sanity in the Montfield family, then Jacob Montfield was your best bet.'

'I don't think you understood,' Tremayne said to Deidre. 'Jacob has died.'

'I heard you the first time, not that it surprises me, the people he associates with.'

'What people is that?' Clare asked.

'The people in the street, fools, all of them, with their petty ways, their drunkenness, their promiscuousness, flaunting their bodies. Those young women, out there getting up to mischief, fornicating and swearing. In my day—'

'Miss Montfield,' Tremayne halted the woman mid-sentence, 'Your brother has been murdered. Doesn't that mean anything to you? Don't you feel remorse or anger, even revulsion?'

'Why? Should I?'

Clare shifted on the sofa she sat on, the plastic cover squeaking as she moved.

To Clare, home meant a potted plant on a window sill, a magazine on a table, a picture on a wall, a pet. But in Deidre Montfield's house, nothing, just somewhere that wouldn't have looked out of place in a 1960s magazine on home decorating.

'It's customary,' Clare said.

'Well, it's not for me. He could have stayed in this house, minded his own business, and then this wouldn't have happened.'

'This?' Tremayne said. 'Are you intimating that his death is only one part of something more?'

'And why minding his own business?' Clare added. 'From what we know, it's not something you practise.'

Clare thought the woman was one of those holier-than-thou people who criticise without forethought, only despising others for not sharing their views.

'Jacob, he lived in the shed at the end of the garden when he was here. I wouldn't have him in the house, not often. I didn't want him soiling the place.'

'You let us in,' Tremayne said.

'If I hadn't, you'd have me in the back of your car, handcuffed, let all the neighbours see my shame, not that I've done anything wrong, only tried to improve the area. And now, Jacob goes and gets himself killed.'

Tremayne knew she was a self-centred bigot, and any attempt to appeal to the woman's higher emotions – her love for her brother, the need to bring a murderer to justice, to help the police in their enquiries – was a wasted effort. He realised another approach was needed.

'Miss Montfield,' Tremayne said, 'your ambivalence regarding your brother's death, the lifestyle he lived, the fact that he was wearing a bulletproof vest, concerns us.'

'If that means you think I killed him, then you're sorely wrong. He was my brother, not that I cared for him, not much anyway, but killing him would have been uncharitable.'

'Miss Montfield, we can either conduct this interview here or at the police station,' Tremayne said. His patience was at an end. 'If you want to play this foolish game, we can relocate to the police station. Your malignancy serves no purpose.'

Clare, whose opinion of the woman was unfavourable, nevertheless felt sorry for Deidre Montfield after Tremayne attempted to break through to the woman. It was, she thought, unnecessarily harsh.

Deidre Montfield looked at Tremayne, her mouth agape, her eyes unblinking, her cheeks a bright red. She did not speak, and then, as if in slow motion, she collapsed on to the floor.

'You've killed her,' Clare said.

'She's fainted. Lay her out on the sofa, give her a few minutes, and she'll be alright.'

Clare could see Tremayne was worried. The badgering of a witness, causing them to lose consciousness, have a heart attack and even die, would be serious, the subject of an internal investigation by the police. Tremayne's career would be sacrificed due to a difficult woman and his temper.

'I'll go and check out Jacob Montfield's place of residence,' Tremayne said as he walked out the back door of the house.

After several minutes, a murmuring from Deidre. Clare held a glass of water to the woman's mouth and breathed a sigh of relief.

***

Tremayne felt easier after Clare's phone call to tell him that Deidre Montfield was sitting up and talking. He stood at the door to the shed, tidy on the outside but chaotic inside. Not sure how to proceed, he hesitated to enter, aware that clues to the man's death could be behind the wooden door.

And why Jacob Montfield came back to the shed rather than the house was obvious. The man's sister was, to Tremayne, the singularly most frustrating person he had met, and he had met a few in his time.

'Is it true?' A voice from the other side of a high fence.

'Is what true?' Tremayne replied as he peered through a gap in the fence, only to be confronted by a stout woman in a dressing gown.

'Her brother, dead?'

'It's true. How did you know?'

'It's on Twitter, a man dead in Salisbury, a supermarket trolley.'

'Is he the only one?' Tremayne said.

'I wouldn't know, but he used to push one. Not that he brought it into the garden, scared of her.'

'Were you?'

'Her! You must be joking, but she was hard work. Pity it wasn't her, instead of him.'

'That much venom?'

'It's not, not to me. We could hear you through the wall, considering we're semi-detached, and the sound insulation isn't as good as it should be.'

Tremayne knew that houses built in the forties were double brick, and sound didn't travel that easily. If the neighbour had picked up details of the conversation between him and Deidre Montfield, it was because she had nipped over the fence, listened up against a window, or else an upended glass on the shared wall. Whatever the truth, it wasn't important, not for now. He was interested in what the woman knew of the dead brother and the difficult sister.

Tremayne walked out through the back gate of the Montfields', another supermarket trolley just outside, and walked to his left, entering next door's rear garden. The woman in her dressing gown was not embarrassed, not that she had a reason to be, as, through the gap in the fence, Tremayne had already seen the dressing-gown open at the top. Naked flesh, if there was to be any, he'd seen before.

'Your name?' Tremayne asked.

'Marjorie Potts. Lived here for twenty-six years, one longer than the Montfields.'

'You're game if she's been on the warpath for all that time.'

'Jacob was a regular person back then, went out to work, dressed well, and always polite.'

'Deidre?'

'She was always difficult, but before, if she had a problem, she'd knock on the door, come in and have a cup of tea. Honestly, back then, it was good to have someone look after the street and make sure no one was parking on the path, safe for the children to ride their bikes up and down. And I'll give it to her, she liked the children, used to give them sweets. But then, people change, and now, Jacob, murdered. Who'd do something like that?'

'Mrs Potts, that's why we're here. What I don't get is why he lived the life he did, and she's so awkward.'

'She fell in love.'

From what he had seen of Deidre, Tremayne found it hard to imagine she would be capable of love. But then, people change as they age, the same as him and Jean, comfortable in each other's company, the passion of youth subsided. Now, holding hands, joking and laughing with each other, their relationship had changed from the volatile to the sublime, although Tremayne, not a wordsmith, wouldn't have put it as succinctly.

Tremayne phoned Clare and checked if she could continue with Deidre Montfield without him. The curt reply told him that she was better off on her own than dealing with his insensitivity.

'It's late. Are you up to this?' Tremayne asked Marjorie, first name at her request.

'Oh, yes. My husband's not here for the week, gone up north, another conference, or maybe he's got a bit on the side.'

'If he has?'

'What's good for one is good for the other. That's what I say.'

Tremayne, unsure where the woman was taking the conversation, perturbed that she had winked as she told him about her husband, stood back. He adopted a police officer's stance and attempted to look more official.

'Mrs Potts,' Tremayne reverted to the formal, just in case. He was unnerved by the woman's apparent ease in discussing matters not of the heart but the physical. 'Deidre fell in love. How did it impact the Montfields?'

'Deidre wasn't a spring chicken, not by any means, but still attractive. No idea why she hadn't found a man before, but I never saw her with one, and then, there she is, dolled up, down the pub, weekends away, acting as if she invented the erotic arts.'

Tremayne thought Marjorie Potts had a colourful turn of phrase.

'What changed?'

'It was over twenty years ago, the details get sketchy, but from what I remember,' Marjorie continued, as they moved towards her house and inside the back door, 'her lover worked with Jacob. I can't say I knew him that well, but occasionally I'd see him out in the street, and he always spoke, mentioned the weather, the cost of things, the normal non-committal banter.'

'And then?'

'I don't know, not really. One minute he's there, and Deidre's fawning over him, and then he's gone. Not long after that, Jacob's gone mad, and he's in the garden shed, and she's crabby and in the house.'

'Shouting, screaming at each other?'

'Not that I heard. And after that, Deidre, the good neighbour, became the monster of Marigold Crescent.'

'What was the man's name?'

'Derek, no idea as to a surname. He was a decent-looking man, skin and bones, no meat on him like you have, Inspector, or should I call you by your first name? I assume you have one.'

'Tremayne, that's what everyone calls me, even my wife.'

'A regular Rumpole of the Bailey. Hilda always called her husband by his surname, but you're not like him. You're not worn out.' Marjorie threw her arms around Tremayne, causing him to stagger back and then to beat a hasty retreat out through the back door of the house.

***

After catching his breath and being spared a fate worse than death, Tremayne re-entered the Montfields' back garden.

'You look as though you've had a fright,' Jim Hughes said.

'I thought you'd send one of your team,' Tremayne said, determined not to tell the crime scene investigator about his encounter with the woman next door. He didn't mind the occasional laugh at someone else's expense, but not at his. And if the police station heard about him and the amorous housewife, he'd never live it down, the constant, neverending hilarity.

'They're wrapping up down at the crime scene. I thought I'd come out here and see what we could find. There's not a lot to be found apart from the man and his trolley, no clear sign of fingerprints, not even a shoe print.'

'The rain?'

'It hasn't helped. We'll check again when it dries out, but for now, you've got a body and not much else.'

'The shed?' Tremayne asked. He needed a drink, but that would have to wait for later. Now it was time to focus.

'One of the team's inside, checking it out. It's not that tidy, just a makeshift bed, an old table, and the typical junk that people store in sheds,' which resonated with Tremayne.

When he and Jean had first married, a garden and a shed seemed important. And at the weekends, Jean would be out in the garden, down on her knees, pulling weeds, planting flowers, and he would be pushing a lawnmower. He had never enjoyed gardening, although he had loved the shed, a place where he could enjoy a cigarette. He had believed that marriage was all about gardening, home decorating and being dragged around the shops on a Saturday morning. It had taken a month for the joy of the first to wane, eight months for the second, and the third, the shopping at the weekend, an instant dislike.

And now, another shed, similar to the one he had had. The Montfields' shed was still standing, whereas Tremayne's had deteriorated after Jean had moved out, eventually succumbing to neglect and the elements, the roof caving in, and him paying for a couple of men to dump it.

Tremayne put his head through the shed doorway. 'Anything?' he said.

A young woman's voice came back. 'Not unless you're keen on dirty underwear, a couple of copies of *Playboy* and something that might have been a meat pie in a previous life.'

'It might have been best if you'd said who you were first,' Hughes said. 'Marilyn's an excellent member of the team, only she's got a wicked tongue, a ready wit.'

Tremayne tried again. 'Detective Inspector Tremayne. Anything?'

'Nothing, Inspector. Sorry about before, but it's not much fun in here, smells awful, and the man's hygiene was not the best.'

'Don't worry,' Tremayne said. 'Murder's a nasty business.'

'It doesn't look like he was here that often,' Marilyn said. 'Probably not for a few weeks, and even when he was, there's no heating. It must have been cold.'

'He used to sleep rough most of the time. The cold he was used to.'

'There are some other papers, not sure what they're about. We'll get them to Homicide; let your people have a look. They might help; they might not. I used to see him around the city, harmless, used to be someone important.'

'How do you know?'

'I've just found a wall plaque, a copy of his degree in engineering, also some award.'

'Make sure they're sent to Homicide.'

'The shed?'

'Send what you've got, not the shed,' Tremayne said. 'I had one once, more trouble than it was worth.'

***

'Miss Montfield, your reaction to your brother's death is disturbing,' Clare said.

'Is it? Are we meant to feign sorrow when we're not sorry? Should I be distraught and crying? What is the correct response, you tell me.'

'He was your brother; somebody murdered him. Doesn't that count for anything?'

'Pilloried, due to my disinterest in Jacob, arrested on suspicion of murder because of my cold heart.'

'The police deal in facts,' Clare said, although the woman was right; Deidre Montfield was her own worst enemy. 'You said your brother lived in the garden shed.' Clare gave up expecting an emotional response from the woman and refocussed her efforts on the facts.

'He did.'

'Did he come into the house?'

'Not often, but I could hardly stop him, could I?'

'You could, considering your hatred.'

'I didn't hate him. I blamed him for destroying my life and my happiness.'

Clare had to acknowledge that it was a step forward. An emotion, even if it was negative.

'Happiness?' Clare quizzed.

'It was a long time ago and not relevant.'

'I believe I'm the judge as to whether it is or not.'

'It's private and will remain so.'

It wouldn't, not if it pertained to the death of the woman's brother, but for now, Clare let it rest, not to put pressure anymore on what was a sensitive subject.

'How often did Jacob come into the house?'

'If he was in the shed, sometimes he'd come into the house, go to the bathroom, heat some food in the microwave.'

'And where were you when he was in the house?'

'He would knock on the back door first, enough time for me to lock myself in my bedroom.'

'And when he left?'

'He'd knock on his way out.'

'Did you ever look out the window, curious as to what he had become?'

'I did once, not that I felt anything other than revulsion.'

'With what? His appearance? His hygiene?'

'It was a long time ago; it's not important.'

It was, but the woman wasn't talking, not yet.

'Did your brother have any enemies? It would seem to be the most viable reason for his death.'

'Jacob had me, not that I hated him.'

Clare, feeling queasy, stood up, patted her belly, said a few silent words to her unborn child, looked through the door to the kitchen. 'Any chance of a cup of tea?' she said.

'I've read about you,' Deidre said as she walked into the kitchen. 'I don't approve of your husband.'

It was, if not an outright repudiation of Clare's husband, the current mayor of Salisbury, at least a begrudging acknowledgement of his importance.

'Not everyone does,' Clare replied, 'but I do.'

Clare followed Deidre out into the kitchen, as neat as the living room had been. Nothing was out of place, stored in cupboards, drawers, or the pantry.

'He wasn't here often,' Deidre said as she looked out of the kitchen window and at a grassed-over garden, a concrete path over to the left-hand side.

'Do you mow the lawn?'

'I pay someone to come in once a fortnight in summer, once a month in winter.'

'You're not a gardener?'

'Jacob used to look after it, but that was a long time ago.'

'No flowers?'

'Sergeant, I appreciate you're angling for information, someone to blame for my brother's death, but you won't find it here, not with me, and not in this house.'

'Why? Your brother died at the hands of someone who probably hated him; you would seem the logical person, except that you were here, and there's no car in the driveway, no buses nearby.'

'Sergeant, this is a house of the dead. It was before Jacob died; nothing has changed. I suggest those people down by the shed finish their work and leave. As for me, I will drink my tea with you and then go to bed. Tomorrow, I will identify his body. Is there any more for now?'

'I believe there isn't,' Clare said, not sure what she was feeling, other than she was in the presence of a person who sapped the energy of everyone she came into contact with.

Chapter 3

Tremayne came through the Montfields' back door and looked over at the two women drinking tea. 'Is there another cup?'

'Miss Montfield's not told me a lot more,' Clare said as she handed him a cup.

'There's not a lot to say. Jacob kept his distance from me; I kept my distance from him,' Deidre said.

'Families fall out with each other, all too often,' Tremayne said. 'However, they don't always live under the same roof.'

'He didn't. He lived in that shed, under a bridge, in the park, anywhere that suited him.'

'Any emotion from Miss Montfield?' Tremayne said to Clare.

'None that benefits us.'

'I've no more to say,' Deidre said.

'And if you knew anything, would you tell us?' Tremayne said.

Deidre poured herself another cup of tea and sat down on a stool in the far corner of the kitchen. 'I would, but believe me, I'm not interested in how and who and why, only that he won't be coming back to this house, and as for that shed, I'll have someone out here tomorrow to knock it down and to take it away.'

'It's evidence,' Tremayne said. 'It stays there for now. Is that clear?'

'Inspector, what about inside?'

'The shed will be locked; your house will need to be checked.'

'For what?'

'Evidence, a motive. Or do you know of one?'

'Only one, the reason I would have killed him, not that I did, but I had the anger.'

'Miss Montfield, I suggest we go to the other room, sit down calmly and talk this through. This holding back, intimating your hatred, and now, your willingness to kill him, but denying that you did. And what about the degree in engineering? What's the truth?'

Clare chose a wooden chair in the other room, not wanting to sit on the plastic-covered sofa, although it didn't bother Tremayne. Deidre Montfield remained standing.

Clare could see Tremayne was pushing hard, and he wasn't going to back off until he got the woman to talk.

'We need the full story,' Tremayne said. 'I've been next door, spoken to your neighbour, found out that you and your brother were friendly in the past.'

'She's no right talking about us.'

'Miss Montfield, Deidre, this is a murder investigation, not a Sunday school get-together. No amount of lying, deception, beating around the bush, and especially feeding us nonsense, is going to make us go away. If you want to be a hostile witness, then that's up to you. As for us, we can take you down to the police station and charge you with perverting the course of justice.'

Clare looked over at Tremayne, a quizzical look. Tremayne gave a slight nod of his head.

Clare knew that Tremayne had something up his sleeve, although she didn't know what it was. The chair she was sitting on wasn't any more comfortable than the plastic-covered sofa. She moved, made herself secure and waited for the fireworks.

'Let me tell you certain facts,' Tremayne said. 'Miss Montfield, twenty or twenty-one years ago, you met a man, who, according to next door, you fell for in a big way. Is this true?'

'I don't want to think back to that time. It's not relevant.'

'It is, and you need to tell us.'

Deidre Montfield sat down on the wooden chair that Clare had just vacated. She looked down at the floor, up at the ceiling, then at Clare, and finally, at Tremayne.

'Derek Sutherland.'

'Marjorie Potts knew his name was Derek, but not his surname. What else?'

'There's not much more to tell. I was younger, foolishly believing that he loved me, that I loved him.'

'Believing, or knew?' Clare asked.

'I thought I loved him, not that Jacob ever approved, not when Derek made himself at home in the house.'

'He was living here?'

'No, but sometimes he'd stay the night.'

'How did you meet?'

'He was a friend of Jacob's. Jacob was involved in scientific research, held a good position.'

'That matches what I know so far, not where Jacob worked, but that you and he were regular people, friendly to the neighbours, liked.'

'And now they hate me.'

'Why not?' Clare said. 'Your behaviour is abysmal, uncaring and downright obnoxious. Why the change? What happened to Derek Sutherland?'

'His wife happened.'

'Which means you didn't know. Did Jacob?'

'Jacob was my brother; we were very close, having grown up together. Our parents were good people, very academic, instilled a strong work ethic into both of us.'

'Dead?'

'Our father, thirty-three years ago; our mother, twenty-nine. Neither of us shed tears, frowned on by our parents, a sign of weakness. I was approaching middle age, an agreeable woman, but not emotional, thought I'd die a spinster, and then Derek came along.'

'The love of your life?'

'Derek was, but then Jacob came home from work, told me that Derek was married, and he wasn't about to leave his wife. And then, that night, Derek's here, pleading forgiveness, said it was only me he loved, and we could be together forever.'

'You let him in?'

'I did, only because I didn't want the neighbours to know.'

'What happened?'

Deidre got up from the chair, paced around the room, sat down again.

'I listened patiently, wanting to believe him, knowing that I could never trust him again, wanting to go and hug him, to smash something hard on his head.'

'Your brother?'

'He came in, saw Derek sitting there, a smile on his face, attempting to put his arm around me. Jacob did what I couldn't.'

'Which was?'

'He picked up that bronze statue you can see in the corner,' Deidre looked over at the only ornament in the room, 'and smashed it down on Derek's head.'

'Afterwards?'

'There was no afterwards. Unhinged from what he had done, Jacob stayed for a couple of days, maybe longer, and then he disappeared. I stayed in the house, barely anything to eat or drink, inconsolable.'

'Derek Sutherland?' Clare asked.

'Don't you understand, Sergeant? Derek was dead.'

'Jacob had killed him?'

'It wasn't intentional, purely in the heat of the moment.'

'You did nothing about it, never reported it?'

'For weeks, there was the shame and the guilt of what had happened. In time, we moved on, me, in this house, Jacob in that shed. No more was spoken by either of us about that night; not possible to look each other in the face. Jacob was a broken man; I was an embittered woman who had seen the man she loved die.'

'Sutherland, where is he now?' Tremayne asked.

'He's under that shed,' Deidre said. 'It was Jacob. He dug a hole large enough for a body, put Derek in there, and then bought a shed, put it over the top.'

Tremayne was stumped about what to say and do; Clare felt a lump in her throat.

As for Deidre Montfield, she was in tears. 'Jacob, my lovely brother. How I miss you,' she kept repeating.

***

Deidre Montfield lay on her bed, barely eating, only sipping weak soup; a home nurse brought in to look after her.

'If she remains distraught, I'll have to commit her to a facility,' the doctor had said. Clare understood the dilemma. The thoughts were playing out in Deidre

Montfield's mind: memories of sweet love confused by the man's betrayal, and then the anger of her and her brother, and then death.

Clare wasn't sure how she would have acted under the circumstances. Would she have snapped as Jacob had? Would she be upstairs in bed, unable to respond? She felt a great sadness at a time in her life when she should be feeling overjoyed.

Tremayne stood with Jim Hughes in the small lane at the rear of the house, close to the shed.

'Not long now,' Hughes said.

'The shed emptied, the contents documented, in evidence bags?' Tremayne said.

'Body or no body, we had to be thorough.'

Tremayne had received confirmation that Derek Sutherland, a former colleague of Jacob Montfield, as well as Deidre's lover, had last been seen twenty years previously. If what Deidre had said was confirmed, his wife was now his widow. However, Sutherland's widow had formed another relationship and borne two children. Tremayne had spoken to her by phone to hear that she didn't care whether the man was alive or not, and no, she hadn't heard of Deidre Montfield, but she had heard of others.

Two of Hughes's team prepared for action, each armed with a spade. Another two seconded to sift the removed soil. A floodlight had been set up, and if needed, the work would continue through the night.

Tremayne intended to stay for as long as necessary, not that he would remain awake; Clare left the site after ensuring that Deidre Montfield was fine and that Jean would bring Tremayne a hot meal.

The situation had been so tense at the Montfields' that Tremayne told Clare how Marjorie Potts had propositioned him.

His sergeant's response was as expected; she burst out into raucous laughter, tears running down her face.

'Don't tell Jean,' Tremayne said.

'I won't,' Clare said.

Tremayne knew she would.

***

Tremayne dozed in his car, waking just before one in the morning. He had a crick in his neck, a stiff back, cramp in one leg. He decided that staying at the site hadn't been such a great idea after all. A warm bed awaited him at home.

He had to smile at what had happened next door, so much so that one of the crime scene investigators asked him how he could be so cheerful, given that the night was perishing cold. As for them, all they got was cold and hungry, with a hefty dose of abject misery.

'Anything?' Tremayne asked another investigator, not so boorish as the other, not as predictable. Sure, it was cold, Tremayne knew, but the crime scene investigators, if there wasn't murder or a crime scene, would be in their office, going home at five in the afternoon, weekends off, which to someone in Homicide was a rarely achieved luxury.

Unbeknown to the CSIs and Tremayne, Deidre Montfield watched in the house.

'If you've found nothing,' Tremayne said, 'I'll be off home.'

'Don't know why you waited,' a female CSI said.

'Nor do I,' Tremayne said, although it had seemed important. As if something was amiss.

It worried him that Montfield's death was complex and that Derek Sutherland would throw the murder investigation or investigations in a hitherto unknown direction if his body were found.

Tremayne glanced up towards the house, saw the movement of a drawn curtain, but took no notice. He looked over at the neighbour's, saw Marjorie Potts looking down at him – she waved, he looked away.

'Call me if you find anything,' Tremayne said to the CSI.

'If there's a body here, it's buried deep.'

Tremayne got into his car and drove home, only to find Jean waiting up for him. She ran a hot bath for him, and even though he had complained, he was pleased.

'Busy day?' Jean asked.

Tremayne didn't like the smirk on his wife's face, knew that his sergeant and his wife had been talking: the two most important people in his life, the two who cared about him the most. He felt he should take umbrage with his wife for the smirk, his sergeant for betraying a secret, but as he lay back in the bath, the crick and the aches slowly easing, he knew he wouldn't.

By one forty-six in the morning, he was fast asleep, Jean at his side. Four hours later, his phone rang.

Jean picked it up and went into the other room. 'He's not awake,' she said.

'I am,' a voice from the bedroom.

Tremayne took the phone from Jean, then listened to Marilyn, the CSI with the ready wit, as she spoke. He phoned Clare and updated her. After that, he gave Jean a kiss on the cheek. 'Thanks,' he said, 'but I've got to go out.'

'A body?'

'Yes.'

'Clare?'

'She's heading out to the crime scene.'

Tremayne showered, even though he had had a bath not long before, while downstairs the kettle was on the boil, rashers of bacon in a frying pan. Jean did not intend her husband to go out of the house hungry, knowing it would be another long day for him, even though he would pop into a pub for lunch and a pint of beer if given half a chance.

Chapter 4

Clare arrived at the rear of the Montfield garden. It was still dark, and she found an eerie calm where the shed had once stood; none of the crime scene team was present.

A uniform stood outside the rear gate. The Montfield residence had become a crime scene. 'They'll be back in a few minutes, went out for something to eat,' he said.

Tremayne arrived thirteen minutes after Clare, confident that the body would be Derek Sutherland.

Jacob Montfield's murder was the primary focus. Discovering another body would be an unforeseen complication. The realisation that either of the siblings could have killed the person buried in the garden and that Deidre, the only one of the two siblings alive, could be a murderer of one or two persons.

Deidre Montfield, uncaring and unemotional at first, had eventually broken down at her brother's death, and once again, when Clare told her a body had been found in the garden.

'What's going through her head?' Clare said.

'Nothing,' Tremayne said, 'and you know it.'

'Denial, unable to grasp the truth, to deal with reality. After all, it's twenty years since it happened. The memory plays tricks, remembers what it wants, not what it should.'

The CSIs returned, said hello to Tremayne and Clare, and ushered them into the crime scene tent.

'That's what we've found,' one of the CSIs said.

'It's not a lot,' Tremayne said as he looked at a radius bone, undoubtedly human. 'How long for the rest?'

'Another team will be here within the hour. We're beyond exhaustion. We'll bag the bone, get it to Forensics, and they'll organise a DNA sample from a blood relative of Derek Sutherland. Subject to it going to plan, they should be able to give you conclusive proof by the end of the day.'

'You went beyond the call of duty on this one,' Tremayne said.

'Either we're keen or stupid, don't know which.'

'Both,' Clare said, 'but thanks anyway.'

Tremayne and Clare left the tent and went over to the house. Clare knocked on the back door. After what seemed an interminable delay, a nurse opened it.

'Sorry about that,' she said. 'Miss Montfield has taken a strong sedative. She's resting now.'

'Emotional?'

'No lashing out, beating of the chest, self-harming, just a quietness about her. You saw her?'

'Was she watching all night?'

'Most of it. There wasn't much I could do. After all, I'm here to help her deal with her brother's death and to see that she comes to no harm.'

'Can she stay here?' Clare asked.

'If it were up to me, I'd say she'd be better off somewhere she can get proper rest. It must be hard, your brother murdered, a body in the garden.'

'She told you this?'

'I knew about the brother before I came. I don't agree to home nursing without a doctor's report as to the person's physical health, dietary requirements, medicines they might be taking, and, it goes without saying, their mental health. I'm not equipped to deal with people who may go psychotic, come at me with the kitchen knife.'

'No doctor could have told you whether Miss Montfield was psychotic or not. As far as we know, she could be blaming her brother for the body in the garden. She could have easily killed him.'

'I took all factors into account, weighed up the pros and cons, decided that Miss Montfield if sedated, was worth the risk.'

Deidre Montfield rested upstairs while Pathology prepared her brother for his autopsy in Salisbury. And at the bottom of the garden, a new team of crime scene investigators removed soil, two of them sifting it for the minutiae that may prove to be relevant, another two exposing the bones, taking endless photos.

Tremayne left Clare with the nurse and walked down the garden.

'Any updates?' he asked one of the sifters.

A short, stocky man in his twenties replied. 'Jim Hughes said you would ask.'

'He was right.'

'He said to tell you that they've found Sutherland's brother in Devon, and a local team down there is organising to take a DNA sample from him and then to drive it up to Salisbury, let Forensics do what they do.'

'Thanks,' Tremayne said, realising he was only getting in the way of people who knew more about extracting a body from its hastily-constructed grave than he did.

He knew that other people in the street, nosey people, might have seen something suspicious, even though it had been two decades ago. And the nosiest person, also the closest to the murder scene, was outside her back door, looking over at him and the CSIs.

A brave man, he had stood down a man pointing a gun at him, threatening to shoot, but Marjorie Potts rendered him a coward.

'Yarwood,' Tremayne phoned his sergeant, never once in all the years they had been together calling her Clare, 'if you're free, I need to talk to the woman next door.'

'Frightened she'll bite?'

'It isn't the bite I'm worried about.'

'If you want me to come with you, I will. But she'll be open with you. She'll see me as a threat.'

'You're young enough to be my daughter; besides, I don't fancy you. Why would she believe that?'

'Inspector, you might be a good police officer, but you don't understand women,' Clare said.

'I know enough to know that you told Jean what I told you in confidence last night. Couldn't resist it, could you?'

'Only Jean, and besides, Detective Inspector Tremayne, Salisbury's very own Don Juan.'

'Okay, stop laughing. I'll go and talk to the woman.'

Tremayne knew she was right, but he was scared of the woman next door, a vulture waiting to grab her prey.

***

Tremayne paused at the crime scene on his way from the rear of one house to the rear of another. He took a look inside the tent, a rib cage exposed, the top of a skull.

'Male, from what we can tell,' one of the CSIs said.

'How can you be sure?' Tremayne replied.

'We can't, not one hundred per cent, not our job. That'll be for Pathology and Forensics. However, the pelvis is taller and narrower than would be expected with a female, and the pubic arch angle is less than ninety degrees. As I said, that's an opinion, not a fact.'

'Thanks, anyway. Phone me if you need me, but give me thirty minutes first.'

'Another five hours, and we'll be finished here,' the CSI said.

Tremayne didn't hear the man. Recognising the inevitable, he picked up his pace, opened the gate at the end of Marjorie Potts's garden, to her delight, and strode up a narrow gravel path to her back door.

'Inspector, you're back. Let me get you a tea, or would you like a beer, maybe a whisky.'

'Tea will be fine,' Tremayne said. 'Your husband?'

'He won't be back for another couple of days.'

'It's important we speak to him. After all, you and your husband have lived here for a long time, since before Derek Sutherland went missing.'

'Is that his name? Is that him at the bottom of the garden?'

'It's not proven, not yet. I'm not in a position to give you a conclusive answer, but there is a high probability.'

The mention of the woman's husband appeared to have acted as a dampener on Marjorie Potts' amorous intent. It had almost killed it when Tremayne insisted on phoning the man, only to find out that he was rarely at the house, only every two to three weeks, for a couple of days.

'Marjorie's got her life; I've got mine. I prefer the quiet life, isolation, at one with nature, but she's more interested in friends and socialising.'

And none too subtle seductions of police inspectors, Tremayne thought but did not mention to the husband.

Tremayne made his apologies and ended the phone conversation. He would get back to him at a later date.

'Mrs Potts, I don't believe you understand the seriousness of the situation. This is an official enquiry. One of your next-door neighbours is murdered. There's a body buried at the end of the garden, almost certainly Derek Sutherland, and Deidre Montfield upstairs, sedated, a possible murderer.'

'Her brother?' Marjorie said.

'How much do you remember? What else can you tell us? After all, you noticed the difference in her, in him. A failed love affair could have unhinged Deidre, especially if her mental state was fragile. But what about him? What did you reckon to his changed behaviour?'

'I didn't. Who would? They were acquaintances who we'd talk to over the garden fence, see down the pub occasionally, nothing more.'

'You've not answered the question,' Tremayne said.

'I have. Deidre disappeared for a couple of weeks, locked herself in the house, only came out late at night, wandered around the garden, and then *that* shed appeared.'

'You emphasised your reference to the shed. Did you have a problem with it?'

'Not the shed, per se, but there was a problem with the fence, an issue with the boundary alignment back then. They were perfectly acceptable neighbours, and if we went away for a few days, we'd give them the key to our house to look after. You can remember the winters back then, the freezing pipes, the flooding if they broke, the ruined carpets.'

Tremayne remembered water pipes in winter freezing solid and breaking, and then, with warmer weather, the ice turning to water, but that was back in the fifties, not the turn of the twenty-first century. Was Marjorie Potts obtuse or just confused?

'What about the shed?' Tremayne asked again.

'He had butted it hard up against the fence. It wasn't the greatest tragedy, and we were willing to give him time to move it over a foot to the right. After all, it was wood, not that heavy. My husband, he understands such things, reckoned Jacob could have lifted the shed at one end with a couple of jacks or a plank of wood as a lever, rolled a pole underneath, repeated it at the other end and then a few strong men could have pushed it. My husband even offered to help Jacob, but he wouldn't talk about it, only grumbled every time we saw him, which wasn't often.'

'What did you do in the end?' Tremayne asked. 'It wasn't on your fence when we moved it.'

'The local council weren't any use, said that garden sheds were not in their jurisdiction and that they could recommend a mediator to deal with it, but we didn't bother. In the end, my husband, he's not one to mess around, phoned up a fencing company, got them to come down, give a quote, not only to move the fence that you've seen but to give the shed a push, which they did. They didn't bother with rollers, just got five of their strongest, two at the back and at the front a big strap around the shed and three men. All over in minutes, not that Jacob was pleased. Not much he could do about it, though. After that, we never spoke again, not to him, only to Deidre when she was causing trouble.'

'The shed, when Jacob installed it, anything unusual?'

'It's not as if I can remember it clearly, only the trouble afterwards. If Derek was under it, then why bury him close to us, why not on the other side of their garden?'

'For that, I don't have an answer,' Tremayne said. 'I'll bid you a good day, and thanks for your help.'

Chapter 5

Clare believed Derek Sutherland to be the villain due to his seduction of Deidre Montfield. And that the affair had precipitated a chain of events that had led to his death, and then Jacob Montfield's murder, and ultimately to Deidre's mental meltdown.

However, Sutherland's wife, Gloria, who he had cheated on, did not see it that way.

'You'd not understand,' she said.

Tremayne didn't, and Clare struggled to understand the woman's logic. They had found her living an outwardly conservative life, a bungalow on a housing estate north of Bath in Somerset.

Gloria Hardcastle, no longer Sutherland, on account of the man she had lived with for sixteen years.

'What wouldn't we understand?' Clare asked.

'Derek, we had this arrangement. It's what they call an "open marriage", although he was more open than me.'

'People get hurt,' Tremayne said. 'Emotionally devastated, some even kill because of it.'

'We never saw it like that.'

'A scorecard, notches on a bedpost,' Clare said facetiously, knowing full well that the woman was about to launch into a speech about variety being the spice of life and where's the harm.

The three sat at a dining table in the bungalow, the family photos on a small cabinet, some more on the wall, even one of Derek.

'Your first husband?' Tremayne said, pointing to the photo.

'My present husband has got a photo of a previous lover. As I said, what's wrong if we're open with each other?'

Clare could have said she was more puritanical in her views, but she was in the house as a police officer, not a judge of right and wrong.

'Did you know about Deidre Montfield?' she asked.

'Not by name, although he would have told me.'

'What she looked like, where they met, made love?'

'We were open about it.'

Tremayne could see his sergeant struggling to communicate, unable to keep it impartial. He thought it might have something to do with her condition, but he couldn't be sure, having never gone through life with a pregnant wife; something he regretted, although Jean's children by another man would often phone, take him out for a drink.

'Aside from your unusual views,' Tremayne said, more for Clare's benefit than Gloria's, 'it doesn't alter the fact that your husband failed to come home. And that you never registered a missing person, nor did you, from what we can ascertain, ever make any attempt to find him.'

'But I did.'

'Did what?' Clare asked.

'I tried to find him. I went through his papers, checked his emails, made a few phone calls, but he was gone.'

'Did you inform the police?'

'No. Do you believe I should have?'

'It's customary,' Tremayne said. 'After all, we're the logical people to find a missing person. If they're in our database, or they reappear, dead as in your husband's case, we don't have to go wasting our time to find the next of kin.'

'I received a letter from him, two weeks after he disappeared, told me that he had met someone else and he was going to live with her, and he hoped I'd be happy.'

'Were you?'

'No. I had loved Derek. It was him that introduced me to life, who educated me in the beauty of the human body, not to be ashamed to express my innermost feelings.'

'Let's get this straight – your husband was a colleague of Jacob Montfield, yet you never contacted him or the place where they both worked?' Tremayne said, barely suppressing his frustration with a woman who continued to babble errant nonsense as if she believed it, which he thought was probably the case. After all, in his thirty-plus years in the police force, he had come across white and black witches, paganists and one person who believed that an alien had committed untold atrocities on him and had told him to go and murder his brother. Although, thankfully, that person had been committed to a mental hospital for life.

'I told you I received a letter after two weeks. He sometimes went away for a few weeks, nothing unusual in that.'

'But he never phoned?'

'As I said, it could have been work-related; he could have been with a woman. What should I care?'

'Mrs Hardcastle, what about his bank accounts, his personal belongings?'

'He said he was breaking away, going to live a simple contemplative life, free from the poison of society.'

'And you believed this?' Clare asked.

'Oh, yes. Why not?'

'You mentioned a letter,' Clare said.

'I still have it. Do you want to see it?'

Tremayne felt like saying, 'Are you stupid? Of course, we do,' but instead, he said, 'It's important.'

Gloria leant behind her, pulled out a cabinet drawer, took hold of a wad of letters secured by an elastic band, peeled it off and handed a letter to Tremayne.

'The others?' Clare asked.

'Some from Derek; some from others.'

'We'll need to take them.'

'They're personal. You might be shocked.'

'I won't,' Clare said. Possibly bemused, probably disgusted, she thought, but she kept her opinion to herself.

Tremayne glanced at the postmark as he turned the letter over. 'There's no return, only a postmark,' he said.

'Salisbury?' Clare asked.

'Where else. It's suspicious.'

'Your husband disappears. You receive a letter with a Salisbury postmark,' Clare said to Gloria. 'You knew that Derek worked with Jacob Montfield, and he lived in Salisbury, yet you never thought to drive there to see him.'

'I did, spoke to Deidre, realised he had been sleeping with her. I could see she was upset, more than I. Derek had said he would live a contemplative life; also, he had money of his own, and I could see it wasn't to be with her.'

'How could you be sure?' Clare said.

'Deidre Montfield was a staid woman, moral, suburban,' Gloria said.

'And then?' Tremayne asked.

'I waited for another letter, but none ever came. Our joint bank account didn't need both signatures. I suppose I just accepted that he'd gone, maybe knock on the door sometime or never again. Life moved on, and then I met Harry, and that was that, and now you're telling me that Derek had been murdered and the woman I had felt sorry for was involved.'

'It's yet to be confirmed, but yes.'

'It will be; I know that.'

'How?'

'Logical deduction. I can see it now, but I didn't think about it back then. And then, twenty years, not a word. There was no reason; I might have been sorry for myself, the way he left, even felt anger, but I never blamed him for leaving.'

'Could you have left him?' Clare asked.

'Derek? Never. He was the only man I loved. You never forget your first love, the man I had hoped would father my children.'

'If he had returned?'

'For one or two years, I might have welcomed him back, but after that, the bond was broken, impossible to repair.'

Regardless of Gloria's unusual lifestyle when younger, Clare had to admit there was a purity to the woman, a common sense about how life and people evolve. And now, Clare with Clive, the comfort of their relationship, an unbreakable bond, united by shared beliefs, a child yet to be born.

***

Tremayne, back in Salisbury, sat in his office; in his hands, Jacob Montfield's autopsy report. Never a great fan of exceedingly complex medical terminology, the detective inspector preferred to get what he needed from Jim Hughes, the senior crime scene investigator, invariably garnering little more from the pathologist. Although, the report showed two interesting additional facts, the first being that Montfield had terminal cancer and would not have lived for more than a few months. Other than that, he took drugs, not heroin, but hashish. Also, the CSIs had found a large notebook under the detritus in the trolley, which was now in Forensics' possession.

Furthermore, Gloria Hardcastle's letter had not been written by Derek Sutherland. Handwriting analysis had revealed a clever forgery and that Jacob had written it.

Montfield's death had been due to asphyxiation by an unknown person. Forensics believed that whatever was in the notebook was important.

However, why the shed had been erected close to the property's boundary was unresolved.

'Yarwood, in here,' Tremayne shouted over to where Clare was writing a report on her laptop, looking at a list of baby names as well.

'Yes, Inspector,' Clare said as she sat down in Tremayne's office.

'Forensics, have they concluded their DNA checks yet?'

'They've passed them over to a company in Southampton. The result should be through soon.'

'What's keeping them? It didn't take this long to confirm the body in that burial mound up at Stonehenge was your brother-in-law.'

It did, Clare remembered.

This letter,' Tremayne continued, forgetting about the DNA, 'was written by Jacob, which means that Deidre must have known and that it wasn't just a case of covering up the murder, but a conscious effort to throw off any further investigation into the man's whereabouts.'

'If Jacob wrote the letter, then the question is, did Deidre know?'

'And the woman's flat out on her bed.'

'She's resting comfortably.'

'That's what I said, but comfortable or not, comatose or sitting up bright and alert, it doesn't make a difference. Deidre Montfield has to answer our questions,' Tremayne said.

***

Even though Montfield had forged a letter to Sutherland's widow, it seemed to have little bearing on his murder.

Deidre could have killed Jacob, so could have Gloria, but neither appeared to have a current motive, and Gloria had only just found out that her husband had been holding up a shed for twenty years.

The nurse opened the door at the Montfields' and held a finger to her mouth, clearly indicating her patient was resting. To Tremayne, resting, sedated, excitable or just plain mad meant nothing to him. Deidre Montfield would answer questions in the next fifteen minutes.

'I don't care what you do,' Tremayne said to the nurse, 'wake your patient, get her down here, or we'll go up there.'

'Doctor's orders,' the nurse replied.

'Phone him up if you want, but this is a double homicide, and the only thing in common is your patient upstairs.'

The nurse phoned the doctor then handed the phone over to Tremayne.

'You can't disturb her,' the doctor said. 'Her mental stability. The woman's had a serious shock, the death of her brother.'

'Doctor, she was also there when her lover died, and she helped her brother put him in a hole at the bottom of the garden. For twenty years, she has seen that grave from her kitchen window, and Jacob Montfield had slept over him for a few nights every week. She will speak.'

'Inspector, I will need to report this. If the woman's condition worsens, if she dies, then it is on your head. You will be answerable to your superiors.'

Tremayne ended the call. He knew he would not be answerable, other than to his superintendent, a man who was a stickler for wrapping up investigations promptly and within budget. One frail woman at this juncture would not faze the man.

The nurse, reluctant to concede, aware there was no option, went upstairs; Clare followed.

The lights were turned down low in the bedroom, and the curtains were drawn; the woman was sitting up.

'We thought you were asleep,' Clare said.

'I woke up.'

Clare could see an iPad on the bed. Whether Deidre Montfield had been sedated or traumatised and resting, it was clear she still retained the faculties to allow her to surf the net, to watch a video, and, more importantly, to answer some questions.

Clare looked over at the nurse. 'Ten minutes,' she said as she closed the bedroom door on her way out.

Chapter 6

Deidre Montfield, her face drawn and stifling a yawn, entered the room. The nurse warned about the woman's delicate state before she left.

'Miss Montfield, according to Derek Sutherland's wife, came here after he had disappeared,' Tremayne said.

Although the room wasn't cold, Deidre sat in a chair and pulled a blanket around her shoulders.

'She did, briefly.'

'Yet you failed to tell us.'

'What was there to say? I don't remember her making a scene, not accusing me of this and that.'

'By "this and that", we assume you mean having an affair with her husband,' Clare said.

'I never knew he was married.'

'If you had known?'

'Then the romance wouldn't have occurred, and he'd be alive, and so would my brother.'

'Let's be precise on this,' Tremayne said, 'do you know that both deaths are related or is this a hypothesis?'

'Cause and effect,' Deidre Montfield said.

'I don't get it; it makes no sense to me.'

'Inspector, if I'd known that Derek had been married, then I would not have allowed myself to become involved with him. If it hadn't happened, then Derek wouldn't have treated me the way he did, nor would Jacob have killed him, and I wouldn't have ended up an embittered old maid.'

'Over my head, too much theory, not enough reality. Miss Montfield, let's get back to when Sutherland's wife was at your doorstep. And let's not go down this road that it was sweetness and light, a couple of women chatting over her husband.'

'What Inspector Tremayne is saying,' Clare felt she should clarify it better for the woman, 'is that the man you loved is dead and buried, murdered by your brother, underneath a shed in the garden that we can see from your kitchen window.'

'I understand your inspector. Should I have been distraught? Derek had been a bastard. I could not grieve for him,' Deidre said.

'Are you telling us that the wife of a man your brother murdered was standing on your doorstep, and you acted as though nothing had happened?

'Yes. The bastard cheated. How did you expect me to react?'

'And his wife? No shame, even if you had believed that he wasn't married, that the woman in front of you was distraught, desperate for answers?'

'No shame, and who said she was distraught?'

Tremayne realised that Deidre Montfield had spoken the truth. Sutherland's wife hadn't been concerned either way about where he was, who he was sleeping with, only that she needed to know, nothing more.

'According to Derek Sutherland's wife, you were upset. What's the truth, you or her?' Clare asked.

'She's lying. I don't know why, but she is.'

'Deidre, we've only got your word for it that your brother killed Derek. What if that's not the truth? It could have been you. What if you were psychotic? Diminished responsibility, mentally disturbed, whether by drugs or grief, we'd not know. It's a good defence; get you a cosy bed in a place for the confused.'

'A lunatic asylum, in with society's garbage. Is that it? Do you want me to plead guilty to something I didn't do, another arrest to your name?'

'Miss Montfield,' Tremayne said, 'we're giving you leeway here on account of your brother's death, but we still have a job to do. Regardless of your doctor's advice and your nurse, we need some truths.'

'Inspector Tremayne's right,' Clare said. 'We can't ignore this and come back in a couple of weeks when you're feeling better.'

'I can't agree with this,' the nurse who had been outside the room looking in through an open door said.

Neither of the police officers acknowledged her and continued with their questioning. If it wasn't murder, Tremayne could sympathise, but that was an emotion he couldn't afford at this time.

'What do you want me to say? That I killed Derek? Then, yes, I did,' Deidre said. 'The bastard deserved what he got.'

Clare realised the woman had been pushed too far, answering questions without forethought for the consequences. It was time to back off, to make sure the woman didn't feel threatened. She looked over at the nurse. 'We'll have a break. Let Miss Montfield calm down,' she said.

Tremayne took the hint from his sergeant, got up and walked out of the back door and down to where the shed had once stood.

***

The nurse checked her patient's blood pressure, then her heartbeat and hydration. As it continued, Clare walked out of the back door and joined Tremayne. She looked at the hole in the ground where Derek Sutherland's body had been, then back at the house and over to the house next door. Tremayne smoked a cigarette.

'Your lady friend's watching,' Clare said, a smile on her face, barely hiding a laugh.

'Yarwood,' Tremayne said, 'what did you reckon?' not rising to the bait.

'Even if we go back twenty years, Jacob and Deidre Montfield were in their forties, and that's a decent size hole for one person to dig.'

'That's what I thought. Not that I was ever one for gardening, but even if I was, I don't reckon I could have dug a hole that deep on my own.'

'Which means he had help.'

'There's only one person.'

'The sister.'

'Are we agreed?' Tremayne said.

'Why build the shed to one side?' Clare said. 'If you're trying to conceal a body, and you have a shed to put over the top, why waste time and effort erecting it in the wrong place, knowing the neighbours would complain?'

'And nosey, at that. If Marjorie Potts was here when Sutherland died, she must know something.'

Tremayne walked out of one back garden and into the next, watched by Clare, who decided to wait another five minutes before returning to the Montfield home.

Clare continued to concern herself with the shed's position. To her, it seemed irrational, nonsensical, but significant. Perplexed, she thought of Tremayne next door, who was now sitting down, a cup of tea in his hand, a woman hovering perilously close.

'My husband won't be home until tomorrow,' Marjorie said, leaning over Tremayne.

Tremayne, who should have been flustered and embarrassed, had to smile. After all, the night before, his wife had given him a ribbing about the woman.

The smile caused palpitations in Marjorie Potts, so much so that Tremayne, sensing the woman's elevated arousal, had to get up from his chair and move to the other side of the kitchen.

'Mrs Potts, this is a murder enquiry, not fun and games,' Tremayne said.

Reasoning with the amorously inflamed woman had little effect.

'We'll need to conduct this interview at the police station,' Tremayne said as he pushed the woman away.

'It's just harmless fun, and yes, I know it's murder, but so what? It's not as if they're coming back.'

Tremayne didn't know what to make of it. This woman who wouldn't take no for an answer, and next door, a cold fish of a woman; a woman who apparently could act dispassionately when a murdered man's wife knocked on the door, and then act similarly on the death of her brother, only to break down later.

'Then, Mrs Potts, I suggest you treat this investigation as serious.'

Tremayne knew she wouldn't. He took his phone out of his jacket pocket. 'Over here, now,' he said.

'Can't keep her hands off your lithe body, is that it?' Clare replied.

'I've just had to remind Mrs Potts as to the seriousness of the investigation, the reason that you need to be here.'

'I can't accede to your request.'

'Important new information?' Tremayne said.

'Yes.'

'Two minutes. I'll be over.'

'Well, Mrs Potts,' Tremayne said, looking back at the woman who was now sitting calmly on a chair on the other side of the room, 'our interview will have to wait. Your husband, here tomorrow?'

'Late afternoon.'

***

Deidre Montfield sat quietly to one side of the living room as Tremayne entered. Compared to the last time he'd seen her, no more than thirty minutes before, the woman's countenance had changed. No longer the drawn face, the pale complexion, the bags around the eyes.

Deidre Montfield had taken ten minutes to walk up the stairs and change, now wearing a tee shirt and a pair of jeans. She had also splashed her face with water, powdered it and applied lipstick.

'Miss Montfield is better,' Clare said.

Tremayne didn't buy it for one minute. He'd dealt with more than his fair share of tragedy over the years, spoken to hundreds of the nearest and dearest. He knew that the severe emotional reaction after the death of a loved one follows a pattern. Initially, the disbelief, then the realisation and the sobbing tears. And then, after a period, not precise as it depended on the extent of the tragedy, the circumstances of how a loved one had died, and the person's innate personality, whether stoic, nervous, quick-tempered or slow, rational or irrational, logical or illogical, the shock followed by normality. What he saw in Deidre Montfield was not characteristic; it was too quick, as though it was an act.

For one thing, she had been stoic about the death of her brother, apparently the same when Derek Sutherland's wife had knocked on the door. However, that was open to speculation, as Deidre and the former Gloria Sutherland differed in their statements. Although the former wife, now the man's widow, had other questions to answer. How come the woman hadn't registered a missing person report?

'That's fine,' Tremayne said, with some scepticism. 'Is she able to help us more with our enquiries? Sutherland's death? His wife's visit?'

'I am,' Deidre said. 'This has been difficult for me, and then with Derek's body discovered, I've not been myself.'

'There is an anomaly,' Tremayne said.

'I'm not sure I understand.'

'Your brother erected the garden shed after Sutherland's death. Is that correct?'

'A week later.'

'Did he erect it or pay a contractor to deliver it ready built?'

'You must have asked this question before.'

'If I have or have not, that's not important. We need to follow this through from start to finish. To find out why you lied about helping your brother to bury the body.'

Clare looked at Deidre, over at Tremayne, and then back at Deidre.

'I didn't,' Deidre said. She crossed her legs, uncrossed them, and crossed them again. She was on edge, unsure what to say or do next.

'Miss Montfield, I spent time down near the shed and the grave. There are anomalies in your statements so far and no doubt in those from Sutherland's widow and your neighbour, Marjorie Potts. All three of you are guilty of something or other, not necessarily crimes, although in your case, witness to a murder and the concealment of a body are criminal. And for those, you will be charged in due course.'

'I couldn't go to prison; I couldn't.'

'Your reason? And don't give me any of this "I've not done anything wrong. I'm innocent".'

The nurse came into the room. 'Miss Montfield is under my care. She has suffered emotional stress, and any further impairment to her condition will be as a result of your investigation.'

'I believe,' Clare said, 'that Inspector Tremayne would say that this is a murder investigation, and that your objection is noted, and that his questioning will continue.'

'Sergeant Yarwood's right,' Tremayne said. 'And may I add that Miss Montfield's brother has been murdered. He was wearing a bulletproof vest, not for comfort, nor did he find it thrown out as rubbish from someone's house, but because he feared for his life, a life now forfeited. Jacob Montfield knew that someone, for whatever reason, intended to kill him, and until your patient tells us the truth, she will remain with us, not with you. Now, if you don't mind, I suggest you do not eavesdrop on what is a police matter and go and busy yourself with checking your bandages.'

It was, Clare had to admit, a remarkable outburst from Tremayne. As much as she felt for the nurse, on the sharp end of Tremayne's tongue, she could understand his intent. He was right; she just wished that he hadn't been so terse with the nurse who was only doing her job.

Clare felt she should go out and talk to the nurse; tell her that the rebuke was for Deidre Montfield's benefit, not for her and that she shouldn't take it seriously or be upset by it, only to leave them alone with the woman for the next hour.

However, she knew that Tremayne was champing at the bit; he was wound up and raring to go, no doubt had had a tense time with the lady next door, another person who concealed secrets, if not from the police, but her husband. And if she were so keen on Tremayne, she would have tried it on with other men, including Jacob Montfield.

'Miss Montfield,' Tremayne said, focussing back on his primary target, 'I've just been rude to your nurse. No doubt she's right, in that you need medical care, but I can't let this rest. Your brother wore a bulletproof vest. Why?'

'I don't know,' Deidre replied.

'Very well. Let's go back to the start. On the night that Derek Sutherland died, you found out that he had been playing you for a fool.'

'It was Jacob who found out. They worked together.'

'Jacob tells you that Derek has been cheating on you.'

'I never knew, not at the time, that he had a wife. I was a Jezebel.'

'You're not, not if you didn't know,' Clare said. 'If Jacob worked with the man, then he should have known about a wife.'

'It was him that told me he was married.'

'Yes, you've said that before. When he told you, was Derek Sutherland here?'

'No. I phoned for him to come over.'

'That day?'

'Yes.'

'Did you mention the reason why?'

'I said it was important, and I was lonely.'

'He agreed?'

'He did, but then that was Derek, and now we know it wasn't only my charms that drew him, but others too, some not as attractive, more statuesque.'

'Marjorie Potts,' Tremayne ventured.

'She was my friend, yet she couldn't keep her hands to herself. I might have been a Jezebel by default, but she was by desire.'

'Do you hate the woman?'

'Not hate, just a loathing of what she did.'

'When did you find out?'

'Three weeks after Derek died. She came over to the house and asked why she hadn't seen me for some time. The conversation got around to Derek. I was highly sensitised after what had happened and what we had done with him. She's an awful tart, known up and down the street. Her neighbours on the other side registered a complaint with the police.'

'But you didn't?'

'It was before Derek, and she was a friend, not that I agreed with her behaviour, told her to her face on many occasions.'

'Her reaction?'

'She used to laugh. "Wait till you find a man for yourself. Then you'll understand".'

'And then you did.'

'She was right, not that the neighbours complained, not with me.'

Tremayne didn't need to hear the salacious details of Deidre Montfield's sex life, not unless they were relevant to the investigation.

'You said that Marjorie Potts was spending time with Derek,' Tremayne said.

'She never admitted to it, but I knew that time we spoke.'

'Did she know you were involved with him?'

'She did. I had always seen her as a friend, someone to talk to, not that we had much in common. I was an old maid, a boyfriend in my teens, but after that, nothing.'

'Why?'

'No reason in particular. I was content with my life, a steady job, enough money to live comfortably.'

'It's not natural,' Clare said.

'I was never emotive, not one of those out drinking in my teens, nor a succession of boyfriends. I had one, as I said, but we had this pact, saving ourselves till we were married.'

'What happened?'

'We weren't religious, not particularly, and his parents had separated after his father had taken off with another woman. It seemed better to start the marriage on a sound footing, to make a lifelong commitment, each to the other.'

'Idealistic,' Tremayne said. 'Not the reality, is it?'

'I thought it was, but a drunken night out with his friends, and he lost what was important to both of us, in the backseat of a car, a friend's sister.'

'What happened to him?'

'I tried to forgive him, but I couldn't. In the end, he drifted away. The last I heard of him was a long time ago. He had married, had a few kids, cheated on his wife, left her for another woman.'

'You were saved,' Clare said.

'Saved for what? We don't always get what we want from life, and then Derek happened.'

'You met him through your brother?'

'Jacob introduced him to me, and then over six months I'd meet with Derek, got to know him better, slept with him. I don't know why; after all, I was set in my ways.'

'Since then?'

'Nobody. I just became a crabby old woman, everyone's worst nightmare, a harridan.'

'Your brother's reaction to Derek sleeping in this house with you?'

'He was fine with it, not that Derek slept here often. He preferred the occasional weekend away; now we know why.'

'Next door?'

'I don't think he spent much time in her house. Otherwise, she would have woken the neighbourhood.'

'It appears,' Tremayne said, 'that your mood is changeable. One minute you're as sweet as pie, and then, almost at the flip of a switch, you, as you say, are either a harridan or emotionally distraught.'

'Quick to temper.'

'You were not so quick to love, and there, in front of you and your brother, the bane of your life, the man who had just destroyed your chance at happiness. Yet you continue to say that it was your brother that killed him. Why?'

'You never knew my brother,' Deidre said. 'He was an unemotional man, solitary, unyielding, a cold heart.'

'Killing a person requires emotion, a hot emotion.'

Clare could see where Tremayne was heading, that it hadn't been Jacob who had killed the man but his sister. And if she had, then her action and subsequent behaviour, her changeable nature, would indicate profound psychological traumas.

'I put it to you,' Tremayne said, 'that it was you, not your brother, that killed Derek Sutherland. How do you answer?'

'Badly. Damned if I do, damned if I don't,' Deidre said.

Tremayne was perplexed. The woman was talking in riddles.

'Deidre,' Clare said, trying a more personal approach, the good cop, bad cop routine. 'If you didn't kill the man, where's the damning?'

'How can I prove to you and others that I wasn't involved and that it was Jacob?'

'Yet Jacob had a cold heart. You've just said that.'

'Did you help him with the body?' Clare asked.

'Not to take it from this room.'

'But you helped him to bury it, and what about her next door?'

'What about her? We took him down there at night, a moonless night. No one would have seen.'

'Except for Marjorie Potts,' Tremayne said. 'She's got an inbuilt radar.'

'For you, she might have,' Deidre said.

'The reason the shed was butting onto her land?'

'That was me.'

'None of this makes sense.'

'It did to me. Derek was in a grave of sorts, and the shed was to cover him, but I couldn't let Jacob do it straight away. I needed to mourn for a few days, and a shed is hardly a gravestone.'

'Inspector Tremayne's right,' Clare said.

'You'd not understand,' Deidre said.

'Try us,' Tremayne's rebuttal.

'I loved him; don't you understand. Derek, for all his faults, for what he had done to me, I couldn't hate him. And there he was, in that hole in the ground, a shed the only marker to his passing. I pleaded with Jacob to give me time to grieve, and then her next door and her husband pushed the shed across, covering Derek. He shouldn't have died that way.'

'You killed him, didn't you?' Clare said.

In a feeble voice, 'Yes, it was me. I should have been honest with you from the start.'

'You better get the nurse,' Tremayne said to Clare. 'Miss Montfield needs a sedative.'

For that night, Deidre Montfield would sleep in her bed.

Tremayne stood with Clare outside the house, a cigarette in his hand.

'You don't believe her,' Clare said.

'I don't know what to believe. She could be telling the truth or what she considers the truth. Whatever happened that night unhinged her.'

'You believed her story about the shed, the reason it was off to one side?'

'That, I did,' Tremayne said. 'There's only one thing we didn't get to the bottom of.'

'The bulletproof vest?'

'Exactly. Sutherland died a long time ago, and those who knew him have moved on with their lives. Both murders are interrelated, or they're not. I'm not sure which I prefer, although it won't be tonight that we solve that dilemma.'

'Nor arrest Deidre.'

'It was a long time ago, and besides, we can only prove it on her testimony.'

'You're certain that she's disturbed?'

'Disturbed, yes. She still needs to explain why her brother was wearing that vest, why he chose to live a life on the street and in a shed.'

'Marjorie Potts?'

'We need to talk to her, find the truth about her and Sutherland.'

'You want me with you?'

'She's had her fun at my expense. From now on, she's got to give serious answers to serious questions.'

Tremayne crushed his cigarette underfoot and kicked the butt into a nearby flower bed. He then got into his car and drove home. Clare followed him five minutes later after checking with the nurse. Deidre Montfield, heavily sedated, was fast asleep.

Chapter 7

It was eleven in the morning, and Deidre was apologetic about her erratic behaviour during the last few days. Neither Tremayne nor Clare mentioned her murder confession. Derek Sutherland's death was history, and charges would be laid later or not, depending on unfolding events.

Every time they spoke to the woman, she revealed additional facets of Jacob. On the street wheeling his trolley along, he had been a solitary figure, causing no trouble other than offending some who felt that Salisbury, a city rich in history and historical sites, didn't need the homeless giving the place a bad reputation. Not that it had ever worried Tremayne. He knew Salisbury for what it was, no better, no worse than any other small city or town in the country.

''What else do we need to know about your brother?' Tremayne asked.

Deidre's changeable mental state perplexed him. But for now, the woman was neatly dressed, even if her clothing was dated, Clare's observation, not Tremayne's, as he wasn't a man to know much about fashion. The woman who had terrorised her street was gone. In her place, a perfectly agreeable, almost charming, woman.

It was an illusion, both police officers knew. A cheerful person does not become morose at the flip of a coin, nor does an optimist become pessimistic due to the prevailing weather, not even when a brother has been murdered.

'Yesterday, you mentioned the reason for the shed not covering the body,' Tremayne reminded Deidre, hopeful that referring to yesterday and the body wasn't going to set the woman off again.

'Jacob wanted to put it over Derek straight away, but I couldn't agree.'

'You've portrayed your brother as an oddball, not compassionate, certainly not the sort of person who would have cared for the dead, not even for you.'

'For me, he would do anything.'

'And yet, after Derek's death, he goes mad, lives in the shed or out on the street, and you become the scourge of your neighbourhood. How do you explain that?'

'I can't. I don't believe we hated each other, only that Derek's death affected us in different ways. It hardened me, destroyed him. He had had a good career, research mainly, satisfied with the solitary aspect of it, and eccentricity wasn't discouraged, not if the results were there.'

'Did Jacob give results?' Clare asked.

'He did.'

'Then, coming back to Jacob and Derek, work colleagues,' Tremayne said. 'Jacob was solitary; Derek was by nature a gregarious man, friendly, comfortable with women. How could they be friends?'

'Do friends necessarily have the same traits? Is it necessary that they are similar in beliefs and behaviour?' Deidre said.

'Not at all. Only that we're trying to form an overview of Derek's and your brother's deaths. Jacob, for instance, believed there was a credible threat to his life.'

'I never knew threats had been made, not that he would have told me.'

'But he's in the shed; you're in the house. You must have communicated.'

'By notes in the kitchen, nothing more.'

'And we're meant to believe this?'

'Sibling love is complicated. Once, about seven years ago, I broke my leg, unable to move far. Jacob made sure I had food and drink, made me warm, ensured I was comfortable.'

'Attentive?'

'Distant. We spoke when we had to, and for a week, he stayed in the house, in his old bedroom, but not once did we talk other than was necessary, and never about Derek.'

Tremayne had one other question to ask. 'Miss Montfield, if, as you said yesterday, you spent time at the end of your garden, tending to where Derek had been buried, why didn't your neighbours see you?'

'Why would they take any notice? It's not as if I was weeping uncontrollably or lighting candles.'

'And in the years since, did you go there on the anniversary of his death, leave flowers?'

'That, Inspector, would be bizarre,' Deidre said. 'Why would I do that?'

It didn't seem bizarre, not to Clare. After all, her first love in Salisbury, Harry Holchester, had been dead for years, and she didn't visit his grave anymore, not since marrying Clive. Still, she would ensure that somebody placed flowers on his grave on the anniversary of his death. After all, even though the man had been a murderer, he had given his life in a selfless sacrifice.

'The only man you loved,' Tremayne said. 'Slain in this room, buried at the end of the garden. To me, it would seem odd if you hadn't.'

'Then, Inspector, that's where you and I differ. He was dead, rotting in the ground. No remembrance or mourning was going to bring him back, nor praying or flowers or self-flagellating, not even you digging him up. After a couple of months, I ceased to care.'

To Clare, Deidre Montfield was emotionally dead.

'Jacob left the shed to one side, upsetting the neighbours. How did he intend to move it? After all, it was the Potts who eventually moved it.'

'What did they say, or should I say *she*?'

'That they arranged for a few strong men to give it a push.'

'Jacob gave me two weeks, no more, and as for next door, we weren't on their boundary. It was a dispute that goes back years, long before either of us moved in. The boundary line was eleven inches over their side. Check with the council; they'll confirm.'

'Even so, there was friction, something you and Jacob wouldn't have wanted, not after you had murdered a man.'

'If he hadn't cheated on me, he wouldn't be dead. Derek killed himself, not me and not Jacob,' Deidre said. Her mood was changing. The earlier friendliness was replaced by a more belligerent, wilder looking woman.

Clare left the room, found the nurse, told her what was happening. Another thirty minutes, and Deidre Montfield was back upstairs and sedated.

'I'm afraid it's more serious than even the doctor thought,' the nurse said.

'Serious psychological disorder?' Clare said.

'That's for others to decide. But this house, the body in the garden, her brother, all of them are contributory factors. I'm not sure if she can stay here, not anymore.'

Clare knew that none of the three mentioned by the nurse was the primary factor; it was the love for a man who had wronged her. Clare knew the feeling, having been there, but she had had Tremayne to ease her through, to push her hard.

Deidre Montfield had nothing, only a memory in the garden, and a brother who eventually rejected her. For twenty years, the woman had suffered.

***

Tremayne and Clare moved next door to Marjorie Potts, unwilling to waste a trip to the murder site.

'Inspector,' Marjorie said, as she opened the front door of her house, 'I knew you would be back.'

The woman's face dropped as Clare came through the gate at the front of the house.

'Pleased to meet you,' Clare said.

'Likewise,' Marjorie replied as she shook hands.

Tremayne observed the interplay between the two women. He enjoyed it immensely.

'You'd better come in,' Marjorie said, which to Clare sounded like defeat, the impending romance dead before it had started.

'We need to ask you a few questions,' Tremayne said.

The three sat at a table, a spread of food laid out on it. Intended for Tremayne, but now it would wait for the husband.

'Mrs Potts,' Clare said, 'we're interested in the shed.'

'I've told Inspector Tremayne all that I know,' the reluctant response.

'According to Miss Montfield, there was a dispute about the boundary between this property and theirs. Is that true?'

'My husband would be able to advise you.'

'Does that mean there was or there wasn't?'

'There was.'

'Resolved?'

'It was Jacob who was pursuing the matter, and then he went mad, or whatever you call pushing a supermarket trolley around.'

'Mad will do for now,' Tremayne said.

'Are you saying the dispute still exists?' Clare asked.

'It was eleven inches, not enough to worry about, and besides, closer to the houses, the boundary was three inches in our favour. My husband dealt with it years ago.'

'No problems?'

'Jacob wasn't an unreasonable man, and Deidre and I were friends once.'

'Yet you had the shed pushed away from the disputed boundary?'

'Not out of anger. It didn't seem that big a deal, and we didn't know about the body.'

'According to Deidre, there were already rollers to one side of the shed.'

'There might have been. Is this important? After all, it was a long time ago, too long to remember every detail.'

'Every fact, no matter how minuscule, is important,' Tremayne said. 'There's also another matter of a more sensitive nature.'

'Say it,' Marjorie said.

'You knew Derek Sutherland?'

'I did, not that I can remember him well. It was a long time ago.'

Selective memory, Clare thought.

'Derek Sutherland was a man who played the field, had more than one girlfriend, a wife sitting at home waiting for him.'

'And was I one, is that what you are about to ask?'

'There are variables with this case,' Tremayne said. 'Too many lies and half-truths. Your involvement with Derek Sutherland might just be one of those.'

'And if I was?'

'We need indisputable facts, not innuendo, sleaze or outright lies. We're not arbiters of morality, and quite frankly, we couldn't care less how many you might have slept with, only if it's relevant to the death of Jacob Montfield.'

'And Derek?'

'Derek Sutherland died a long time ago, but yes. Only two people could have murdered Sutherland, either Jacob or Deidre. With Jacob Montfield's death, we have no other suspects at this time.'

'Do you expect others to die?'

'It depends on what Jacob was frightened of. Do you know?'

'I'm just the next-door neighbour. What should I know?'

'Did you see Deidre down by the shed, on her knees, crying, laying flowers?'

'When? Back when Derek died?'

'Yes.'

'If she had been, how would I have known what she was there for. I'm not the nosey neighbour, not that you will believe me.'

Clare thought the interview was getting out of control. 'Mrs Potts, the first question. Were you involved with Derek Sutherland?'

'He came over the once.'

'Did you have a physical relationship with him?'

'I did.'

'You said Deidre was your friend. Why would you do that to her?'

'Deidre might have been the great innocent, a never-been-kissed virgin; I wasn't.'

'You knew.'

'That he was married. Of course I did.'

'So you saw yourself as doing Deidre a favour.'

'You make me sound as though I was a charitable institution. I'm not, just a bored housewife. He never told me, but married men wear it like a badge.'

'How?'

'How they look at you, their tongues hanging out, as though they haven't been with a woman for a long time.'

'Yet you chose to sleep with him,' Tremayne said.

'Deidre might want to believe in eternal love, in soppy fairy tales, I don't. Derek was a man who liked to pass the joy around; I wasn't the woman to stop him.'

'Was it joy?' Clare asked.

'Not that much. It served its need, and what my husband and Deidre never knew didn't matter either way.'

'Did you tell her that he was married?'

'Why? Why tell a woman blinded by love? And besides, it did her more good than harm, cheered her up, brought a smile to her face. As long as no one was hurt, where's the harm?'

Clare wasn't sure what to make of Marjorie Potts. She decided to give her the benefit of the doubt, to admit that disapproval of her actions was one thing, dislike was another.

'It would have hurt the man's wife,' Tremayne said.

'Would it? Or did she know about her husband?'

'You spoke to her?'

'I saw her leaving Deidre's. I waved over to her, careful to make sure that Deidre didn't see. Gloria came into my house, sat down and told me about her husband, the type of man he was, and that she wasn't upset, wouldn't be if he never came back.'

'She admitted to knowing of her husband's affairs?' Clare said.

'I suppose the wife of Salisbury's mayor would be shocked,' Marjorie said.

Once again, Clare's position as the wife of Clive Grantley impinging on a murder investigation.

'I was a sergeant in Homicide long before I married my husband. There's nothing that you or anyone else can say or do that will shock me.'

'Sensitive subject. I suppose I'm not the first one that's brought it up.'

'You're not.'

'Getting back to murder, not my sergeant's marital arrangement,' Tremayne said. 'We still have the issue that you spoke to Gloria Sutherland. We need to know what was said.'

'She drove her car around the block, parked further down the street, walked up and knocked on my door.'

'What did she say?'

'She knew what her husband was. She felt sorry for Deidre, knowing she'd been fed a line.'

'Did she know her husband was dead?'

'I'm sure she didn't. She wasn't concerned where he was, other than he needed to deal with the separation if that was what it was.'

'If it wasn't?'

'She had an open marriage; she told me that. He had other women; she had other men.'

'The same as you,' Tremayne said.

'Not with us. My husband is strait-laced, more Deidre's style than mine. He knew that when we married, but men, they're all the same, think they can change you.'

'I thought that claim was levelled at women, not men.'

'Whatever. Anyway, Gloria told me to let her know if I saw her husband, but I never did, and now we know why. Have you confirmed that it was Derek under that shed?'

'Yes.'

'So near, yet so far. It just shows what a woman crossed is capable of.'

'Deidre said she killed him.'

'What else?'

'Jacob,' Tremayne said. 'According to his sister and our research, he was a solitary man, no long-term relationships, none short term either.'

'Asexual.'

'That's what it appears to be,' Clare said. 'No interest in any form of sexual congress.'

'Not for me, the life of a celibate, but then, it takes all sorts to make a world, doesn't it?' Marjorie said.

'It does,' Tremayne said. 'It still doesn't explain why you didn't see anything.'

'I wouldn't have been looking, would I?'

Clare wasn't so sure, but there were no more questions for Marjorie Potts for now.

Chapter 8

Tremayne was unsure whether Jacob Montfield's death in Salisbury and Derek Sutherland's were related. The logical assumption would be that they were, but there had been twenty years between the two deaths, enough time for those involved with the first to have moved on, to have compartmentalised Sutherland's disappearance, or as it was now known, his murder.

Although, as Sutherland's widow had said, his disappearance wasn't the issue. Only that she would have preferred some closure as to where he had gone, the ability to get on with her life, to find someone else, none of which rang true to either Tremayne and Clare, the reason the former Gloria Sutherland received another visit at her home.

Gloria Hardcastle, previously Sutherland, sat in a comfortable chair, too confident for Tremayne's liking. However, the woman wasn't under suspicion, and as his sergeant had reminded him, it had been a long time since she had seen her husband, and what did he expect from her: remorse, sadness at a life lost? Besides, Gloria had found herself another man, a new husband. Deidre had been an innocent soul; nobody could accuse Gloria of that virtue.

'We're perplexed,' Clare said.

'About what?' Gloria replied. 'After all, I've been more than open with you, told you all I know.'

'It's not you specifically, but why would someone kill Jacob Montfield?'

'I can't answer that, or do you expect me to?'

'Did you ever meet him?'

'Once, a couple of days before Derek disappeared.'

'How?'

'Derek introduced me. A function where he worked. I'd been to a few in the past, but I'd never met Jacob before. I can't say that he impressed me, didn't say much, but he was polite.'

'Is that it? Could that have been when Montfield found out his work colleague was married?'

'I can't remember discussing that I was Derek's wife, but it was a long time ago, although logical for Derek to have introduced me as such. I didn't intend to make small talk with the man, although I was probably polite, made my excuses and moved on, found someone more chatty, ready for a laugh and a drink, a dance maybe.'

'From what we know, he had limited contact with women, no relationships that we know of.'

'Not something I would have spoken to him about, and he never came along to any of the places that Derek and I used to go to.'

'Such as?'

'Clubs for open-minded people.'

'Swingers,' Clare said.

'I don't think I've been reticent in telling you this,' Gloria said. 'No reason to be, not really. Not the sort of place for Deidre, her belief in unrequited love, but what did she expect? Did she think she was Derek's first love? How can anyone be so stupid?'

'Do you think she was?'

'Emotionally, yes, but realistically, how could she be so naïve?'

'Did you know about her before he disappeared?' Tremayne asked.

'We've been through this before. I received a postcard, a Salisbury postmark. I knew that Jacob Montfield lived there, and he was in the phone book. I phoned the number, Deidre answered.'

'You never mentioned that before.'

'Maybe I forgot.'

'People remember significant events in their lives and where they were: Kennedy's assassination, when Lady Di was in a car crash, when they found out their husband had been sleeping with another woman, whispering sweet nothings.'

'Sweet nothings, beautifully put,' Gloria said. 'He would say them to me, no doubt in the same mellifluous voice. He was a charmer, and she wouldn't have been the only one.'

'Was Marjorie Potts one of those?'

'The next-door neighbour?'

'You met her.'

'I did, but I have to ask you, what do you expect me to remember after so many years? Deidre, yes, and I did speak to someone next door, wondered why she called me over.'

'Why did she?'

'Maybe she was concerned about Deidre.'

'Mrs Hardcastle,' Tremayne said, 'don't play us for fools. You and your dead husband might have played the field, enjoyed sexual gymnastics with numerous partners, some of whom you wouldn't have known the names of, but don't treat us as plodding police officers.'

'We've been through all this before,' Gloria said, more annoyed than previously.

'And we'll go through it again and again until we start to get answers,' Tremayne said. 'Gloria, was your husband emotionally involved with Deidre?'

'He could have been, but I never considered it at the time, nor would I now.'

'You were tired of your marriage?'

'It was good timing on his part, and if he was in love with the woman, so much the better, but I still don't see where this is heading.'

'You visit Marjorie Potts, someone you can identify with.'

'Can I? Why? What's so special about her?'

'She slept with your husband.'

'And you expect me to be upset. Inspector, not based on fact, and it appears to be a criticism of Deidre's neighbour and me.'

'Then you, Mrs Hardcastle, do not understand where I'm coming from. You know your husband was involved with Deidre, and Marjorie Potts was also sleeping with your husband.'

'Okay, I suspected it. After all, why invite me into her house?'

'Asked about you and Derek?'

'Not in as many words, but she knew about him and Deidre.'

'We believe she knows more than she's telling us about the night your husband died.'

'Former husband. I dealt with his abandonment a long time ago and went through legal. To me, he died a long time ago.'

The day he left you, or the day he fell in love with Deidre?'

'Neither.'

'What does that mean?'

'Exactly what I just said. Our marriage was over before then, and you were correct, our lifestyle wasn't conducive to marriage. The body might be willing, but the mind is confused. We both knew it, Derek more than me.'

'If he intended to make an honest woman of Deidre, would you have been surprised?'

'I can't believe he loved her. Although he would have liked children, a conventional life.'

'You didn't?'

'Not back then, but I was younger than him, more liberal in my views. And if Derek wanted to settle down, why was he with the woman next door too? The man was incorrigible; he would have made a poor husband for Deidre.'

***

Clare arrived at the police station at 11 a.m. after visiting the gynaecologist. She had taken Clive with her, who was nervous as he sat in the waiting room. He was known in the city and older than the other men in the room. Two of them, young enough to be his sons, pretended not to notice but occasionally cast a glance at Clare and then at her man, one with a snigger, the other smiling.

Clare was attractive, Clive was greying and dignified, but to the younger men, he was a ladies' man, especially after it had become known that he had fathered a child in his twenties, and now in his fifties, his daughter was not a lot younger than his second wife.

He would have preferred not to have accompanied Clare, but she had been adamant, and she intended to take him along to the antenatal classes too. He hoped she was joking, but regardless, whatever she wanted, he would comply.

Tremayne sat at his desk. There were reports to prepare, another memo about professionalism and how to treat the public, the accused's rights, to respect the individual regardless of colour, religion and gender identity.

Disregarding all the above, which he would grant were important but distracting, he took a piece of paper and wrote the names of those that had died, those that lived, those that he suspected would be capable of murder.

After five minutes, he scrunched the paper up and threw it into a bin close to his desk. To him, anyone could be capable of Jacob's murder, even Marjorie Potts and Gloria Hardcastle, although he couldn't see why and how, and that concerned him. It wasn't a problematic murder investigation, not on the face of it. Derek Sutherland's murderer had to be either Jacob or Deidre, and time would resolve the identity of the guilty person.

Tremayne got up from his chair, put on his jacket and walked out of the door. There was one person he intended to catch up with, the person who had discovered the body, someone he said had been a friend, when, in truth, he hadn't liked the man.

'Tremayne,' Christine Maloney said as she flung her arms around his neck, 'Jerry said he'd met you. We have to get together, the four of us. How's Jean?'

Tremayne wracked his brain, thought back to a short, dark-haired young woman and Jerry Maloney, tall and upright, a spring in his step, a slap you on the back joviality, and realised that time had had its effect.

Even so, he wasn't prepared for the change in the two. It had only been a short time together on the night of Montfield's death, and in the half-light, he had only seen a silhouette, not had a clear look at Jerry.

Christine Maloney, aged, with round shoulders, blonde hair and a ruddy-red complexion, limped as she walked, and as for Jerry, he was stooped and grey-haired. Tremayne realised that the years had done their damage, knowing that Jean and he probably looked equally tired and aged. It wasn't a cheerful thought.

'Jean's fine,' Tremayne said. 'How much longer are you in Salisbury?'

'We're going back tomorrow. Come to the hotel tonight, you and Jean. We can have a meal together, talk about old times.'

'At 9 p.m.'

'Nine it is. Children?' Christine asked.

'We broke up, got divorced. That was years ago. Jean had two, then her husband died, and we got back together, got married again.'

He would have preferred not to have spoken about his and Jean's past, but it was best to mention it now rather than for Jean to receive the grilling.

'Don't worry,' Jerry said. 'We broke up for a while, realised it wasn't much fun on our own. Mind you, running a hotel out in the sticks puts a strain on a relationship.'

'Not as much as policing,' Tremayne said. 'We need to talk, Jerry.'

'Do you have Jean's phone number?' Christine asked. 'I could pick her up, get in some shopping, talk about old times.'

Tremayne remembered that his wife and Maloney's hadn't been friendly years before, but he thought wisdom and forgiveness came with maturity. He was sure they would be fine, and that although Christine had been mouthy in her youth and Jean had been quick to take offence, they were traits that mellow with age.

'She'd like that. If you could make sure she gets here tonight, I'd appreciate it,' Tremayne said. 'We've got another murder to solve; it keeps us hard at work.'

'Your sergeant, I heard about her. Jerry said she was attractive.'

'I don't give her compliments, don't want to spoil her, but yes, she is.'

Making small talk wasn't Tremayne's forte, and he was glad when Christine walked away, talking on the phone to Jean.

Tremayne and Maloney sat down in the hotel bar, each man ordering a pint of beer, Tremayne paying.

'I haven't told Christine about your sergeant. She's keen on celebrity.'

'I don't think Yarwood would regard herself as such, nor would her husband.'

'It doesn't mean much to me, but your sergeant's married to the mayor.'

'Up to you. If you want, I'll make sure they meet. Jean can set it up.'

'I read up on her, had a rough time a few years back,' Maloney said.

'Don't let Christine know. Yarwood doesn't talk about it, neither do I.'

'Don't worry. I can keep a secret.'

'Can you?' Tremayne said. 'What were you doing in the Haunch of Venison? Where was Christine?'

'A policeman's mind, always looking for a reason.'

'It's a valid question. You're the closest we've got to Montfield's death, although we're sidelined by another body.'

'The sister's lover.'

'The internet?'

'Where else?'

'You were a police officer once. What do you reckon?' Tremayne asked.

'I made sergeant, and not for very long. I don't see how I can help you.'

'Let's go back to the Haunch. Follow through from when you left the place.'

'Christine was tired after the trip down, wanted an early night. Not that I can blame her, but I was back in Salisbury. I was excited; it brought back memories. She understood, and I was only going out for a couple of pints, but once in the pub, one thing led to another. Instead of the two, I had six. Most days, I don't drink at all, and then it's only a pint or two. Anyway, a few drinks, a few laughs, a chance to reminisce, and I staggered out of the pub. If I hadn't met you, told Christine about it, she would have torn a strip off me.'

'No more than would have happened to me,' Tremayne remarked. 'Carry on with your story.'

'I crossed the road outside the pub and walked up Silver Street, looking this way and that, trying to recollect the shops from back then. Some have stayed the same; some haven't. Anyway, I walked past a man sitting down, looking lost to the world. I thought he was probably drunk, the same as me, although I couldn't be sure. I gave him a prod, if only to wake him up and to get him to move somewhere warmer, but he didn't respond. A little more sober by then, the cold air had done that, so I leant in closer, studied him, the police training kicking back in. I could see he was dead; that's when I phoned emergency services. Then you and everyone else turned up. Apart from that, there's not much I can tell you.'

'There must have been other people in the area.'

'If there were, I didn't see them, but then again, that's not unusual. My eyesight's good enough to find my way, not bump into things, but not so good on the detail. Close up, I'm fine, but at a distance, not as good.'

'Who did you meet in the pub?'

'Houghton. You must remember him. A tall piece of misery, or at least he was back in the past, but now he's doing well for himself. He bought himself a house, got his own business, doing well, even a boat, although who'd want to go boating around England in the summer, let alone the winter, beats me. But then, it takes all sorts. Anyway, he's not the misery he was, positively agreeable. We had a good talk, a few too many drinks, and then I left. He'll corroborate what I just told you.'

Tremayne had no reason to doubt Maloney's testimony; however, it would need to be checked, as he felt that more time at the Montfield residency was leading nowhere, just a collection of contradictory explanations and shaky memories.

'Tonight, 9 p.m.,' Tremayne said as he shook Maloney's hand.

Chapter 9

Deidre Montfield, sedated, did not sleep the sleep of the just, but she dreamed, not of pleasantness and love and happy thoughts, but the past, of Derek Sutherland, a man she had chanced to love. Of his death, fresh in her mind, her brother carrying the body in an old blanket down to the end of the garden, her crying but with no more tears possible.

It was the nurse who found her at four in the morning, her mouth agape, gasping for breath, her hands to either side of the small bed. The woman had suffered a stroke, and by five fifteen in the morning, she was in the hospital, and then by six twenty, enough time for both Tremayne and Clare to get there, she was dead.

Clare could only feel sorrow for a woman tainted with tragedy, a woman who had lived an unsatisfying life, destroyed by a man she had loved but who had not loved her with equal passion in return. A woman who may have been a murderer or complicit.

Tremayne summed up the situation: 'She was damned.'

It wasn't insensitive, Clare knew, just acknowledging the reality. No matter how much the two of them could sympathise, no matter the weight of public outpouring of emotion as the woman's life unfolded, no matter how much others might cry, she was by her admission involved in a murder, although whether she was the murderer or not was moot.

Derek Sutherland had been a philanderer, a man who regarded fidelity as of little worth, a man who cheated on his wife, a wife who cheated on him; his murder was still punishable, but of the two who could have killed him, both were now dead.

Tremayne and Clare sat in the cafeteria at the hospital. It was just after eight in the morning, and there would be no relatives to come and mourn the dead woman, no one to identify her. The last of the Montfields was dead. It was then that Clare cried.

'Not like you to get emotional,' Tremayne said.

'Sometimes the injustice gets to me, even to you,' Clare said.

'Not often, but you're right. Jacob, mad due to Sutherland's death; a body in the garden. And then the sister dead in her bed, no one to care or to say a kind word about her at her funeral, reduced to a headstone in the cemetery, assuming someone comes forward to pay for it.'

'If that. Who's going to deal with it? More likely cremated, their ashes scattered in the crematorium's gardens.'

The two walked back to where the woman's body had been taken, spoke to the person in charge, ensured that the pathologist was informed. Even though the cause of death was apparent, a criminal autopsy would be needed.

***

Tremayne went back to the police station; Clare drove out to the Montfield house. On her arrival, Marjorie Potts was outside the front of her home.

Clare did not want to speak to the woman, but she was still a police officer, and there were questions.

'Deidre?' Marjorie asked.

'She passed away this morning, never regained consciousness,' Clare said.

'It's strange, isn't it? At times like this, I remember her friendship, not the bitch she became.'

'A tragic end to a disturbed life.'

'Stress-related?'

'The pathologist will be able to tell us more, but it would be a reasonable assumption. Who knows what went through the woman's mind, and then her brother dying tragically?'

'My husband's taking me down to the coast, a restaurant we know down there.'

'A special occasion?'

'It isn't, just a chance to get away from here, from next door.'

'It wasn't your fault.'

'Maybe it wasn't, but I can't help feeling guilty. After all, I did sleep with Derek on one occasion.'

'What you did might be reprehensible, but it's not as if you turned a faithful husband into a monster. What if Jacob hadn't worked with Sutherland, then Deidre would never have found love, only to have it thrown in her face, to find out that he was married. Minor circumstances, all have consequences.'

'If your husband's brother hadn't died, you would never have met him, become pregnant,' Marjorie said.

'How did you know?' Clare said, not comfortable with an unpleasant memory, conscious that her life had turned out fine, Deidre Montfield's had not.

'People talk.'

'Which people?'

'You'd better take it easy; no point endangering your health and that of the child. A friend's daughter at the gynaecologist saw the two of you there.'

Clare hadn't thought about it before. Her mother had worked until a month before giving birth, but she had been the manager of a hotel, behind a desk most of the day, not out at crime scenes. She could see a few more months, then light duties in Homicide, which didn't appeal, or extended leave until the birth, and then after several months, back at work again.

'Does anyone else in the street know about Deidre?' Clare asked.

'Some would have seen an ambulance, couldn't miss it, but I've not spoken to anyone about it.'

Clare couldn't believe that Marjorie Potts hadn't been on the phone with others, but it wasn't important.

In the Montfield house, Clare had a key; a silence pervaded the place. It had never been a house of joy, but now it felt as though it was the haunt of the dead. Clare, not a suspicious person, nor of a morbid nature, found she was walking softly, trying not to make a noise, as if she'd disturb something she didn't want to; as if she would open a door, and someone or something would jump out.

Unable to stand the emptiness of the place, she switched on a television in the corner of the kitchen. An interminable soap opera that had been on the television nightly ever since she had been a child. It had not interested her then; it didn't now, but it had the desired effect, in that Clare could walk freely, the sound of the television bringing life back to the house.

She climbed the stairs and entered Deidre's bedroom, the medicines lined up on a cabinet to the side of the bed, the nurse's bag in one corner of the room, an iPhone on a small table.

Clare phoned Tremayne and told him where she was. The house had been checked before by the crime scene investigators. They had been looking for evidence where Derek Sutherland had supposedly died: strands of hair, a blood sample, an item that could have fallen from Sutherland's clothing before his naked body had been buried in the garden, his clothes burnt, according to Deidre. After twenty years, the CSIs had come away empty-handed, stating that conclusive evidence of foul deeds was almost impossible to find. And where the murder had occurred, the carpet was now dark blue, when before it had been beige, the wallpaper removed, the bare walls painted.

Clare opened another cabinet on the other side of the bed and withdrew an old shoebox, a ribbon around it, tied in a knot. It was what she had been looking for.

Downstairs, Clare opened the box, took out various papers, thought them unimportant, a couple of postcards, one from a friend in Italy, the typical 'wish you were here' message that people always say but don't mean. After all, the friend was on her honeymoon, clear enough from the other words on the postcard.

She found eight letters at the bottom of the box, all with the same handwriting on the front, all addressed to the same person, to Deidre. Clare opened the first, read through it, felt as though she was invading the dead woman's privacy, involving herself in the secrets of two lovers. It wasn't the first time she had felt such emotions, but with murder comes intrusion and then unpleasantness, an unravelling of the tenuous cords that tie one person to another, to the truth of death.

The first letter's sentiment was romantic and mushy. Even if Derek Sutherland had been a total bastard, Clare had to admit that the man had had a poetic bent, an understanding of a woman's psyche, of Deidre.

Clare knew Clive would never write such letters, and whereas she could be dismissive of their content, she couldn't help but be moved by the strength of emotion that Sutherland's writing conveyed.

Putting the first letter down, she opened the second, more direct than the first, in that it was no longer only emotion conveyed but a remembrance of the night they had spent together, the longing for it to continue.

Each letter was only two to three pages. The postmarks showed a time period extending over nine months, the tone of the letters progressively becoming more sombre, less childishly romantic. Absorbed for close to an hour, noticing the intensity of first love, then the gradual decline; letters sent in a time before email had started to supersede.

The nurse entered the room as Clare was about to read the last letter.

'I saw your car outside,' the nurse said. 'I was at the hospital with Deidre.'

'I didn't see you.'

'I was there, in with the doctor, discussing Deidre.'

'And what did you decide?'

'I don't think we decided anything. Deidre had been under a lot of stress, and he needed to write a report, considering the woman's involvement in a murder.'

'You were aware of her condition, had taken her blood pressure, checked her pulse.'

'Deidre was in her sixties, not in the best of health.'

The nurse was acting defensively, attempting to protect her reputation. Clare had already taken photos of the room, especially the medicines. She would pass over what she had seen to the pathologist and ask him to check for overdosing of prescription drugs. She was confident it would prove to be a wasted action, but Deidre Montfield deserved more than to be discarded with no one to mourn her.

'I'll be off,' the nurse said after she had gone upstairs, picked up her bag, pulled the iPhone's charger out of the wall, and taken her phone.

'Yes, bye,' Clare said without looking up. She held the last letter, dated ten days before Derek Sutherland's death. Apart from the writing as the letters progressed, the opening line of 'honey' and then 'sweet', before settling into 'darling', the final letter opened with 'Dear Deidre'.

Clare read the letter. It was interlaced with romantic assertions, an arrangement to meet up in a couple of weeks, a trip to London, take in a show, a night at a hotel, recollections of past times together, a reinforcement of the love between the two of them, their future together. Clare knew what it was – it was the letter before the end, the trip to London, the death knell of the relationship. The journey never occurred, and a couple of weeks never arrived: Derek Sutherland had died before then.

Clare put the box and the letters into an evidence bag. She then left the house, switching the light off in the bedroom and turning off the television on her way. She closed the front door behind her. She felt sad.

Chapter 10

Tremayne mulled over the facts. Jacob Montfield, an educated man, had turned his back on his career to embrace homelessness, but even so, sometimes, he slept in a shed at the bottom of his and Deidre's Garden. Derek Sutherland, his death the supposed catalyst for Jacob's unusual lifestyle; Gloria Hardcastle, Derek's widow, and a subsequent partnership with another man, bearing him two children. Somewhere, Marjorie Potts came into the equation, more so than they knew so far, although he wasn't sure where and how and when.

With his sergeant out of the office and at a loose end, Tremayne left the office. Two people concerned him, the flirtatious and easily excitable Marjorie and the promiscuous Gloria, although with her first husband's approval when he had been alive.

Gloria Hardcastle sat in the kitchen at her house. Clare had joined Tremayne after she had finished at the Montfield house. It was late afternoon, and in another room, the short and overweight Jim Hardcastle, the new man in Gloria's life.

Both officers had sensed the false interplay between the man and the woman on their arrival, the pretence of affection, the arms around each other, the smiles. However, there was insincerity on Jim's part, a screwing up of Gloria's face as he left the room.

'Trouble in paradise?' Clare's first question after Jim had left the three alone.

'He's upset by this whole business, and your coming here every other day doesn't help.'

'He's aware of your past?'

'He is, but he doesn't like it rammed down his throat, not like this.'

'Not like what?' Tremayne said.

'You two turning up here unannounced, disturbing the peace, resurrecting the past, what I was, what Derek was.'

'Why Derek? What's it to do with him? It's you he's with, not your former husband.'

'You don't get it, do you?'

The mood in the kitchen had changed. The formerly agreeable Gloria, now taking umbrage, was aware that she was treading on thin ice and about to fall through.

'Are you and Jim strait-laced, exclusively monogamous,' Clare said, 'or is it that you, Gloria, are still active and Jim is sitting at home while you screw around?'

'Jim knew about Derek and me. After all, he was one of those we swung with.'

'Spin a bottle, car keys in a bowl,' Tremayne said.

'It wasn't postman's knock,' Gloria said. 'More a free-for-all, a few too many drinks and then pairing off. Jim was into it, so was his wife, and another three or four couples.'

'Where is his wife?'

'She found religion and started spouting Sodom and Gomorrah, pillars of salt, damned for eternity. She became a bore, and when she's around here, not so often these days, she's threatening me with fire and brimstone.'

'She sounds a bundle of fun,' Clare said.

'It was at first. We used to laugh at her, but after so many years, it's become tiresome. She still wants Jim back, and sometimes I reckon I could give him to her.'

'Not much fun?'

'He's slowing down, but I'm not. Derek was a better man than him, although I suppose I shouldn't say that.'

'Did you suspect that Derek was keener on Deidre than you would have liked?' Tremayne asked, ignoring the slight to Jim Hardcastle.

'I didn't know about her, not at first.'

'Was that unusual?'

'We were honest. Both of us had chequered backgrounds, and I'd been the town bike in my teens, and Derek, well, he could charm the birds out of the trees. He had had a succession of women before I met him; I'd had more than my fair share of men.'

'Why marry?'

'Shallow, both of us, interested in pleasure without complication, thought that married love was better than what we had experienced before.'

'You married without love. Hoped it would come along?'

'I think we were in love. After all, we spent all our time together.'

'Even when you slept with others?' Tremayne said.

'Even,' Gloria replied.

'And your current partner was one of them?'

'Husband. I dealt with Derek's absence a long time ago. I was free to marry Jim.'

'Let me be clear on this,' Clare said. 'When Derek was alive, your current husband was one of your group of libertines?'

'For such a young woman, your contempt is palpable,' Gloria said.

'There is no contempt, just a need to understand the psyche of a woman who could profess love to one man, have sex with another.'

'Spare me your psychological BS. I know contempt when I hear it, heard it all my life.'

'Have you? From whom?'

'My parents when I was younger. They used to argue, clear that they hated each other, but would they separate, find another partner? Not them, too holy they were, going on about one man, one woman, marriage was forever. What's the point in that? You may as well be dead, that's what I reckon, and then Derek, screwing anything that moved, and him wanting me to be there when he came home.'

'You said he wasn't jealous, accepted that both of you were unfaithful.'

'More open for him. And then there was Deidre, virginal and innocent, fruit ready for the picking.'

'He fell for her?' Tremayne said.

'More than he should have. I could see it, even if I didn't know who it was, and that's the truth.'

'How did you know?' Clare asked.

'When he ceased to be angry with me, not so concerned about the meal, not wanting me.'

'He satisfied both pangs of hunger with Deidre.'

'Not only satisfying, getting fat on both. Derek, he was a glutton, kept the weight off through exercise, and he was inexhaustible, and there's this woman, Deidre, who was tiring him out.'

'Was Deidre?' Clare asked. 'All we saw was a tired and troubled woman. Granted, when Derek was alive, she was younger, but a femme fatale, we never saw that.'

'You wouldn't have, nor did I that time I met her,' Gloria said.

'Gloria, you're the only one apart from the next-door neighbour that can shed any light on your husband's murder, and even so, it's not the most important. We still have the death of Jacob Montfield to deal with.'

'He was a strange man.'

'Derek had liked him.'

'Liked his sister more,' Gloria said, a sneering tone.

'Tell us about Jacob Montfield, the time you met him.'

'Forgettable, that's all I can say. He wasn't there the day I called on Deidre.'

'Only the one time?'

'Only once.'

'We've found out that you had been there on several occasions,' Tremayne said. He was not telling the truth, throwing a diversion, hoping to break the woman's practised replies. He had his suspicions, not that he wanted to reveal them yet, not even to his sergeant, but the more he listened to the woman, the less sure he was of her.

'It was only the one time,' Gloria said without the degree of conviction required.

'We can prove this,' Clare said, sensing Tremayne's tactic.

'Only once when I knocked on the door.'

'That, Gloria Hardcastle, is a deviation from your previous statements,' Tremayne said. 'I suggest we reconvene at the police station, formally caution you, and then settle down for a long night, you telling us all you know, instead of this nonsense.'

'I've told you the truth. You asked me how many times I knocked on the door. You and your sergeant are indulging in semantics, attempting to confuse me.'

'You seem well acquainted with interrogation tactics,' Tremayne said.

Clare called for time out, a break in the proceedings. Gloria had revealed a hitherto unknown fact; she would tell more, but it was best to let her mull over the situation, to allow her to speak in her own good time.

Tremayne, more bluster than his sergeant, willing to pressure the woman, initially displeased that his train of thought had been interrupted, took out a cigarette packet from his pocket. 'I need five minutes,' he said.

He disagreed with his sergeant, but as the lighted cigarette calmed his nerves, he conceded that a woman's intuition was a mighty force, never more potent than when focussed on another woman.

Chapter 11

There was always someone not revealing all they knew. Not that Tremayne believed it was always intentional, some regarding the minutiae as unimportant, some forgetting, and others not registering what they had seen or heard. That belief did not, however, extend to Gloria Hardcastle. Tremayne knew she was hiding facts for a reason, and what those facts were and for what reason was significant. After all, she was the only direct contact between two murdered men and a dead woman, apart from Marjorie Potts. However, Marjorie Potts wasn't deemed as significant as Gloria Hardcastle, not for the present.

'Gloria,' Clare said on her and Tremayne's return from outside, 'why didn't you tell us the full story the first time?'

'What story? I knocked on the door once, watched from outside on another couple of occasions.'

'Before your husband's death?'

'I knew about Deidre; hard not to when you lived with the man.'

'How? And more importantly, why did you choose to lie?'

'Embarrassment,' Gloria said.

'Gloria, you have sex with other men for pleasure, you cheat on your husband, or at least, you did with Derek. You looked the other way to his previous dalliances, and you're telling us that you are embarrassed.'

'Ashamed. Is that a better word? Derek and I were always honest with each other. It was the only way our marriage could endure. As for the lifestyle, it's not all it's cracked up to be. Sure, sometimes it's great, but occasionally you meet someone and feel drawn to them. It plays hell with the emotions, and I met Jim at one of these events, and there's his wife, sweet as pie, sitting there, watching us.'

'Derek, why didn't he take her?'

'I'm not sure. Normally, he would have, but he had changed, met Deidre, I suppose. Although I didn't know about it that night.'

'Did you fancy Jacob?'

'He was strange, more interested in talking to Derek about work and politics. Jacob was a man you instinctively trusted, not the sort of man to tell. Once, Jacob slept over at our house. I was game, so was Derek, and a threesome was on the cards, but Jacob, he wouldn't take the hint, not until Derek was forthright, told him the score, and that I was there for him, no questions asked, no complications.'

'His response? And equally important, previously, you told us that you'd met Jacob once. Now it's two times.'

'He listened to Derek, nodded his head at the right time, shook it at the other. It was surreal. No man resists, not if it's on a plate, and I was still attractive, able to turn a man's head, but with Jacob, nothing, not even a look of disgust, more a benign indifference.'

'And why haven't you told us about this before?'

'No woman wants to be rejected.'

'Jacob wasn't shocked by you and Derek?'

'He thanked us for our consideration.'

'Did he give a reason?'

He told us that he had committed to a celibate life. That he enjoyed the peace of being one with himself, perfectly content to go through life unencumbered by extraneous pulls on his intellect and his academic pursuits.'

'Were you offended?'

'To some extent, I was, but Derek said later that evening, long after Jacob had gone to bed, that the man's eccentricity was becoming more extreme, although he was a brilliant scientist. He called him a boffin, not a term you hear much these days, but it summed up Jacob.'

'You told us that you found out about your husband and Deidre after his disappearance, and now you're telling us that you knew. How does this tally? What did you imagine our response would be when the truth was revealed?'

'I never thought about it, but yes, I knew about Derek and Deidre, although I hadn't met her, not then, no idea what she looked like, not until I saw her come out of the house one day.'

'Your impression?'

'I couldn't understand what he saw in her. She was nothing special, the sort who had a cat and watched the television every night.'

'A lot of men might want that sort of life,' Clare said. 'Who was the more promiscuous, you or your husband? As you've said, it was fun, but did you ever consider that he might have changed, craved stability, the love of another.'

'How could he? What sort of man would reject me for her?' Gloria said.

Tremayne could see that the woman was incapable of seeing the flaws in her character and that she had an unhealthy sense of self-worth. She was, he believed, a potentially dangerous woman if crossed.

'Deidre was adamant she had killed Derek, that Jacob hadn't,' Clare said.

'Does it matter?' Gloria responded.

'It matters a great deal,' Tremayne said. 'Jacob Montfield's life was threatened; he knew this. This means he had received direct and recent indication, or else, he had an increasingly paranoid concern that Derek's death had perpetuated a chain of events that had been brewing over many years. A hidden threat, a need by someone to right the wrongs of the past. Are you Jacob's murderer, considering that the man had rejected you and his sister had killed Derek?'

Clare knew it was typical Tremayne to throw in an outrageous and unsubstantiated question. Although she had to admit that Tremayne had hit on a possibility, not clearly postulated at present, but worthy of consideration.

Gloria Hardcastle shrank visibly in her chair, pulled her feet in under her and looked down, not wanting to make eye contact, as though she wanted the floor to open up and swallow her.

After what seemed an eternity but was closer to two minutes than five, she spoke. 'I would have killed Derek.'

'Did you?' Tremayne asked.

'You don't understand. We had a libertarian view of sexuality and sex. That doesn't, however, make a person devoid of emotion.'

'You loved Derek, and he had disappointed you, spent his emotions on another,' Clare said.

'He had. With Deidre, it was different. I grew to hate both of them.'

'Kill is a strong word, easily bandied around,' Tremayne said. 'Are you saying that "killing" was metaphorical, a rolling pin over the head, a slap to the face, or do you mean something more?'

'I had the anger,' Gloria said.

'A distraught lover, not one who truly loves, thinks like that,' Clare said. 'Are you sure it was your husband falling for another woman that made you want to kill him, or had you met another man?'

Tremayne knew that if a person could kill one, they could kill another. Pandora's box had been opened; he wasn't sure what else was to tumble out. He did not believe she had killed Derek, all evidence pointed to the Montfields, and intent is not a crime.

Tremayne sat quietly, not saying a word, knowing he had trained his sergeant well. He was concerned that Gloria Hardcastle, a woman who had a casual approach to love, could also hate. Could she have killed Jacob Montfield? And if so, why the city centre, and why after so many years? Anger and hatred, even love, dissipate with the years of separation from the object of veneration or loathing.

'It's been such a long time since Derek vanished, but now we know Deidre and her brother had known the truth,' Gloria said. 'What makes a person do that? How do they live with themselves, knowing what they had done?'

'We're police officers, not psychiatrists,' Clare said. 'Don't you, Gloria, ever have any compunction about betraying your husband?'

'Jim?'

'Have you betrayed him?' Tremayne said.

'It was never betrayal with Derek. We were kindred spirits, free of petty jealousies.'

'But Derek was with Deidre.'

'That was a betrayal. If he had been honest, I would have understood.'

Clare could not agree with the woman's libidinous behaviour and beliefs but would only use them against her if necessary. She left Tremayne to it, observed where he was heading, would intercede if she could see an advantage.

'Tell us about Marjorie Potts,' Tremayne said. 'Did you recognise her as a kindred spirit?'

'It wasn't something we talked about, and I only met her the once, judged her to be the nosey neighbour, and we've had our fair share of those.'

'You and Derek? Parties at your house, the neighbours with binoculars?'

'And calling the police, not that we made a noise, nor did we clutter the street with cars.'

'Only the grunting and groaning of heaving bodies,' Tremayne said.

'Your disapproval does you no justice. You're here to question me about murder, Derek's murder, not to condemn me.'

'Condemnation does not concern me, the truth does, and you are not telling the full story. Why?'

'What more do you want? Coming in here, badgering me with pointless questions, going over again and again what I have already told you.'

'One more time,' Clare said, 'from the beginning.'

Tremayne pulled back and left it to his sergeant.

'Very well,' Gloria said. 'Derek was missing, and I knew where he was or was likely to be. I drove over, confronted Deidre, spoke to her about my husband, got nowhere.'

'You thought he was hiding out in the house?'

'I didn't know what to think. He hadn't reported for work, and they were concerned.'

'And he hadn't touched your bank accounts?'

'He hadn't. It was strange, but he had a separate bank account, and Deidre had money. I thought that at some stage, he'd appear, make his peace, come back to me, or stay with her.'

'Which did you prefer?' Clare asked.

'I had no preference, honestly. I suppose I should have, but there was tension in the marriage.'

'Not helped by your lifestyles,' Tremayne said.

'Nothing to do with it, Inspector, if you must know. We'd been trying for a child, and it was Derek who was the issue, not me.'

'The solution?' Clare said.

'Wasn't it obvious?' Gloria said. 'We had friends who would help.'

'No need for a sample in a vial, was there?'

'No need, but Derek was against it, said he didn't have the paternal instinct, but that wasn't true. For some reason, casual sex wasn't the problem, but a child from someone we knew, someone I would have slept with, aroused emotions in him that I didn't understand. Not sure if he did, either.'

'Is it possible that Derek was tired of the lifestyle?'

'It may have been, and then, Derek's gone, and I'm with Jim. Two children with the man since then. God's will.'

'That's the first time you've mentioned God,' Clare said.

'What else could it be?' Gloria said. 'It could have been a punishment for my licentious ways, not worthy of bringing a child into the world.'

'You previously mentioned Derek as a problem. Or was it that multiple partners, deviancy, and whatever else you practised at these get-togethers could have caused internal damage. I assume it wasn't just missionary.'

'We never had proof, one way or the other, that it was Derek. He wasn't interested, never wanted children. And you might be right, but it was fun, even if it was transient and selfish. I see it all now, but it's too late, no reason to poke in the ashes of a past life, better to live in the moment.'

Tremayne could see that within Gloria Hardcastle, there was a malignancy, to love with a passion, to hate with a vengeance.

From another part of the house, the sound of a door opening.

'That'll be Jim,' Gloria said. 'He's upset that this is taking too long.'

'He'll get angry with us, not you. Call him in,' Tremayne said.

Gloria shouted out; Jim Hardcastle entered.

'You've been here long enough. Why you continue to question my wife is beyond me,' Jim said.

'It's murder,' Tremayne said, 'not one of your spin-the-bottle nights out.' He was irritated and not afraid to show it. He'd met the type before, their determination to ride roughshod over others. Hardcastle had met his match in Tremayne. 'Mr Hardcastle, you might think you're Napoleon ordering his generals around, but to Sergeant Yarwood and me, you are a minor functionary in this investigation.'

'You can't come into my house and talk to me like that.'

Tremayne looked over at Clare. She understood.

Clare took out her phone and dialled the police station, 'Interview Room, twenty minutes,' she said.

'Okay, you win. What do you want?' Jim Hardcastle said as he sat down.

The number Clare had dialled was not the station but a bogus number that sometimes came in handy.

'The truth would be a good start,' Tremayne said.

'What can my wife tell you that she's not already told you?'

'The truth.'

'If you're somehow trying to correlate our past activities, reprehensible to you, abhorrent probably, with her involvement in the death of either man, you will be sorely disappointed.'

'We're not accusing your wife of anything, not yet. Only that originally she had told us she found the Montfield's address after Derek had failed to come home. Then it comes out that she had staked out the Montfield house on a couple of occasions previously, and she had seen Deidre coming out of the house, as well as chatting with the next-door neighbour.'

'What else do you want from her? She feels guilty she didn't pursue his disappearance, didn't take it to the police.'

'Would the police have acted?' Gloria asked.

'They would have registered Derek's disappearance, visited the Montfields and your friends, formed a profile of him, his movements, who he spoke to,' Clare said. 'Assuming that his disappearance was out of character and you had a reason to be worried, proof of possible violence against him.'

'And how long would that have taken?' Jim Hardcastle asked.

'Four or five days. After all, he was an adult, no criminal record, no reason to believe he was dead.'

'Filed in the not-interested basket.'

'Interested, but where's the evidence? After all, your wife has told us she was angry enough to have killed him, which raises an interesting possibility, would explain a lot of what we're talking about here today.'

'Such as?' Gloria said.

'Whether you were outside the Montfield house on the day he died. How did Deidre come to know that Derek was married? Whether you saw something or had your suspicions. Jacob had known, but he had chosen not to tell her, not sure why, or maybe he believed that her life had been miserable enough, and a man in her bed would have cheered her up. We know he was morose, hardly the life and soul of the party, and he had chosen celibacy as a lifestyle, not that we'll ever know.'

'I'd not know. How could I? I only met Deidre once.'

'It's your word we're forced to believe, only because we don't have any contradictory information. Is it a possibility that you, obsessed with your husband's betrayal, saw the conflict inside the house? Maybe you were peering through the curtains, saw what had happened, but were transfixed, unable to shout out, to do something, to call the police?'

'This is crazy talk,' Hardcastle said. 'My wife is a gentle person, wouldn't harm a fly.'

'We're not talking about a fly,' Tremayne said. 'Your wife admitted he was a rat, and she had the anger, if not the opportunity or the will to follow through, and Deidre was doing it for her, or maybe it was Jacob.'

'If you're attempting to make me admit that I was there, I won't. Nor will I be bullied by two police officers who feel that intimidation of a poor defenceless woman is acceptable,' Gloria said. 'My morals and those of both of my husbands are inconsequential. Deidre professed piety, yet she was a confessed murderer. I am not guilty of any crime, other than a poor taste in men.'

Anger, at last. Tremayne sat back, pleased that the woman was revealing herself and her emotions. He'd leave it to his sergeant to continue.

Clare knew Tremayne preferred people to be testy and on edge, ready to make a mistake, lie, and speak without forethought. And now, the woman had admitted to her poor taste in men.

Jim Hardcastle paced around the room, cast steely glances over at his wife, scowled at Tremayne, ignored eye contact with Clare. The insignificant little bullying man was seething. It was a good state of affairs, long fought for and not to be relinquished, not before new facts were revealed.

'Is that directed at me?' Jim said.

Family conflict, even better, Tremayne thought, although it made Clare uncomfortable. Her parents would bicker, say things in the heat of the moment they'd later regret, and Gloria was travelling down that road.

'I was talking about Derek, not you,' Gloria said. 'It's the police; they're confusing me, trying to get me to lie.'

'We don't need lies,' Clare said. 'Only the truth. What were you doing spying on the Montfields? Were you in with Derek on this seduction of Deidre, the deluded brother thinking he was bringing joy to his sister? This woman who had led a spinsterly life, devoid of pleasure, probably content. Was it a challenge, even a bet between you two? And what about your current husband? Another person to dangle a carrot in front of, and these parties, no consideration as to the psychological damage you were inflicting.'

Gloria was out of her chair, flaming eyes, hands outstretched, looking for a neck to wrap them around. Tremayne moved faster than he thought possible. Jim

Hardcastle lunged forward, grabbed his wife by one arm, pulled her back, put her back in her chair.

'You bitch,' Gloria said. 'Coming in here, disrupting my husband and me, accusing me of murder, of being a voyeur, watching Derek fall in love with another woman.'

Clare, startled at the woman's ferocity, the speed at which her true colours had been revealed, took a handkerchief out of her pocket, wiped her hands which had become sweaty. Even though she regretted that she had raised such intensity of emotion in Gloria Hardcastle, she did not intend to lose the advantage.

'That answers one question,' Clare said, attempting not to sound shaken, aware that she was not making a good job of it.

'What question?' Jim Hardcastle said. 'Is this acceptable, what you've done to my wife?'

'Probably not, but that's not what concerns you or us now. Your wife has shown that she is capable of violence. She is also disparaging of her former husband and you. You heard her. Have you long suspected?'

'That's between a man and his wife, not outsiders who barge into our house, berate my wife, cause dissension and conflict.'

'You're right,' Tremayne said. 'We can always reconvene at the police station.'

'What you want can be said here,' Gloria said.

'Then the truth. How many times spying on the Montfields?'

'More than two, less than six. I can't remember the exact number, and that's the truth. Derek intended to walk out on me; whether it was with Deidre or not, I wouldn't know.'

'According to letters he had written to her,' Clare said, 'the impression that I got was that the relationship was weakening. Deidre wasn't the issue; it was you.'

'It's called marriage,' Gloria said. 'My husband had tired of our life. He wanted a more conventional lifestyle, more like my sister and her brood of five children, more like my brother with a docile mouse of a wife and two smart-arsed, know-it-all kids.'

'You said he wasn't capable of fathering a child.'

'He hadn't been interested, or it might have been me. And that's the truth. Back then, children had been anathema, not that you'd understand.'

'I wouldn't,' Clare said.

Jim Hardcastle felt the need to intervene, to go to his wife's defence. 'This interrogation is not balanced.'

'What do you mean?' Tremayne said. 'We're here asking questions, getting verbiage in return, slowly drawing out the truth from your wife. And besides, where do you fit into this?'

'I don't. Only that I think you're unfair to Gloria. If she saw nothing wrong with the human body, nor with sharing it, it doesn't make her a murderer.'

'It doesn't. However, your wife was aware her first husband was involved with Deidre Montfield. If your wife accepted that, that's fine if it didn't upset her, but then her husband disappears. She had a chat with Deidre, knowing full well that the man was keen on her, more so than her, and then she adopts this persona of not caring, only leaving the door open if he came back, getting on with her life.'

'Looking to the future is not a crime, nor what I believed back then, what I believe now,' Gloria said.

'Your behaviour after Derek died is not suggestive of innocence. You knew something, and we intend to find out today, one way or the other. Jim, how long before you took up with him?'

'Six, maybe seven months.'

'Perilously short,' Clare said. 'Derek could have walked in at any time, found you with Jim, created a scene, thrown him out.'

'Not Derek; he was a pacifist, mild-mannered.'

'So were you until we got you riled. You carried the anger and hatred for the two of you if he was indeed as harmless as you say.'

'Anger and hatred do not equate to murder.'

'Ordinarily, we'd agree,' Tremayne said, 'but Sergeant Yarwood's correct. You, Gloria Hardcastle, knew your first husband was dead. That was why you didn't contact the police.'

The reaction was slow in coming. Ashen-faced, the previously resolute and determined Gloria started to sob. Clare could not help but be moved by the emotions of a broken woman; Tremayne was impassive. Whether they were crocodile tears or not didn't concern him, only the truth did.

Jim Hardcastle stood dumbfounded, unsure what to do or say. His life, such as it had been with Gloria, was shattered. Tremayne looked at him and saw a man who didn't know the whole story; he was almost certainly innocent of any wrongdoing other than loving a woman with psychological issues.

'I knew,' Gloria said. 'I was there that night.' Her voice was weak, and she was gulping, almost as though she was attempting to suck in air, suffocating in her grief.

Clare, a sensitive woman, placed her hand on the woman's arm. 'The truth is always the best.'

'In the house?' Tremayne asked.

'Not there. I was outside in my car. It was late, and I could see Deidre with Derek upstairs when the light was on, and then Jacob coming in the house.'

'What then?'

'I was obsessed; I'll admit to it now. I loved my husband.'

Tremayne disregarded the last statement, the defence of a possessive woman, professing that her actions were motivated by affection.

'Gloria, what did you see?' Clare asked.

'In the front room of the house, the three of them, their silhouettes through the curtain, close together, the raised voices, Jacob accusing Derek of maltreating his sister, spinning her a story about how he intended to leave me for her; Deidre leaping to Derek's defence, saying words of love to Derek, her arm around him.'

'Through the curtains?' Tremayne said. 'You saw all this?'

'I snuck around the back of the house and crouched down, a crack at the bottom of a side window, a clear view in.'

'You didn't intercede,' Clare said.

'I was transfixed, not sure what to do, and that's the truth. A man I loved, a woman he loved, a man that Derek admired. I should have acted, made my presence known, but I couldn't. My mind was blank, or it was going at a hundred miles an hour. It was an impossible situation, complicated by my presence, but it wasn't violent, not then. And if Derek had stormed out, he would come back to me, and I wanted to be rid of him, even though I still loved him, to move on, nothing wrong in that.

'The situation was fluid, one person playing off the other, Jacob getting progressively angrier, Deidre unsure of what to say or do, not sure if Derek loved her or not, hating her brother. And if he intended to come back to me, I didn't want him.'

'Then why outside the house?'

'I needed to know, and I was curious.'

'Regardless,' Clare said, 'you've not committed any crime.'

'Later, I did.'

'You killed your husband?'

'Jacob told Deidre that he didn't believe that Derek was serious and he was married. Deidre hadn't believed her brother the first time, only the second. And then Derek, weak-willed, had confessed, admitted the truth, that he intended to come back to me, not out of love, but because I wasn't the clingy type, and that the illusion of a normal marriage, which is what it would have been with Deidre, didn't suit. Besides, he wanted a child, and she was getting older by the day, and he doubted if her health was up to it. All of which made no sense to me, as she was still young enough to carry a child.'

'Deidre's reaction?'

'Initially, nothing. Just stood there, saying nothing, looking at Derek and then at her brother. That was when she grabbed something off the mantelpiece, slammed it down on his head.'

'And you did nothing?'

'I couldn't.'

'Is that because you were pleased?' Clare asked. 'One problem solved.'

'Sergeant, you've seen bodies. Have you ever seen a murder?'

Most police officers would have replied negatively, but Clare and Tremayne had both been in the forest up above Avon Hill that fateful night when men had died, when Clare had come close to being killed.

'Yes,' Clare said.

'Then you know the reaction, the paralysis, the mind unable to comprehend, the body unsure what to do.'

Neither Tremayne nor Clare could counteract the woman's statement. Neither of them on that moonless night had acted rationally, although the selfless action of another had saved their lives, especially Clare's.

'Yet, a few days later, you're there at the Montfields' door.'

'I managed to get away from their house that night, not sure how. For a few days, I couldn't believe what had happened, not sure even today as to what I had seen. I had to know the truth; that's why I confronted Deidre.'

'You accused her of murder?'

'No. I only asked about her and Derek. She was polite, so was I; told me she hadn't seen him.'

'You didn't go to the police?'

'With what? Who would have believed what I've just told you?'

'It would have been investigated.'

'A chat to Deidre and Jacob, a cup of tea, a piece of cake with them, and then a report filed. Would they have checked the house, issued an alert for Derek's car?'

Tremayne knew they wouldn't have. People, young and old, disappeared every week, and a mature adult male with no criminal record would have only been of cursory interest.

'Did you see them bury him in the garden?'

'No. It would have been best if he had never been found.'

It was a callous statement, but it had a ring of truth. Tremayne knew that Jacob Montfield's death was still far from being solved.

Chapter 12

Back at Homicide, Tremayne and Clare mulled over the case, the direction going forward, postulating on the variables, what they knew, what they didn't.

'I don't like it,' Tremayne said.

'What don't you like?' Clare replied, knowing that her inspector was thinking out loud, going through the investigation in his head, trying to understand what was important, what was not.

'Too neat, this story that Gloria Hardcastle fed us.'

'It sounded plausible.'

'Plausible, but was it true? She sees her husband murdered. Fine, we'll go along with that, but she didn't kill him. If she had reported what she had seen, her lifestyle would have come out, the resulting scandal.'

'Not something to be proud of.'

'Being berated for her behaviour wouldn't have been the worst thing in the world for her. A couple of months, three at the most, and forgotten.'

'You think there's more to what she told us?'

'I do. She hooks up with Jim Hardcastle, although he was married when Derek died, divorced later. But we've got Gloria, a woman who didn't love strongly, although she says she did with Derek, which appears contradictory to the truth. And then she's in love with Jim. It's not as if he's anything special, not compared to Derek, who by all accounts was charming and attractive,' Tremayne said.

'Love isn't quantifiable,' Clare said.

'If it was, his numbers don't add up. A most unimpressive man, hardly the great lover, and that seems to be what interests Gloria.'

'Did. He's not so young, nor is she. Hardly the young vixen.'

'Even if the body's not as willing, the mind is, and with Jim, she'd not get a lot of joy, and it's clear their marriage is on the rocks.'

'Not important, not now.' Clare reminded Tremayne that Jacob Montfield's death was their primary focus.

'I'd agree, but if Gloria saw Derek die, what about next door? There must have been some noise, and Marjorie Potts can be nosey.'

'Phone the woman, find out when Simon Potts will be home; better still phone him directly. You've got his number?' Tremayne said.

***

'On my way home,' Simon Potts said on his arrival at the police station. 'I understand there's been some drama.'

The husband of a woman who had made overtures to Tremayne and had slept with Derek Sutherland by her admission was not as expected.

'Thanks for coming,' Tremayne said.

'I didn't see any point in rushing home. Marjorie's more than capable of handling any drama,' Potts said. In his mid-fifties, a tall, robust man with a full head of hair and a commanding voice, he was impressive. It was incongruous to Clare why Potts' wife strayed, but it was clear she did.

'It's hardly just a drama,' Clare said.

'Marjorie's capable, and I can't say we were ever close to the Montfields, although Deidre could be sociable, or at least, she was before Sutherland gave her the brushoff.'

'You knew him?'

'Derek? Not well, but he'd be around there on occasions. He used to park his car a few streets away and then sneak in; no idea why.'

'What does that mean?'

'Nothing in itself, only that we knew what the two of them were up to, no doubt half the street did, but who's criticising?'

'Maybe Deidre was.'

'A pious woman, butter wouldn't melt in her mouth, or maybe that was the impression she wanted to give. But where there's good, there's bad.'

'What does that mean?' Clare said.

'Yin and yang, two sides to a coin. What I reckon is those that profess one thing are often the other.'

'Do you have strong opinions?' Tremayne asked. 'A man who has an answer to all the world's ills?'

'I like to read if that's what you mean?'

'Isn't this the pot calling the kettle black, throwing doubt on the good name of a dead woman?'

'I don't see how. Deidre was neighbourly, even if she could be difficult, and with Sutherland taking her to paradise and back every so often, she positively mellowed.'

'And then the man disappears, and Deidre's back to crabby, causing trouble in the neighbourhood, which brings up another subject.'

'Which one? My wife, is that it? Has she been talking, telling you that she's easy with her favours and that Sutherland had planted his seed there, sowed where he should have left fallow?'

'Something like that,' Tremayne said. 'It's hardly helpful unless you've got facts to back up whatever you're about to say next.'

'And what makes you sure I've got more to say?'

There was a cockiness about Simon Potts that Tremayne didn't like. Smart arses didn't appeal to him, made him suspicious, determined him to delve deeper.

'You've just defamed your wife, hardly the attribute of a loving husband.'

'And what makes you think we're loving. Just because we live together doesn't mean we're fond of each other.'

'The Sutherlands had a liberated approach to marital fidelity,' Clare said. 'You and your wife included?'

'My wife's a larger-than-life character, always gilding the lily, making out that she's something she's not, and yes, I know about her sidling up to your inspector, getting him hot under the collar.'

'I suggest you take this seriously,' Tremayne said. 'Homicide is not a laughing matter, nor is it a time for obstructing the police, and that's what you're doing, Mr Potts.'

'Am I?' Potts said. 'Jacob Montfield's dead, so is his sister, and as for Sutherland…'

'What about Sutherland? Any truth in your wife's statement that he had spent time upstairs in your marital bed?'

'No truth at all.'

Simon Potts was either a good liar or a deluded and naïve fool; Clare wasn't sure which. To her, Marjorie Potts was guilty, not of an actionable crime, but a suspect morality, and the husband, if not condoning, was accepting.

'Then why your ambivalence towards Sutherland?'

'If you intend to give me a lesson on morality, love thy neighbour, figuratively or not, you're wasting your time,' Potts said. 'If Sutherland wanted to spend his time taking Deidre on a flight through the cosmos every time he came over, that was up to her and him.'

Clare found Simon Potts dislikeable, a crudity about his speech which sounded like velvet but grated like sandpaper. She almost felt sympathy for his wife and her flirtatious manner.

'So far, you've spoken a lot, said nothing,' Tremayne said. 'Either your wife was sleeping with Sutherland, or she wasn't. It's the truth we're after, not this skirting the issue. And why Jacob Montfield died and why Derek Sutherland was buried in the garden next door. Was he involved with your wife or not?'

'I never killed him; you can't pin that on me,' Potts said.

'The first true words you've uttered today. Not that we can prove which of the Montfields did, but then if you had done it, why bury the man's body in the Montfield's garden.'

'Did Deidre claim to have killed him?'

'She did, but that may be misguided loyalty to the memory of her dead brother, or she believed that her involvement with the man led to confrontation and death.'

'I wouldn't know either way, and besides, is it relevant? The man's dead, no great loss to society.'

'Why do you refer to Sutherland in such a manner, and the truth with the shed would come in handy?'

'Okay, I knew he was making a play for Marjorie, not that she wouldn't have encouraged him.'

'Yet you believe that your wife was no more than a flirt?'

'I suppose I do.'

'I'm afraid we don't believe you,' Clare said. 'Your wife is not the innocent that you make out, and further denial does you no credit, and if our enquiries lead us to the conclusion that you are somehow involved in any part of this charade, it will not go well for you.'

Simon Potts sat quietly. He was in reflective mode, thinking through the facts, what to say next, feeling nervous, shaking a little.

Tremayne and Clare observed him. They understood the body language, the posture, the quietude of the man; they waited for Potts to speak.

Potts realised that unpardonable sins once spoken about could never be forgotten, the memories of the past coming back to haunt, to transform, to distort, to be misinterpreted, to destroy.

'Marjorie has strayed,' Potts said. 'No man wants to admit to the truth, but she's wired that way, and because I love her, always have, always will, I can forgive and forget as long as I am not reminded of it, but now, here, in this police station with the two of you, it is too painful. I don't believe I can continue.'

'With Marjorie or with us?' Clare asked.

'It wasn't long after we married that I found out that her nature was amorous, whereas mine was sedentary and measured.'

'Is Sutherland and your wife true?'

'It is a question I've never asked my wife, but I believe it is probable.'

'No proof?' Tremayne asked. He did not feel empathy, an emotion that did not sit strongly within him, but he sensed the truth. And that the man might have within him facts that would turn the investigation of Jacob Montfield's death upside down, leading the investigation in a hitherto unknown direction, to a place that might get murkier, more muddied, more soulful. It was something that he, as a detective inspector, was prepared for, a direction he wanted.

'I never went looking, just accepted it the first time, and it wasn't often. A happy home was more important than raising tension by an open accusation, hoping that in time she would change.'

'She's older now, less enthusiastic,' Clare said.

'No less enthusiastic, just less frequent, and if you ask me, honestly, if she was after your inspector, then I believe she probably was.'

'But you denied it before, came in here dismissive of us and the murders of Montfield and Sutherland,' Tremayne said.

'Feigned sorrow serves no one. I knew of Sutherland, despised him for the time he spent with Marjorie, admired him when it had been Deidre.'

'An ambiguous statement.'

'We all admire the successful person, as long as their success is not a result of our sorrow. Sutherland crossed that line; I hated him for what he had done, as I did Jacob, the reason for the conflict over the boundary between our properties.'

'You grant that arguing over a sliver of land was unimportant?'

'It was. After all, it had been the council's planning department that made the error in the first place, but I was pig-headed, unwilling to listen to reason, and that caused the conflict to escalate with Jacob.'

'Why the antagonism against him?' Clare asked.

'I caught him with her once.'

'With your wife?'

'Yes.'

'We've found no evidence of a woman in his life,' Tremayne said.

'Jacob Montfield, are you certain of this?' Clare asked.

'I admit that Jacob seems an unlikely contender.'

'Let's come back to Sutherland and Deidre,' Clare continued. 'If he's sleeping with your wife, then it would be at the same time as he was with Deidre. She, naively as it appears, had believed it was eternal, and there he is, nipping next door for desserts or maybe the main course. She must have known.'

'Shakespeare penned it, "Love is blind", and that's what it was with Deidre, a lovesick puppy, totally besotted with the man.'

'How come you know so much about him?'

'It was Deidre, waxing lyrical with Marjorie over the garden fence, or in our house or theirs, and Marjorie is nodding her head, agreeing with the woman, congratulating her on her choice of man.'

'Deceitful?'

'Is it? Marjorie didn't want the man, not in the long term. Quite frankly, she didn't like the man too much, thought he was a bore, talking about Deidre. Strange isn't it, two people who had little in common: a man who put it about and a frustrated and timid woman in love for the first time in her life, and it's Sutherland who feels more for her than she for him.'

'Maybe it was the first time he had known purity,' Clare opined. 'After all, his wife was the more enthusiastic in attending wife swaps, and then your wife, hardly pure as the driven snow.'

'I never evaluated it that closely, but you're right. There's Deidre, up on a pedestal, unplucked fruit, ripe and ready for eating, and Marjorie, bruised and fast approaching her use-by date.'

'It was a long time ago; she was nowhere close to that date back then.'

'Literally, I would agree, but figuratively, she was.'

'How do you know so much?' Tremayne asked.

'I used to talk to him sometimes, out in the street, occasionally down the pub if he invited me.'

'Taking into account all that you've said about the man, you were willing to have a drink with him.'

'I haven't said anything about him, only what others thought, good and bad. You can't blame a man, can you?'

Clare could, but she was a police officer, personal opinion accounted for nothing, only what Potts was saying, and he did appear to be speaking the truth. Even so, there was more depth to what he had revealed so far. Clare knew that her inspector wouldn't rest until he had drawn every last bit of concealed information from the man.

'Let's get to the crux of the matter,' Tremayne said. Clare knew she had been right, and her senior was preparing to up the tempo, to make Potts feel the heat, to make him sweat, to push him into a literal corner from which the only way out was by talking.

'I've given you all that I know,' Potts said.

'Let us lay the facts out before us.' Tremayne drew a phantom spreadsheet on the table with a finger, a way of reinforcing the mental process. 'One, you tell us you know nothing; you don't care who's died, a strike against you. No one's disinterested when there's a murder, so why didn't you come home straight away to assist your wife, to express your condolences to Deidre over the death of her brother.'

Tremayne traced his finger down one line on the phantom spreadsheet. 'Two, when we drag you into the police station, you sit there and tell us your wife was pure, that Sutherland was a person you knew only in passing.'

'Spousal privilege. I do not intend to condemn my wife.'

'It doesn't apply, not unless either you or your wife have committed a crime.'

'We haven't.'

'Then what's all this nonsense about Jacob Montfield taking liberties? Why are you trying to protect your wife?'

'I'm not. It's me, don't you understand?'

'Understand what?'

'You're meant to be the investigators. Marjorie's not the problem.'

Clare started to understand, but she was sure that Tremayne hadn't.

'Medical?' Clare asked.

'Neurological. A car accident disturbed a part of the brain, rendered me neutered.'

'Literally?'

'Marjorie's still got her needs. I can't solve mine, but she can hers.'

'She has your permission?'

'With discretion, in the family home, not outside, and never blatantly. Deidre knew about it, so did Jacob, but no one else.'

'How did they know?'

'I told them, asked Jacob to do us a favour. After all, neither Marjorie nor myself wanted to separate.'

'What the hell are you both talking about?' Tremayne asked.

'I believe that Mr Potts is telling us that he's medically impotent, the reason that he tolerated Marjorie's indiscretions,' Clare said.

'Why didn't you say so in the first place?' Tremayne said, looking over at Simon Potts.

'It's not something a man is proud of.'

'Are you saying that you invited Jacob to share your wife's bed?'

'You make it sound clinical. It wasn't that, but I loved my wife, still do, and I couldn't begrudge her.'

'As for you?'

'I distract myself with work and exhaustion. That's why I spend so much time away from home, not playing the field, not attempting to be apart from Marjorie, just because I have to. Marjorie understands, as did Jacob.'

'He was a reluctant seduction?'

'Somewhat. Apparently, once he warmed up, he was fine, but it wasn't for long, and then after that, there was one Sutherland or another.'

'Not only Derek?'

'Not often, and most of the time Marjorie would meet somewhere discreet, casual sex, release the pent-up emotions and then come home.'

'And you were fine with this?'

'The hell I was. I hated it, but what could I do? Life is about compromise. Marjorie with me, even under such circumstances, was better than the alternative.'

'Why didn't Marjorie tell us?' Clare asked.

'Out of respect for me. It may have been wrong of us to keep this hidden, but it's not something either of us wants to talk about; I'm sure you understand.'

'You can prove this?' Tremayne said.

'I can give you copies of my medical records, the name of a neurologist who will confirm.'

'Sorry I pushed you, but we needed the truth.'

'I understand. I only wish it had remained secret.'

'It will,' Clare said, 'but there remains the deaths of Jacob Montfield and Derek Sutherland.'

'I can't help you there, nor can Marjorie.'

After the man confessed his medical condition, Tremayne no longer had the heart to press him further. He wished Simon Potts well, shook his hand, and walked out of the police station with him.

Clare remained seated, awaiting Tremayne's return, aware that questions remained but that they would wait for another day. For now, she could only feel sorry for Marjorie and her husband.

Chapter 13

Marjorie Potts sat in the chair that her husband had recently vacated. The flirtation that she had exhibited at her house was no longer present. Her dismissive attitude to the deaths next door was gone. She was, Clare thought, contrite, aware of her lackadaisical approach to two murders, conscious of the fool she had made of herself.

'My husband's told you?' Marjorie said.

'He did,' Tremayne's replied. 'Unfortunately, we had to probe.'

It was a remarkable admission by Tremayne, something that Clare didn't often see, that the man felt sympathy for the woman and her husband. Unusual it may have been, but she was pleased to see it.

Regardless of his medical condition and her needs, Marjorie Potts and her husband, Simon, had reached a compromise. Others would criticise, call Marjorie wanton, her husband a snivelling wretch of a man, but they would be wrong; Clare could see that. Happiness was an illusion, a construct, more suited to fairy tales and movies. In life, the reality is that people need to make the best of what they've got, strive for more, accept what is unattainable, and be content. And that was what Marjorie and Simon Potts had, an arrangement that allowed them to be together.

'You want to know about Jacob?' Marjorie said as she shifted uneasily on her seat.

Clare called out to a young constable walking by the door. 'If you could, three teas,' she said.

The room's atmosphere was emotional, not only for Marjorie, who was dressed conservatively and wore a navy-blue coat, but also for Clare. The evening before, watching a movie on the television, she had broken down when the heroine walked out on the hero.

In the past, a dead body, a sad story about why someone had killed another, and she would have been impassive, but that was real life, not a movie. But now, with Marjorie, Clare could understand the Potts' dilemma and imagine the emotional trauma they must have gone through.

'In your own time,' Clare said.

Marjorie took a sip of her tea; her hand was shaking, and her face was pale. 'We'd been married for a few years by then, no children, but we had come to terms with that. After the accident, not Simon's fault, he was a changed man, not the easy-going nature as before, but still loving; still the man I married.'

'Yet incomplete,' Tremayne said.

'It wasn't as if he didn't care, but he never felt the need for that closeness again. He had tests, and you can lead a horse to water, but you can't be certain it will drink. And that was how it was with Simon. It's neurological, and after that, he'd spend more time away from home, avoiding the inevitable.'

'How did you resolve the issue?'

'It was Simon who suggested it. He could see how sad I was, and our bond convinced him a solution needed to be reached. That's when the idea came up. I hated it at the time, but that was when he approached Jacob.'

'How did you feel about that?'

'Jacob wasn't my type, never was, but any ship in a storm and discretion was important to both of us.'

'You agreed?'

'Eventually, although it took more convincing Jacob for him to be a party to it. You see, Jacob wasn't interested in me or anyone else. He was solitary, friendly if you met him, social even, but a person content with himself, reclusive if life would let him.'

'He became your lover.'

'In time, and even then, to him, it was passionless, to me, unsatisfactory, but it's true, I did have a relationship with him.'

'For how long?' Clare asked.

'No more than six or seven months, and then he would only come over every other week, a Thursday night.'

'Deidre's reaction?'

'Not that it was important, but she was non-committal. Remember, Deidre had her issues, but even though she wouldn't admit to it, a more measured woman than me, more able to control her emotions, she was jealous. Not of Jacob, you would understand, but of life in general, of my ability to rationalise, to get on with it, to put the morality of it to one side, to deal with the status quo.'

'After Jacob ceased to come over?'

'Life moved on. Every few months, there had been someone, not that I ever became close to them. I still wanted my husband, but he wasn't there, not in that way, and he did try, visited specialists, went to psychoanalysis, even electric shock treatment. He was sexually dead, yet we remained together and will do so.'

'Derek Sutherland?' Tremayne said.

'Deidre never knew, and it was only the once. He appeared on her doorstep one day, expecting her to be there, but Deidre had gone away, a friend in London to visit, or that was what she said. Derek had thought her to be at home for whatever reason, but she wasn't. I saw him outside, called him over, not that I intended to seduce him.'

'One thing led to another?' Clare asked. Marjorie's description of what had transpired had been clinical, not base, as if she was discussing a plumber fixing a leaky tap in the kitchen rather than sexual congress with the next-door neighbour's lover.

'I'm certain that Derek cared for Deidre, and I never knew the history of his wife and their philandering.'

'Would you regard yourself as promiscuous?' Tremayne asked.

'A good Catholic schoolgirl, not at all. My appetite is healthy, no more than others, but circumstance cause people to do things they would not normally consider, even murder, I assume.'

'Murder is often committed by those closest to the victim, even their next-door neighbours, and from what you've told us, your relationship with Jacob could well have caused psychological damage to his well-being.'

'I believe, Inspector, that you are melodramatic. I slept with Jacob, that's all, no romantic dinners with candles, no sweet words. I can't even remember us looking at each other, and then Jacob's out of the house and over the back fence.'

'Your husband?'

'He wasn't in the house when Jacob came over. Simon would spend more time away from home, not that I blamed him, who could. It wasn't something we talked about, and when Jacob ceased to visit, nothing was said.'

'Why was Jacob murdered?' Clare asked.

'I don't know. After he stopped coming over, I don't believe we spoke again. And then, Derek Sutherland's friendly with Deidre, and she's beaming ear-to-ear like a Cheshire cat. That's when I spoke to her the most, and then, he's gone, no idea where.'

'You slept with him. Didn't you keep in contact?'

'It was only the one time, and even though you might not believe me, I did feel guilt afterwards.'

'The issue with the shed?'

'It was Jacob, not us. Eventually, his attitude changed, no longer the neighbourly chat, only antagonistic. As if he was punishing us for destroying his ordered life, the disciplined regularity of it.'

'He could have said no to you,' Clare said.

'I've thought about that since he died,' Marjorie said.

'What did you conclude?'

'I think he was more curious than interested. It's unnatural not to want affection, to feel a closeness to another human being. He was, after all, a scientist with a scientist's enquiring mind, and there I was, a test subject, a chance for him to find out what it was about life that he was missing, that he had never felt desire for.'

'Are you certain?'

'About what?'

'You being the only woman he had known.'

'I was certainly the first.'

'Apparently the last,' Tremayne said. 'I get the feeling you're holding something back. Are you trying to protect your husband?'

'It was a long time ago,' Marjorie said.

'Love, as with hate, transmutes over the years; one becomes more intense, the other, inconsequential, or as could be the case with your husband, more vengeful, taking root in his psyche, in his subconscious, the memory of you and him, nightmare visions of you with

Jacob. Who knows what goes through the troubled mind?'

Marjorie took a sip of tea, even though it had gone cold. 'I'm frightened for Simon,' she said.

'Do you believe he killed Jacob?'

A tremulous voice, almost a whisper. 'I can't believe it, not of Simon, but you're right. Simon's hatred of Jacob has become pathological over the years, not because of me, but Jacob was whole, whereas he was not. You see, Simon has improved mentally over the years. It had been a physical impairment caused by a mental condition, but while the mental has waned, the physical has not. He's still physically incapable. That may also be due to age or poor health, but when he saw Jacob, a man who had it all, shuffling along the way he did, and then, there was Simon, upstanding, hardworking, a credit to society. He saw himself as a eunuch in a harem.'

'Then I'll repeat the question – did Simon kill Jacob Montfield?'

'He could have, but I hope I'm wrong.'

'Loyalty to your husband is one thing; homicide is another,' Clare said.

'I know, so does Simon. He is guilty of love and hate, pride and despair, possibly of violence.'

'Even after Jacob had died, and with our questioning, you still made it uncomfortable for me,' Tremayne said.

'I was only teasing; you must have known that.'

'Were you?'

'Inspector, I'm sure you're a good man, but you're not my type.'

Clare could see the putdown, but she didn't believe the woman for a moment. Marjorie Potts was a woman who needed attention, and Tremayne had been her target.

Chapter 14

Tremayne, tired of trying to make sense of the imponderables, got up from the chair in his office, put on his jacket, checked his cigarettes and walked out of Homicide, only pausing on the way to tell Clare to meet him in the pub in fifteen minutes.

She would have preferred to have gone home to Clive but knew that Tremayne needed the ambience of a pub and a pint of beer, a willing ear to bounce ideas off, to formulate, to debate, to contradict, to see past the forest and out into the green pastures beyond. The investigation needed clarity, a paring away of the superfluous, to focus on what could be believed with a high degree of certainty, what couldn't.

Before leaving the office, Clare phoned Clive to let him know that she would be a couple of hours more.

On more than one occasion in the office when writing reports, she had surfed the internet, read up on baby food and cots, even on breastfeeding, and postnatal depression, something her mother had experienced, according to her father.

She doubted she would; after all, she had dealt with the violent death of a previous lover, and even though she had been obsessively sad, it had not manifested itself as anything more than a natural reaction to a traumatic situation. Since then, she had seen the fragility of humanity, the basest of emotions, the inevitable aftermath of violent crime.

Besides, she intended to return to work after a few months, be back with Tremayne, and become a police inspector, the same rank as her senior. But she also knew that life is not static, and a child changes a person, as does time.

In the office, the vultures were hovering, waiting for Tremayne to falter, for him to fail, to suffer a medical emergency from which there was no coming back.

The superintendent had made it clear that the senior investigating officer's position in Homicide was hers once Tremayne retired, as was her promotion to an inspector. But there was still the office politics, divisive and corruptible, open to sycophancy and underhanded actions, the inevitable embellishing of an applicant's work record, qualifications and experience, and careful crafting of the CV to obscure the negatives.

Clare, not a skilful political animal, knew there was misogyny in the station: the pushing past her in the corridor, the rudeness, the leering eyes, the sexist comments; none of which had caused her to lodge an official statement, aware that the resulting ostracism would achieve nothing, only ensure a reputation as a troublemaker. If Tremayne weren't in the station, she'd still have to fight for his position, regardless of the superintendent.

Clare arrived at the pub to find Tremayne enjoying a pint of his favourite beer, a glass of red wine for her on the table. She pushed it to one side and ordered a glass of orange juice. There would be no more alcohol while she was pregnant.

'I've been going over it,' Tremayne said. Whereas he wasn't smoking in the pub, no longer permissible by law, Clare could tell as he spoke that he had had a cigarette before entering. She didn't like the smell, but although she had become used to it, now she felt nauseous. Excusing herself, she went outside the pub, a balmy night, warm enough not to be wrapped up in a heavy coat, and took in the fresh air.

She knew she would continue to work up until the last month before her child's birth, if possible, but there would be fewer late nights out when there was a frost on the ground, no more trekking across a water-sodden field after heavy rainfall to look at a body, and she would need to spend more time in the office. There were changes afoot, a certainty that she and her inspector knew was coming. On the last day before she took maternity leave, Clare knew that the usually unemotional Tremayne, especially with her, would put his arms around her and wish her well.

To Clare, Tremayne was almost as important as her father, more so than her mother, with whom she had a troubled relationship.

Tremayne came out with his pint and sat down on a wooden bench with her.

'It makes no sense,' Clare said as she sipped her juice.

'Which part?' Tremayne said.

'All of it.'

'I would agree, but we need to focus on a particular aspect, drill down deep, tighten up on it or dismiss it. Remember, it's Jacob Montfield's murder that we're interested in, not Derek Sutherland's, nor Deidre's death.'

'You can't separate one from the other,' Clare said.

'There's an interconnecting thread, but it's weak.'

'Are you suggesting that Jacob's death is unrelated?'

'If it is, then it presents a new set of issues for which we have no motive.'

'We didn't before. Killing the man for something that happened two decades ago has no validity, and besides, if Jacob had slept with Marjorie, then why the anger from Simon Potts. She's not let the grass grow beneath her feet since then, and Potts has been aware of that, even if not fully cognisant of the details.'

'Marjorie said her husband was pathological in his hatred of Jacob.'

'And Jacob wasn't the only known lover of Marjorie.'

'And you weren't interested in her?' Clare said, indulging in a sarcastic retort.

'Never,' Tremayne said, a scowl on his face, the previous spring in his step as an object of desire sufficiently deflated now.

'A random killing?' Clare said. 'Someone passing through the city, a local nutcase taking the opportunity to make his mark?'

'The local idiots, and there's more than a few, don't go around killing someone just for the fun of it, and if they did, they would brag about it one way or the other. And besides, you're missing one fundamental fact.'

'The bulletproof vest, I know,' Clare said.

'We know it was new, and according to Forensics, it hadn't been worn by the man for more than three or four days, even though he might have bought it in the last year.'

'Important when it was bought?'

'It could be, although we haven't found where nor a date. Online shopping has dealt us a blow; it could have come from anywhere in the country or overseas.'

'Except that Jacob Montfield didn't use a computer, not in the last few years.'

'Do we know that? Have we found a computer?'

'Deidre never had one, and there wasn't one in the house.'

'But there are in the libraries. Have we checked?'

'No reason to, not until now.'

'And if he had bought the vest, it still doesn't explain why and who had threatened him. After all, the man didn't have a lifestyle that guaranteed a long life, even if he wanted it.'

'We've accepted Jacob's lifestyle, clearly the result of trauma, but what was it? It hardly seems that spending time with Marjorie was enough to turn him, but then, the death of Derek would,' Clare said.

'It doesn't explain the shed; why it wasn't in the right place. Even if we agree that Jacob was antagonistic towards the Potts, why not put the shed in the right place? After all, there's a body that needs covering, and what about the story that he had done it so Deidre would have somewhere to say her farewells, to get down on her knees and pray, to put flowers, or whatever someone does after they've killed the love of their life.'

Clare, tired from a long day, wanted to be back home. She yawned. For some reason, she wasn't interested, not in the Montfields nor the Potts, especially not in the Hardcastles.

'I'm boring you, aren't I?' Tremayne said.

'A day with people I don't particularly agree with leaves a sour taste in the mouth.'

'Give me an honest criminal any day. Someone who doesn't attempt to deceive us with half-truths?'

'Honour among thieves?'

'You know it as well as I do. Catch a thief, and once the proof's indisputable, they're singing like a bird.'

'They accept their punishment, albeit reluctantly, but those we're dealing with don't. They think they're above it, justified in thinking that killing Jacob Montfield was not an issue, and they'll be answerable to a higher court when the time comes.'

'Or they're stark-staring mad.'

'Who's mad? Who's not?' Clare said.

'The most unlikely.'

'Simon Potts?'

'He sounds plausible, spun us a tale about how he's struck low, an unfortunate event in his life.'

'It's hardly castration.'

'Isn't it? A man in the prime of life, separated from what made him whole. No man can remain sane, and the idea that work and career are substitutes is just that. Potts is a marked man,' Tremayne said.

***

The purpose of a ballistic bulletproof vest, the type that Montfield had been wearing, was to give protection from a handgun, a knife, also a syringe and blunt trauma. It was not designed to protect against all weaponry, nor was it invincible. The type that the man had worn was similar in construction to that worn by the police, not cumbersome and weighed less than six pounds.

The number of suppliers in the country totalled no more than twelve; Montfield had bought his brand and type of vest from only a possible three. Clare, who had arrived in the office not feeling as well as she should, was concerned that she should have taken the day off but couldn't concede the possibility.

She found out from the first company that it wasn't illegal to wear body armour in the UK without authorisation and that Montfield's vest was mid-range.

However, they had no record of a sale to Jacob Montfield or anyone else in Salisbury.

The second company, not as helpful as the first, advised that a private individual wearing a ballistic vest served no purpose given the country's low level of violent crime. However, it would have helped keep the wearer warm during a cold night. As with the first, they had not sold the jacket.

The third company, a pleasant woman on the line, had gone through the selection process with Clare, the reason a man who lived on the street would have chosen the vest that he had. Clare didn't need to be told the ins and outs of the relative merits of the product range, but the woman on the other end of the phone was keen to talk, and Clare wasn't willing to ask her to stop. After all, how often had someone's ramblings revealed a hitherto unknown fact or focussed on an area previously overlooked.

'Yes, that's the one I would have bought,' the woman said as she wrapped up her talk.

'But did the man buy one from you?' Clare asked, finally getting to what interested her most.

'We've sold ninety-four of those in the last month – fifty to a security company up north, another twenty to a police station in the West Country. Sometimes police and prison officers buy their own, not wanting someone's hand-me-down, especially those in the prisons. Not much demand from the homeless, as you've no doubt gathered.'

'The man in question was educated and articulate. He bought a vest for a reason; as to why we don't know.'

'He could have been neurotic, read too much on the internet, watched the negativity on the television, believed it's coming to a street near him. Statistically, it's not.'

Clare needed to end the phone call; she required the woman to focus. 'Vests to Salisbury, a one-off in the last couple of months, one year maximum, assuming the man had kept it packaged,' she said.

'We sold one, a credit card, delivered to an address in Salisbury, name of Montfield.'

Chapter 15

Jacob Montfield and Derek Sutherland had worked together in scientific research. Montfield had been the senior in rank, and what they had worked on was top secret and would remain so, a fact emphasised by a well-meaning woman in HR when Tremayne and Clare visited the research establishment where the two men had worked.

Gustav Kempler, the director, who they finally got to, after Tremayne had protested that it was murder, and they wanted the person in charge, said, 'Sutherland was a solid and dedicated man; Montfield was the genius, but it was before my time.'

'Jacob Montfield and Derek Sutherland, precisely what were they working on?' Tremayne asked. He wasn't in the mood for another lecture on official secrets, nor did he want to hear it was cutting-edge, state of the art, and not in the national interest to reveal what the two men were involved in.

Although his English was impeccable, Kempler had a solid German accent. 'Jacob Montfield was a brilliant man. Eccentric, as they often are. His behaviour after he left here did not surprise many.'

'Derek Sutherland?' Clare asked.

'A different type of person. Not of genius calibre, but an impressive analytical mind, able to take Montfield's ideas and research from the theoretical to the practical.'

'And after Montfield left?'

'I'm not sure the question has relevance,' Kempler said. 'You must realise this was a long time ago, and I had only been here for a short while, a minor functionary back then, not in this elevated status that you find me now.'

'Solving the murder of Sutherland has proven to be difficult, although we know for a fact that Montfield buried his body, possibly dealt the blow that killed him.'

'I'm aware that Sutherland had a wandering eye,' Kempler said.

'Here, in this building?'

'His lifestyle was known.'

'How did you come to know, and who would have told you?'

'It was general knowledge. Not sure who, probably Sutherland, but for two men, seemingly with little in common apart from their work, he was good friends with Montfield.'

'Montfield's sister?' Clare asked.

'I'm certain I never met her, no idea how she came to be involved with Sutherland. I did hear she was matronly.'

'She was, but it appears that Derek Sutherland swayed her; a changed woman for a while, up until he died. After that, she became the bane of the neighbourhood.'

'As I said, early days for me here, so I'm not the best person to talk to, not sure who would be better.'

'This research they were working on?' Clare asked. 'It seems important for us to know. And besides, it's been a long time. Surely it can't be relevant now.'

'It's still secret, and if I told you, then I'd leave myself open to censure, a possible criminal charge.'

'We've got two dead people, both murdered, and Montfield's sister, dead as well. Our patience is wearing thin, and quite frankly, Mr Kempler, your reticence is counter-productive.'

Kempler picked up his phone, explained the situation to someone at the other end of the line, raised his voice in frustration before ending the phone conversation, and looked across at the two police officers.

'That was a lawyer we employ, advises us on patents, legal matters, interpretation in this instance on the Official Secrets Act. He's not satisfied, but he'll go along with me.'

'Now? All that you know?' Tremayne said.

Kempler opened his laptop, checked his emails, and closed the lid.

'Approved?' Clare asked.

'I asked for a confirmation email from the lawyer. Not that he'll back me up if it goes pear-shaped, and he's written that he's advised me, told me that it still needs further clarification before speaking to the police.'

'But you intend to,' Tremayne said.

'Permission won't be forthcoming, not this year, and besides, as you said, a long time ago. Still pertinent, though.'

'Your career is at risk if you tell us more?' Clare asked, uncomfortable as the office was too hot for her. But she was a serving police officer, and in Homicide, you didn't show weakness, the same as Tremayne would not, although there was a tiredness in his face that was undeniable.

'A reprimand, rap over the knuckles, probably shown the door,' Kempler said. 'But let's not dwell on those, not now, and besides, politics and secrets go hand in hand.'

'Similar to the police force,' Tremayne said. He had a reluctant liking for Kempler, a man after his own heart, willing to bend the rules, not controlled by the politically correct brigade, not shy of taking a position, even at the cost of his job.

'Internal politics, can't get away from it,' Kempler agreed. 'But that's not why you're here. You want to know if their work has any bearing on the death of one at the hand of another.'

'We do,' Clare said.

'Montfield was always eccentric, genius verging on madness, and Sutherland, more practical, a bon vivant, lover of life. A charming man, very popular, but everyone deferred to Montfield. He was the star.'

'But precisely what was it that they were doing here?' Tremayne asked, not wanting to hear anymore what a wonderful person Montfield was. To him, the man was a murderer, and that wasn't wonderful, but the complete opposite.

'Research as I said, highly secret, defence of the nation.'

'Specifics?' Clare said, frustrated with the evasive Kempler. It wasn't the first time they had encountered the brick wall of bureaucracy and the Official Secrets Act, but to her, it was a murder enquiry, and certain easings could be agreed upon.

'A tactical advantage,' Kempler responded, 'not that I can tell you much, not sure that I understand the depth of what they were doing.'

'You're the director,' Tremayne said.

'Silos, don't you understand? So secretive that many people didn't know the whole.'

'Spies?'

'Not spies, but surveillance, updated tracking technology and monitoring equipment, satellite-based, some terrestrial. The need for each nation to be ahead of the other, to maintain the edge, just in case.'

'The cold war was over even before I reached puberty,' Clare said. 'It's passé, espionage, the fodder of fiction stories, dashing men in flash cars and buxom women.'

'I wouldn't know too much about the cold war, I grew up on the other side of the wall, but the game continues. Assuredly, it's conducted differently now, no longer men in big coats, hat-wearing, ready to kill or be killed. It's technology now, the ability to zoom in on a room from a distance, to tap a mobile phone conversation. I grew up, as I said, on the other side of the wall, no more than five kilometres from it in East Berlin; I remember those hapless fools dying as they crossed, desperate for the freedom of the West.'

'You're here,' Tremayne said.

'Those of us who lived under repression never embraced it. I was never a communist, nor was my family, but we lived by the rules, kept our heads down and survived. I'm here, the director, a loyal subject of this country.'

'Patriotism aside, the extent of Montfield and Sutherland's work? Technologically superior to others?'

'For a while, it might have been, and Montfield and Sutherland had their faults, but they had been security cleared, no concern there. Due to his lifestyle, Sutherland could have been open to blackmail, but it was an open secret, and he wasn't ashamed either. I know about his behaviour, full dossiers on both men's backgrounds, financial status, marriages, health, whether they got drunk or not, who they slept with.'

'Due to the nature of their work and their obvious skills, peccadillos were tolerated,' Clare said. She looked around the room, bookshelves along two walls, a window in the third, a door in the fourth. Kempler, she judged to be competent, not evasive, but a bureaucrat, a stickler for paperwork, no doubt a man who knew the cost of running the establishment and gained satisfaction from doing so. However, she wasn't sure he had been open with them, not out of duplicity, but because specific facts had to be swept under the carpet.

Tremayne ended the interview. 'We'll be back with additional questions,' he said to Kempler. A brief handshake, and they were out of the room and walking across the car park to Clare's car, the nominated driver, whenever it was the two of them.

'I don't reckon Kempler is open with us,' Clare said.

'He's not. You noticed he averted his eyes when he was lying?'

'It could have been a habit, thinking through what he was about to say.'

'Lying through his teeth. No doubt growing up in East Germany, you would have had to,' Tremayne said as he took out a cigarette from a packet.

'How old back then?'

'Late teens, early twenties, old enough to have been seduced by the propaganda, and probably, not that we'll find out, a solid party man, willing to run errands, commit acts of treachery, all in the cause, and that would have brought certain benefits.'

'But he's got security clearance in England?'

'Has he? I suppose he has. Montfield, the genius, keeping it to himself, letting Sutherland in on some of it, and then Kempler, a junior back then, fretting, trying to get closer, possibly not understanding even if Montfield had given him a guided tour.'

'It opens possibilities,' Clare said.

'Montfield's death, officially sanctioned?'

'Almost impossible to prove, and if it was, why now? Technology doesn't stand still, obsolete even before it's released.'

'Unless it's cutting-edge, not easily replicable.'

'Beyond our understanding,' Clare said, stating the obvious.

***

The possibility that Montfield's death might not have been a random killing and could be due to his research strengthened. Although there remained Sutherland's murder years earlier, and if someone had found out the story of his death, even where he was buried, it could also be a reason for Montfield's demise.

Sutherland's widow opened the door to her house. The man she had subsequently married was not there.

'We've got three possibilities for Montfield's death,' Tremayne said.

'Which are?' the widow said.

'A random killing, someone who gets kicks out of killing vagrants, but that's not likely, statistically rare in this country.'

'And the second?'

'Were you aware of their work, Montfield and your first husband?'

'Highly secretive, complex, cutting-edge. No more than that, and he rarely spoke about it. Sometimes elated when it was going well, discouraged when it wasn't.'

'We can't dispute that,' Clare said. 'We came away from the place where they worked none the wiser, although more than you knew.'

'He might have said more, but I'm not technically minded, not that well-educated, and it would have been over my head.'

'We'll accept that for now, which brings us to the third option.'

'Which is?'

'That you or someone close to you killed Montfield, a delayed response which could only mean that Montfield or his sister had revealed the truth to a person or persons unknown and that it had filtered down to the murderer.'

'How dare you?' the woman replied.

'Statistically, a loved one is the most likely murderer,' Tremayne said. 'But that's not the case here. However, Montfield's death brings us to another matter. Not a difficult man to kill, not in his condition, the life he led.'

'But why?' the woman remonstrated. 'His sister killed my husband. Why kill the man?'

'It's not relevant, one or the other, a long time ago. It could be that his sister mentioned it to you; women sometimes talk, and how was she to know it was you at her front door?'

'I told you, a long time ago, I knocked at the door, received courtesy, nothing more. And besides, disappearing was out of character, but I didn't give it much thought, not after receiving the letter.'

'But you already knew Derek was dead,' Clare said. 'You told us that before.'

The woman was confused, transposing fact with fiction, a sign of stress, confusion, or delusion. Tremayne could see the woman's blood boiling, her face reddening, arms starting to flail.

'And what would you know, Sergeant? Married to the mayor, a man old enough to be your father. What is it, flat on your back, get him to give you a child, gain the prestige, the wealth when he keels over?'

Shocked by the woman's venom, Tremayne looked over at his sergeant. 'Don't let it rile you,' he said.

'It won't,' Clare said. Although it had, and if she weren't a police officer interviewing a possible suspect in a murder enquiry, she would have slapped the woman hard across the face. Instead, she held her composure, focussed on the woman, and delivered a well-aimed retort.

'Better than what you do, screwing any lecherous pervert. Not that it matters, but I didn't marry for prestige but for the love of a good man who doesn't go sleeping with every bit of stray he can find.'

Tremayne, aware of the animosity and anger, neither conducive to an interrogation, both damaging in a trial if revealed, withdrew, taking Clare with him.

Outside the house. 'Hardly textbook,' he said.

'Sorry about that, but I couldn't take it,' Clare admitted. 'It won't happen again.'

Tremayne knew that it would. He knew he should recommend that she take leave, effective immediately, but wouldn't, not yet.

They were a good team, each playing off the other, and the day she left Homicide for the birth of her child would be, for him, a sad day. The future would not be the same as before. Suddenly, he felt that her time away from policing would sound the death knell to his career and that retirement would beckon and it would be unstoppable.

His sergeant's absence would instigate his, and he wasn't sad for the first time in a long career. He relished his retirement: leisurely drinks down the pub, a chance to sit comfortably at home with Jean, his feet up on a cushion, a warm fire in the corner of the room.

Although he knew that the one reality, pleasant as it might be, came with another, that his generally poor medical condition, coupled with retirement, would mean death. Even that did not concern him, not as much as it once did.

Chapter 16

As with all murder enquiries, Tremayne knew an inevitable lull would occur when all the characters were in play, and there was a surfeit of evidence. It would be when he and his sergeant would need to sit down and go through the facts, one by one, endlessly sifting, attempting to make sense of what they had.

Montfield's death was proving to be complicated. Whether Jacob or Deidre Montfield had committed the murder, Sutherland's death wasn't the primary focus, although it was essential to the station's superintendent. 'Looks bad on the key performance indicators, sloppy police work, poor reporting,' he had said on one of his visits to Homicide.

Not that it concerned Tremayne, not for now.

It was, Tremayne thought, the swansong of him and his sergeant and the current murder enquiry might be his last. However, he knew that his sergeant, better educated than him, was still young enough, would rise higher than him in the police force, chief inspector at least, a probable superintendent.

It was such a mood he took to the Red Lion Hotel that night, the get-together with Jerry and his wife, and yes, Jean still didn't get along with the man's wife; too full of herself, overbearing, a know-it-all, Jean's comment once she and Tremayne were free of the other two.

Even so, they enjoyed the night out, a couple of bottles of wine drunk, a few more pints of beer, and the truth from Jerry that life in Scotland wasn't all heather and thistles and that the climate played havoc with ageing bodies. If they could have afforded it, they would retire to

Spain, allow their bodies to bask in the warmth and shake off the pains.

The philosophical Tremayne would have agreed with Jerry and his wife, but as the night wore on, the previously sombre mood that had beset him started to dissipate.

'You were a good police officer,' Tremayne said, 'capable of more.' By this time, the evening was drawing to a close. Jean was chatting to Jerry's wife, laughing aloud about when they met their husbands, two men both fit and with bushy heads of hair. And now, at the bar, two ageing men. Tremayne with one hand in the small of his back, attempting to alleviate the soreness, and Jerry, his beer gut perilously close to overlapping the top of the bar.

'I should have stayed, felt that policing was a vocation, more than a job. But then, with the money I won, it seemed illogical not to take advantage of it.'

'Wish you hadn't won it?'

'Now I do, but when you're young, you're full of yourself, see yourself as invincible. I could see myself as entrepreneurial, the money to achieve greatness, but what did I achieve? Precious little. Even so, life's what you make of it, good or bad. Nothing certain in life, is there?'

'No,' Tremayne said, thinking of Jacob Montfield, the genius of the man, out on the street pushing a supermarket trolley, wearing a bulletproof vest; of Deidre, ecstatic in love, murderous when crossed, dead in her bed.

Maloney and his problems paled into insignificance.

'You're right there, Tremayne. No doubt your life has been better than mine, a middle-of-the-road police officer.'

Tremayne realised why he and Maloney had never been more than drinking pals in their early years. The man was a master of the subtle putdown, and it jarred. Tremayne knew what he was, and it wasn't the middle of anything. He was, by his admission, and without arrogance, stating it to himself and others, as good an inspector as any other, more diligent, more determined, never one to let a person or a clue get past him.

'It's been great, but we need to go, early start in the morning,' Tremayne said.

Hugs and kisses, promises to meet up soon, a week in Scotland when the weather got warmer.

Outside the Red Lion, Tremayne turned to Jean. 'I smell a rat,' he said.

***

Clare's first job the following day was to conduct a detailed investigation into Jerry Maloney. As Tremayne explained, and memory played a part in it, Jerry might have been a good policeman in his time, but he wasn't always factual in his reporting, and a conviction was more important than the truth.

And then, a financial windfall and the man was gone, not to somewhere sunny and idyllic, but to Scotland, not to a life of luxury, but to strive with a business that wasn't going as well as it should, a remoteness that didn't suit the man's personality.

'I thought he was a friend of yours,' Clare said in the office.

A cold, overcast morning, just her and Tremayne. Early starts were how they liked it, 6 a.m. at the latest, although Clare preferred later in her condition. It concerned her that she wasn't sure if policing would be the primary focus in her life with a child, but she already knew the answer – it wouldn't. Her child would be the main focus.

'A friend of sorts at the time, similar interests.'

'Beer, cigarettes and women, and not necessarily in that order.'

'The order's just about right, but Jerry was more successful with the ladies back then. Apart from Jean, I had no one, but he had plenty, and then he met Christine, and that was him done for.'

'You make it sound as if it was a prison sentence.'

'He used to joke about it at the time, and why Christine, I don't know. She wasn't the easiest back then, mouthy, used to boss him about, and Jean was never keen on her.'

'And now?'

'Jean kept up the pretence last night, but the two women have little in common, other than one's married to a police inspector and the other's married to an ex-police sergeant. Jerry could have gone far. He had the intelligence, thrived on station politics, knew how to make himself look good with the superintendent we had back then.'

'Was the win that much?' Clare asked, not sure what to make of Tremayne's conversation. Two men who had feigned a friendship; two women who got on because of their men, nothing unusual in that.

'Jerry finds the body. Convenient, wouldn't you say, throw us off the scent?'

'But why? What's the point? Why would he come to Salisbury to kill a man, and even if he did, then who knew about him?'

'Someone in Salisbury would be the assumption, but he's been gone a long time. I can't imagine anyone would remember him, and how do you contact a person in Scotland to kill someone back in their home city?'

Clare thought Tremayne's logic unsound, although the man often worked on instinct, as well as evidence. If her inspector thought it was an avenue worth pursuing, that's what she'd do.

In the meantime, while Clare stayed in the police station, Tremayne met with Jerry for a liquid lunch, the type that both men enjoyed.

'Good to get together last night,' Jerry said. 'Christine thought Jean was great, got on like a house on fire, the two of them.'

'That's what Jean said,' Tremayne replied, aware that he hadn't told the truth, and probably his drinking pal hadn't.

Memories came back, Jean and Christine arguing, the two men with fists raised. It had been foolish, Tremayne reflected, but both he and Jerry had been drunk, and Jerry, lecherous, even though he was with Christine, had misbehaved with Jean, touched her backside, a gentle pat. Tremayne, defensive when sober, aggressive when drunk, had grabbed the man and dragged him out of the pub, Christine unaware of the reason, attempting to be the buffer between them, Jean trying to pull her back.

In the light of day, two hungover police officers in the police station, an inspector reprimanding them, and as for the two women, an uneasy get-together for lunch, uncomfortable and stilted conversation, attempting to brush off what had happened.

Tremayne realised why he had been pleased to see Maloney the night Jacob Montfield died. It wasn't because he was a friend but because he reminded him of his youth.

'There's something up, isn't there?' Jerry said.

'You're a suspect.' Tremayne could see no way other than to tell the man. After all, an ex-police officer should have realised the possibility.

'It wasn't me, not that it would have troubled me too much to have killed him.'

'Unemotional?'

'It wasn't that good, the early years in Scotland. Sure, Christine and I were fine, no money problems, but we were frustrated with the move.'

'Not paradise?'

'I enjoyed policing, part of the team, the uniform even, the respect we got.'

'It's changed, not a lot of that nowadays.'

'I realise. Even so, running a hotel wears thin, especially during the winter months.'

'Why Salisbury? Why come back after so many years?'

'Nostalgia, the body tiring, the mind not so robust. Christine's not well, another year, maybe two before she won't be able to travel. She wanted to see the old place again, so did I. Didn't expect you to be here still.'

'Nor did I,' Tremayne said. He downed his beer and nodded to the barman to bring two more pints.

'Ambitious?'

'Not particularly, although chief inspector would have been good; now, it's the degree-educated, wet-behind-the-ears who are the future.'

'Your sergeant?'

'She's got the degree, but she's competent, trained her myself.'

'A couple of bad years when we separated. Christine's looking after the business, and I'm at a loose end, not sure what to do with myself.'

'You had enough money to do nothing, get drunk every day, laid more than most.'

'Not what I wanted. I wanted my wife, but that was out of the question. I ended up in security, third-world, high-end, protecting one corrupt leader after the other.'

'As they stole whatever they could.'

'Whatever, made out they were saviours, but they were grubby hooligans who had made it big. The last one was lynched, not that I was near him at the time, but a couple of colleagues were killed as well.'

'Money good?'

'Unbelievable, but it was more than that. It was exciting, with no restraints, reporting, and the money into an offshore account. It made the money I won pale into insignificance.'

'Kill anyone?'

'In the line of duty. It was the president of a country in Africa. We were protecting him, me and Jamie Barnsworth, Geordie, salt of the earth, do anything for you. Rough and tumble sort of guy, ran with a gang in Newcastle in his teens, lost half an ear in a knife fight, and then he served in the army, behind enemy lines.'

'You sound under-qualified compared to him.'

'I was, but I was a quick learner, tough as nails, tall, and besides, I doctored my CV, told a few lies, as to how as a police officer in the UK had to be handy with their fists, willing to pull the trigger when needed.'

'Neither of which we're allowed to do.'

'The second, I'd agree, but a smack in the face we'd get away with back then. As I remember, you were handy with your fists.'

'I was,' Tremayne said.

'As I was saying, I'd doctored the CV, and the security company knew the guy we were to protect was slime. They gave me a crash course on what I was lacking and sent Barnsworth and me out to Africa, another four as well. We were living in a mansion, swimming pool, food and drink, girls on tap.'

'Christine?'

'Separated, and besides, it's a long way from Scotland. Not that I was into it, not the same as the others, but if you're part of the team, you need to play along. Anyway, to cut a long story short, this guy we're protecting likes to mingle with his people, genuinely believed they loved him.'

'An assassination attempt?'

'I could see the crowd milling around him, patting him on the back, singing his praises, as long as he was handing out money in one hand, a bag of rice in the other. Jamie saw him first and gave me a nod. I look, and there he is, in his twenties, his hands to his sides, not out front and grabbing. To me, that's a weapon he's holding or a grenade, certainly not a lei of flowers to put around the man's neck.

'I get alongside, look down on him. I could see the knife in his hand, a pistol in his belt, a grenade dangling from a belt. He's determined but not too bright.'

'Why do you say that?'

'If he had been brighter, he would have known tall white guys mean security, ex-military and trained to kill, and we weren't inconspicuous.'

'You weren't a killer.'

'Not then, but this guy, he's wiry, small, able to nip through the people in front of him, whereas we would have had to barge.'

'If you did, he'd pull the pin on the grenade.'

'Something like that, but the instructions weren't to neutralise, not from the company nor the president. Our instructions were to kill. Jamie couldn't get to him, nor could the others. It was up to me.'

'You killed him?'

'Had to, no option. I grabbed the knife from him, turned it around and stabbed him, put a cord around his neck for good measure.'

'The crowd?'

'Pandemonium for a few minutes, but they see death too often there. One more wasn't about to faze them.'

'How did you feel afterwards?'

'Ashamed and disgusted. I got drunk that night. I did what I had been paid to do.'

'Someone could have paid to kill Jacob Montfield,' Tremayne said.

'Kill someone in Africa, and they give you a medal. In England, it's a prison cell.'

'That still doesn't mean that you could have killed Montfield without emotion,' Tremayne said.

'After Africa, death meant nothing to me, not even my own.'

'Which means if someone wanted Montfield killing, and they knew of you and Salisbury, you could have done it if the money was sufficient.'

'Tremayne, you're trying it on with me. I wouldn't have done it, not for any money. The man I killed had a wife and four children, grafted eighty hours a week for barely enough to put food on the table.'

Tremayne was willing to give the man the benefit of the doubt, but his sergeant would continue with her investigation, regardless.

Chapter 17

Jerry Maloney had admitted that he was capable of killing another human being. However, Tremayne had to acknowledge the link between his visit to Salisbury and Montfield's murder was tenuous. Whereas it seemed plausible initially, Tremayne discounted it for now and decided to focus their efforts elsewhere.

Clare was to focus on Gloria Hardcastle, and he was to focus on Simon Potts, the dutiful husband of an unfaithful wife, which seemed too good to be true.

Also, more information was required on the research that Montfield and Sutherland had been working on and how it could be relevant twenty years later. Not technologically savvy, even Tremayne knew that it moved fast. As a beat policeman in his day, a two-way radio, but now smartphones. Even he, much as he had resisted, had learnt how to send rudimentary texts, and his sergeant loved the technology, the chance to buy online, to talk to friends around the world, to video conference with a police inspector close to where Jerry and Christine Maloney lived.

The inspector confirmed that the couple were popular and caused no trouble, and their modest hotel was financially viable even if it wasn't full a lot of the time. And yes, the Scottish inspector had admitted, there were marriage difficulties, and the pair had separated for a few years. Apart from that, she had no more to say, and as to why they were in Salisbury, she had no idea.

Tremayne saw the Scottish inspector's response as appropriate, but he had more knowledge of the man, in that Jerry had killed, been in places where others could have killed him, and that he had dealt out violence, received it in return.

'Okay, Yarwood, none of this hiding in the office,' Tremayne said. 'Gloria Hardcastle, push the woman, get under her skin, do whatever.'

Clare took no offence at Tremayne's quip, always appreciating them. 'As long as you don't want me to go with her on one of her night's out.'

'Not in your condition, but…'

'Not for you or anyone else. I disapprove of her, and you know it.'

'So does she. Anyway, get out there, push, cajole, squeeze. She's holding back, so is Marjorie Potts and her husband, and for a motive, it's something to do with what Montfield and Sutherland were working on, I'm sure of that.'

'What if Montfield had something important?'

'Such as?'

'An innovative approach to weapon guidance systems.'

'A long time ago, technology has moved on since then.'

'Maybe it has, but Montfield had a notebook, and his mind was still active. He could have come up with something that people or governments would pay a lot of money for. Just an idea, thinking out loud,' Clare said.

'Not a bad idea, although I had someone look over the notebook, someone who should have found it if there was something of interest.'

'Not if it was coded or too complex,' Clare said.

'Which means, if you're right, that Montfield intended to do something with what was in the book, either to patent it or to sell it to the highest bidder.'

***

Tremayne had to agree that Simon Potts did keep himself busy, constantly on the phone, setting up appointments. He found the man in a hotel room thirty miles from his and Marjorie's house, close enough to drive home of a night, far enough away to allow each to get up to whatever they wanted.

'Bad timing, Inspector,' Potts said. He was dressed in a suit, his hair combed back, his tie straight, in contrast to Tremayne, who, Jean had told him on more than one occasion, looked as if he'd been dragged through a hedge backwards.

'It always is,' Tremayne replied. Inconveniencing someone during a murder enquiry didn't concern him.

'Did you expect me to have a woman with me?'

'It depends, doesn't it?'

'On what? Whether I'm a dud?'

'Whether you are or not, or if you have a bevy of women at your beck and call, doesn't interest me. It's the truth we need.'

'I've already given you that. What more do you want from us? After all, we're not murderers.'

'I'll grant that you aren't, but our investigation depends on total honesty from all parties, no matter how insignificant it might be to them. You knew about your wife and Jacob Montfield?'

'Marjorie's a tactile woman, needs love and closeness, not that I didn't try.'

'Unsuccessfully?'

'Sure, drugs can deal with the physical, but not the mental. I just wasn't interested, not anymore.'

'Still not?'

'You know.'

'I don't, but carry on.'

'Before the accident, it was a great marriage. But afterwards, when I was incapable, we agreed. We didn't want to be apart, nor did we want to end the marriage.'

'So, you agree with your wife to allow her to have affairs.'

'Not affairs, just the occasional dalliance. In all the years since, she's not altered in her love for me.'

'Hypothetically,' Tremayne said, 'if the mental blockage lessened, and you felt a longing for your wife, could you forgive her or forget the other men she had slept with?'

'It's a moot point, but if you need an answer, then probably not.'

'Most men wouldn't.'

'That's what I imagine. It does upset me, stuck in a hotel, attempting to keep busy.'

Tremayne looked around the room. He saw brochures scattered, an open laptop, a framed photo of the man's wife. Tremayne understood the inner trauma, thought back to when he and Jean had separated, and then she had remarried. Wasted years, and for Simon Potts, no respite.

'Marjorie appears to enjoy it,' Tremayne said, not sure if the man had been sincere.

'Maybe she does, and I can't blame her. Who could? We're complex beings, driven by passions, and hers are intact; mine are not.'

'Were you aware of Montfield's research?'

'Something to do with the military?'

'Precisely, and he was a genius.'

'I knew that. Pleasant enough, before he went mad.'

'Before he killed Derek Sutherland, you mean?'

'He was mad before that, a couple of years, although the dates are vague. I had some knowledge he was working on something secret, although he wasn't precise in what it was. Not sure if I would have understood, anyway.'

'Likewise,' Tremayne said. 'He had a notebook with him when he died, It made no sense to me, and I showed it to someone more experienced, a friend of mine.'

'What did he reckon?'

'He thought it could be important, but Montfield might have used a code.'

'Deciphered?'

'Not yet.'

'And you've not managed to pin anything on any of us?'

'A few too many skeletons in the cupboard, but we're used to that. No clear motive, although you could have hated him on account of Marjorie. Did you?'

'Not hate.'

'What word then?'

'Ambivalent, troubled. As for Jacob, I knew he didn't promise her that much. I reckon that was part of his madness.'

Tremayne made himself comfortable on a chair; Potts leant back on his bed, his head on the pillow. For a police interview, it was informal in the extreme. Tremayne chuckled to himself at the scene in front of him: Potts on the bed, his shoes off, as if he was on a psychiatrist's couch.

'This madness, what did you reckon?'

'Unsure, not my area of expertise, and besides, I didn't concern myself, had enough problems of my own.'

Tremayne knew the last part of the statement to be accurate, reflecting on those years without Jean.

'The best you can.'

'Jacob was always eccentric, absent-minded. It was humorous, though, and he was agreeable, as was Deidre. She was always fretting over him.'

'Single?'

'Deidre, up until Sutherland. Then she became remarkably sanguine. Marjorie wanted to tease her about it, but I told her to be careful.'

'Was she?'

'Careful? Up to a point, but the women used to talk, although I doubt if Deidre said too much. Whatever Sutherland was up to, it cheered her up.'

'Let's leave Sutherland to one side for now,' Tremayne said. 'Focus on Jacob. Sutherland's death is not our immediate concern, and it's either Jacob or Deidre who killed him.'

'No way to prove either way?'

'Even if we said it was one or the other, although our money's on Deidre, based on testimony and Pathology, angle of the blow that killed him, that sort of thing, it would still be open to contention, an expert arguing for or against the conclusion.'

'No one's going to be tried for Sutherland's murder,' Potts said.

'No one. Let's get back to Jacob. The man's eccentric, and with genius comes madness. Or is there more?'

'Even before he took to the street, he'd spend hours in the garden, pacing up and down, mumbling to himself.'

'Mumbling or working through issues?'

'Not sure, but he'd be there, sometimes in the rain.'

'He knew the man was married, yet he didn't tell Deidre.'

'Sorry for her, I suppose. Brotherly love, he didn't want to be the one to tell her that Sutherland was a bastard and married.'

'Was he a bastard? According to his former wife, the man acted to character, spread cheer around, and did not get emotionally involved.'

'Marjorie would understand, the man's wife, no doubt, but Deidre wouldn't have. After so many years alone, she would have seen it as love, pure and sweet, a sentimental view of the world. Marjorie used to tell me how Deidre thought. A childish view of the world, goodness and love and bright lights.'

'Whereas it's mostly shades of grey. The question is, where do you place yourself in the colour spectrum?'

'Bland grey, not black or white.'

Tremayne opened the room's window, strictly non-smoking, a sign on the door to that effect. He took out a cigarette and leant out, lighting it and taking a drag.

'I don't approve of smoking,' Potts said.

'More credit to you. At least it shows that you're capable of a firm view on something, not the nonsense you've just fed me.'

'Nonsense!'

Tremayne sensed irritation, the reason for the cigarette, to invoke a reaction, good or bad.

'Yes, precisely that. No man accepts that the woman he professes to care for sleeps with other men. Marjorie must have become emotional with one or two, Jacob, for instance.'

'Yes, she was fond of him, but it wasn't love, and then he stopped coming over, and Sutherland dies, not that we knew that, and he's out on the street.'

'Did you or Marjorie talk to Jacob after that?'

'Not for some years, but sometimes I'd see him near the shed or walking around Salisbury. He'd talk indirectly.'

'What does that mean?'

'He'd never look me in the eye, and then he'd talk about the city, the weather, never about Marjorie or Deidre, the life he once had.'

'Content?'

'Disinterested.'

'A death wish?'

'If you mean he was pushing that trolley to his death, then no. If he was keen on dying, there are easier ways.'

'Yet he was working on something in his notebook, possibly valuable, and then, a bulletproof vest. What about the vest?'

'I've no idea.'

'Marjorie, still incapable, and the truth this time, otherwise I'll have you examined by experts.'

'Not incapable, but you're right. I can't forget or forgive.'

'Other women?'

'Not often, casual.'

'Does Marjorie know?'

'No, please don't tell her.'

'I won't,' Tremayne said, although it wasn't a promise that he would necessarily keep. It was a murder enquiry, and Simon Potts had revealed a motive: jealousy.

Chapter 18

'It's clear you don't like me.' The statement was combative, and Clare couldn't disagree with the woman's anger. It was four in the afternoon; Gloria Hardcastle was ready to go out, a clutch handbag in one hand, a set of keys in the other.

'Inconvenient time?' Clare said, not by way of an apology. She had learnt policing under the tutelage of the best interrogator in the business, Detective Inspector Tremayne. He preferred his people on edge, especially when he was going for the jugular.

'Do you think I sit here all day waiting for the lady mayoress to knock on my door, a visit from Salisbury's aristocracy?'

Again, Clare thought.

'I'm the wife of the mayor, not the lady mayoress, and certainly not aristocracy.'

'It makes no difference to me, but I'm going out, and you're not stopping me. If you've questions, make an appointment.'

As Gloria made for the door, Clare put up her arm and blocked the way.

'You can't do that. I've committed no crime.'

'Fifteen minutes, no more, and this time, answers, open and direct, and yes, I disapprove of your behaviour.'

'A function at my husband's company, not an orgy.'

'Irrelevant,' Clare said. 'Too many people are hiding facts from us, not stating their true feelings. Others have revealed their innermost feelings under pressure. You, Gloria Hardcastle, are about to do the same, and you've got fifteen minutes to do so, or we'll sweat it out of you.'

'Sorry about the lady mayoress.'

'You're not the first.' Clare waited until they were both sitting down. 'You saw your husband die; traumatic?'

'Do you know the emotions of the moment, the inability to believe what the eyes can't deny?' Gloria said.

'I saw a man I loved die,' Clare said, not sure why she had revealed that truth and why to a woman she disapproved of, knowing full well that Gloria Hardcastle was not necessarily the most discreet.

'Avon Hill?'

'Yes.'

'Tragic. I read about it, but it was a long time ago.'

'So was Derek's.'

'Then you know the feeling: disbelief, shock, unable to grasp the reality, not sure what to do.'

'Derek's car, did you register a check on it?'

'I went to Deidre's house, spoke politely to her. I could see she was calm, and I thought I had been delusional.'

'Do you have a medical condition?'

'None that I know of, but you've experienced similar. Did you believe the reality?'

'Not for a long time, but I was a police officer, hard to deny what was obvious. You must have felt the same, and what about his car, the bank accounts?'

'I've already explained the bank accounts on one of your numerous other visits. As for the car, he parked it two streets away.'

'When did you find it?'

'Two days later. I had a spare key, and the car was registered in my name.'

'That was the proof that he had died, that you weren't delusional or in shock, and you've already said he didn't touch his bank accounts after that day. Jacob and Deidre were there when Derek died, but how did Deidre know he was married. We've always assumed Jacob, and that's what Deidre told us.'

'It wasn't Jacob, it was me, a blazing row at the door when I caught him with Deidre. I told her, not that she believed me, and then Jacob came in the back door. He's confronted by Deidre and Derek's trying to get the man to shut up, but Jacob's cornered. He blabbed it out to her, the whole sordid story.'

'And where were you?'

'Outside, peering in through a window, but you already know this. I didn't want to be there; I had said my piece, and so angry, I could have killed Derek.'

'Did you? After all, you've changed your story a dozen times now.'

'I didn't. I could have, but it was those two in the house.'

'Afterwards?'

'As I said, shock, and then the realisation after I found the car. From then on, I fluctuated between rational and madness, thought to go to the police and then decided against it.'

'Did you know where they buried him?'

'Yes, I knew, looked over the back fence a few years later, saw the shed, put two and two together, came up with four.'

'And you kept this quiet for all these years?'

'What was I to do? Time had moved on, and I found another man. Why rake up history?'

Clare could have said it was her duty but thought it an inadequate response.

***

Tremayne was angry, not with Clare, who had done well in making Gloria Hardcastle reveal more, but with the whole mess. People continued not to tell the entire truth. Simon Potts had lied out of embarrassment, but Gloria Hardcastle had out of malice and self-interest. However, it didn't make either of them murderers or explain the reason for Montfield's bulletproof vest.

'Without the reason for the vest, we're flying blind,' Tremayne said.

'Where it was purchased hasn't helped, although the work that Montfield had been working on might,' Clare said.

'Only one person who can help, not that I trust him, not totally.'

'Kempler?'

'No one else, although he might have a vested interest, feed us nonsense, slap the Official Secrets Act on the notebook.'

'And then a visit from men in dark suits who'll confiscate the notebook, our investigation down the tube, case closed.'

'Over my dead body,' Tremayne said.

'That might not concern them. I'll take copies of the notebook, take one to Kempler, keep the original and the other copies in various locations.'

'Hardly by the book, although I can't see another option. Kempler can't be trusted, not if the notebook is so important. Either he'll claim credit, wouldn't put it past him, or he'll sell it to the highest bidder.'

'Not something to debate now, only to do. What about the others?'

'Not important, although one of several could have killed Montfield, the vest is crucial, so is the notebook.'

Due to the seriousness of their actions, Tremayne realised he needed some assurances. Not for himself, too far advanced in his career to matter, but for his sergeant. He didn't want her career blighted by the accusation of tampering with evidence, which would be the charge if the visit to Kempler went wrong. Also, he had encountered the men in suits before on a previous investigation, knew they didn't leave loose ends, and that security at the cost of lives would be tolerated.

The station superintendent, someone Tremayne kept his distance from, too ready to discuss his eldest inspector's impending retirement, was surprised when the man sat down across from him in the office.

'Off the record,' Tremayne said.

'I can't do that, and you know it,' the superintendent said.

'Okay, but discretion then.'

'That I can give, but I'll not commit to an illegal act.'

'Depends on the definition, but that could be construed.'

'What are you intending?'

'Jacob Montfield. We've got motives, one or two strong enough for him to be killed, but…'

'You don't reckon those people are the murderers.'

'There are two reasons we don't, and until we understand the detail of why and what, we can't proceed. Montfield was wearing a bulletproof vest. Why? Important to know the reason and who he feared. Secondly, which could be central to the enquiry, we found a notebook in the man's trolley. It was hidden under rubbish in his trolley, but the writing's recent.'

'Have you read it?'

'Looked at it, but it's formulas and diagrams, almost certain it's coded.'

'You need someone to look at it.'

'There's only one person, and we're not sure if we can trust him.'

'Dishonest? A low-life?'

'No. Gustav Kempler, director of where Montfield and Sutherland worked. He might feel obliged to report the notebook to his superiors, get brownie points, or else take Montfield's work and expand on it. We can't risk an official request to hand over the notebook.'

'Critical to the murder enquiry?'

'I don't know, but I think it could be. It's the bulletproof vest that continually throws us, the reason why Montfield was wearing it.'

'Those that killed him, why didn't they take the notebook at the murder scene? If they are who you think, they won't hesitate.'

'They might have been disturbed by Jerry Maloney. He's ex-police, sensed something was wrong with Montfield. Others, drunk as him, would have walked past.'

'No more details,' the superintendent said. 'How many days' grace do you want, assuming the worst?'

'Five days, if the suits come knocking. If they don't, then we're fine, but I don't want them getting the notebook, not yet.'

'I hope you know what you're doing.'

Tremayne didn't respond, only shook his superintendent's hand. The notebook would remain secure, and Kempler would receive a visit.

***

Clare did what they had agreed, although she had concerns over removing evidence and secreting it in a location known only to her and Tremayne. Most in the police station had gone home for the night, and she was photocopying the notebook page by page, careful to ensure no damage, making four copies.

They would show the first copy to Gustav Kempler, the second they would place in the evidence vault, the third would be Tremayne's responsibility, and the fourth would be with Clare. For the notebook, a location had been agreed upon by the two. It would be safe, impervious to the climate and in a hermetically sealed bag. Clare had serious reservations but understood the logic. If the notebook's contents were dynamite, not literal but actual, and Montfield had come up with a revolutionary approach in his research, it was worth a lot of money. The government or governments could be interested.

The second morning after they had made the decision, they were ready. A nod of the head had informed the superintendent when he and Tremayne had passed in the corridor. Clare, concerned she was about to get involved in something risky and concerned for Clive, informed him in generalisations as to what was happening.

His comment was to be careful and not bite off more than she could chew. That was what she loved about him, his total trust in her.

When confronted with the photocopied pages of the notebook given to him in the afternoon of the next day, Kempler sat back on his chair, scratched his head, studied what was in front of him.

Tremayne and Clare sat still, watching for tell-tale signs of body language, more of a skill to Clare than Tremayne.

'Interesting,' Kempler said. 'Very interesting. And you're saying that Montfield had this with him?'

Tremayne spoke. 'We believe it may be the reason he was killed.'

'And now that it's in your possession, and now mine, makes us potential victims.'

It hadn't been considered before, but Tremayne and Clare realised the man had made a valid point. If the notebook was so important, why hadn't those who wanted it made an official request to the police if they had the authority, and secondly, if the contents were so important, why hadn't whoever, indeterminate at this time, infiltrated the police station, accessed the evidence room and removed the notebook?

It occurred to Tremayne that the notebook might not be as relevant as first thought and that it was back to the nearest and dearest for Montfield's murderer.

'If it's that important,' Clare said in response to Kempler's statement.

'Did you try to get it deciphered by others?' Kempler said. Tremayne sensed a nervousness about the man.

'I ran it past an educated person I knew, a scientist,' Tremayne said.

'No doubt it made no more sense to him than it does to me.'

'You just indicated that it was dangerous.'

'I might not understand it, but I can see the hand of genius. If it was important to Montfield and to whoever killed him, then we need to understand it.'

'Yet you can't,' Clare reminded Kempler.

'I can deduce.'

'Then what does it tell you?' Tremayne thought Kempler was edging around the facts. He could understand the man's reluctance to say aloud what he was thinking.

'I think this is bigger than any of us,' Kempler said.

'And dangerous?'

'To us, yes. Valuable to others.'

'We've come to you, not as our first choice, but because we have no one else who might be able to tell us what it is,' Tremayne said.

'You're concerned that I can't be trusted to maintain confidentiality in what is a murder investigation.'

'Yes.'

'You are right, of course. The contents, if validated, will be confiscated under the auspices of the Official Secrets Act, and your investigation will be finished.'

'That's not what we want,' Tremayne said.

'Excuse me,' Kempler said as he picked up a phone on his desk. 'I need someone else to look at this.'

It was what Tremayne feared, that the contents of a seemingly innocuous notebook were taking on a dimension of their own and that others were becoming interested. He realised that his suspicions were correct and that he and his sergeant would lose control of the murder enquiry. If necessary, they would be isolated or ostracised.

He shuddered at what he was thinking.

In the office, two more people. One, a man in his late fifties, greying hair, a sour appearance as though he had never smiled once in his life, and a pleasant young woman in her thirties, barely up to the sour man's shoulder.

'You found this?' the man said.

'We're police officers conducting a murder enquiry. We don't find, we investigate,' Tremayne said. Clare sensed an immediate antagonism between the two men.

'Apologies, I didn't mean to imply.'

'Accepted.'

Tremayne had made his point; the discussion could continue. 'It was in the bottom of a supermarket trolley he pushed around. Jacob Montfield lived a dishevelled life, one that none of us would understand.'

'I'm security here, and subject to what you've shown to Dr Kempler, then I'm afraid it can't leave here.'

Clare nudged Tremayne; he understood.

'We fear the enquiry will be halted and vital evidence suppressed,' Tremayne said.

'It will, unfortunately.'

'That doesn't concern you?' Clare asked.

'My function is the security of the realm; yours is policing. Sorry to be so blunt, but what's contained here might prove to be more important than any of us, and as for the murder, that I can't answer.'

'Officially sanctioned.'

'Melodramatic, but others might be interested. By the way, both of you need to sign the Official Secrets Act before you leave.'

The woman who had come into the office sat down in one corner of the room. In her hand were the photocopied pages that Clare had prepared.

Kempler continued to look around as she read, glancing at Tremayne and Clare, looking up at the security director, shifting eyes darting between the two men.

'What's the problem?' Tremayne said.

'It depends on our colleague,' Kempler said. 'Dr Baxter, Maureen, any comment?'

'It's complex. It will take time to understand and then program.'

'Could it be significant?'

'It could be a breakthrough, but I can't be sure, not yet. The coding and some diagrams are confusing as if the writer has altered key pointers.'

'Is that unusual?' Clare said.

'Not when you're involved with cutting-edge technology. Everyone wants to protect their work, and professional jealousy is paramount, apart from the accolades. I don't think the code here is too difficult to break; a couple of days, no more.'

'And in the meantime?' Tremayne asked, his eyes directed towards the security director.

'Nothing. You continue with your investigation, and we'll keep you posted.'

'The notebook, where is it?' Kempler asked. 'You've given us a photocopy.'

'The notebook is secure in our evidence room. You have a copy of the book, no need for the original.'

'That's our decision, not yours,' the security director said.

'For now, it's ours,' Tremayne responded.

Chapter 19

With the confusion caused by the visit to Gustav Kempler, Tremayne and Clare were unsure whether to pursue their previous inquiries or wait and see.

They had signed the Official Secrets Act, the security director hovering over them as they filled in the form, and he had explained the penalties for any breach.

Out of the man's office, Kempler had apologised for railroading their murder investigation but explained that national security took precedence over the deaths of a few individuals.

Clare had wanted to respond that the individual was more important than the state but had not. She knew how the system worked, the reason she had omitted one page from the notebook.

Tremayne warned his sergeant that she had taken a risk and hoped she wouldn't regret it, although he congratulated her on her forethought.

The station's superintendent kept his distance, a cursory nod occasionally in passing, and the days stretched out, some in the office, some in the field.

Marjorie Potts' husband was still keeping his distance from her. Gloria Hardcastle busied herself with her social life, and her husband, apparently not the charismatic force of her first husband, maintained the appearance of a contented husband.

The investigation continued, contact was maintained with the key players, but the interviews had been tepid, with no further information gained.

Jerry and Christine Maloney were in Scotland, Tremayne had phoned a couple of times as a friend, but the conversation always got around to the night when Montfield had died. Tremayne's concern was that Maloney had disturbed the murderer, the reason the notebook was still in the trolley, although why in the centre of the city when the man could have been killed in his shed made no sense. But then, what did, and now the research establishment was trying to decipher Montfield's notebook.

On the ninth day, a phone call from Kempler for them to be in his office at six o'clock that night. When quizzed by Tremayne, the man was vague but adamant that it was not a request but an order, enforceable under the Official Secrets Act, and had more weight than the police.

When told by Tremayne of developments and that rapid escalation was possible, the superintendent took to his office. He busily started writing down all that had occurred, the misinformation fed to him, a clear indication that Detective Inspector Tremayne was operating contrary to police procedures and that his sergeant, Clare Yarwood, was an accomplice, willingly or not.

Tremayne did not follow the superintendent's lead, not that he knew of it, as he had done nothing other than to drive their investigations, although he worried for his sergeant.

'The matter's serious,' Kempler said. Also in the room were the sour-faced security director, the pleasant young Dr Maureen Baxter, who had left the first meeting with the photocopies, and two others. One of them was a woman in her sixties with a stern face and a poorly-cut business suit. The other was a man in his late thirties, immaculately dressed, his hair cut short, a tattoo on his neck. Clare could see the outline of a gun secreted at his waist.

Clare thought this was it and that she and Tremayne were in serious trouble.

The woman spoke. 'Do either of you understand what you gave to Mr Kempler?' she asked.

Tremayne replied. 'Not in detail. Due to the nature of the work at this establishment, we assumed it to be related to weapons research. Apart from that, nothing more.'

'That's fine if it's true.'

'I don't understand,' Clare said. 'Would it be possible to have introductions first?'

'Designations only, not names,' the woman said. 'I'm the government, a branch that prefers anonymity. My colleague is from the same branch. I'm administration; he's not.'

'Thank you,' Clare said, aware that was the most they would receive.

The gun spoke. 'We need the original notebook and any other photocopies.'

'The notebook is evidence,' Tremayne said.

'I suggest you comply,' Kempler said. 'These people have absolute power over all of us.'

'Mr Kempler is correct,' the woman said. 'The murder enquiry can continue, in concert with us.'

'How? A police investigation and what you're referring to are distinct and separate. Our role is to disseminate information as we see fit in an attempt to solve the case; yours is to conceal it.'

'I agree, and whereas I can sympathise, I must enforce my demands. The copies and the notebook, where are they?'

'In the evidence room,' Clare said.

'The notebook is not there, only another photocopy,' the gun said. 'May I remind you that obfuscation and attempting to derail an investigation of this magnitude will be treasonous, the penalties I'm sure I don't need to state.'

'Comply, Sergeant, please,' Kempler said. 'These people have control here, and whereas I've no doubt they are decent people, they will not hesitate to apply the full force of their law to this matter.'

Clare looked over at Tremayne; he nodded, affirming no alternative.

'We are not convinced that he died because of the notebook,' the woman said. 'Your murder enquiry can continue, albeit without the notebook and any reference to it.'

'If it's crucial?' Tremayne protested.

'If it is, then tell us, and we'll deal with it. Consider this a joint investigation, although we're the senior partner.'

'That's not how I work.'

'We're aware of your record, also your superintendent's efforts to retire you, and that your sergeant is pregnant and married to the mayor of Salisbury.'

'If you know so much,' Clare said, 'how do you know the notebook is not in the evidence room.'

'I've checked,' the gun said.

Tremayne knew the man was not someone to cross, and if he had murdered Montfield, he would never come to trial.

'The notebook and all copies,' the woman reiterated, this time banging a fist on Kempler's desk.

'If we're to go along with this,' Tremayne said, 'we need some assurances.'

'You don't, but say them anyway.'

'An indication as to what's in the notebook, no action taken against us for removing the notebook from the evidence room, a clear run at the murderer if he or she is not of interest to you.'

'Agreed. Dr Baxter, a précised account of what Montfield was working on.'

Maureen Baxter went over to where the gun stood, a clearer view of everyone in the room. 'Tracking, or more precisely, the tracking and control of weaponry. His approach is innovative, a breakthrough in the algorithms utilising satellites.'

'Surely that's been done before,' Clare said.

'Remote from his peers and this establishment, he went off on a tangent, back to basics, rebuilt the system from the ground up, found a better way, a breakthrough.'

'Important to England?'

'To anyone who could get their hands on it, worth a fortune to some.'

'Enough to kill?'

'Ten times over, and these people, if they are not English, wouldn't hesitate to kill everyone in this room if needed.'

'Nor would you,' Tremayne said, looking over at the suited woman.

'We wouldn't,' the gun said.

'All copies and the notebook, how long?' the woman asked.

'Three hours,' Clare said.

'Don't keep one for yourself,' the gun said. 'The repercussions would not be to your liking.'

'If we need to contact you?'

'Phone Kempler. He will contact us, and we will decide whether we should meet or contact you.'

The gun followed Tremayne and Clare as the two of them visited the places where they had secreted evidence. The two police officers breathed a sigh of relief as the final piece was retrieved and the man drove off.

'He could have killed us there and then,' Tremayne said.

'I know,' Clare said. 'I've never been so frightened.'

Tremayne hadn't the heart to tell her she had been that night in the woods up above Avon Hill.

***

Clive was distraught when Clare came in late that night. All she wanted to do was to snuggle up next to him, her head on his shoulder, aware that stress wasn't good for the mother or impending child.

Tremayne, not used to the treatment they'd received, briefly kissed Jean on the cheek, went to the fridge and took out a bottle of beer. 'I'll need a few of these tonight, no complaints, okay.'

Jean recognised the signs and responded. 'Bad day,' she said.

'The worst,' as he gurgled down the first bottle, another primed to go.

Clare slept poorly that night, and for two days, she was absent from the office. Tremayne made it in the day after the ordeal and gave his superintendent a brief synopsis of what had happened.

Tremayne knew that a government employee's gun was more dangerous than any gangster or hired assassin. The man was impervious to reason, only responding to a directive. The woman intrigued him, but he wasn't about to try and find out who she was.

Clare returned to Homicide on the third day.

'How are you?' Tremayne asked.

'Don't talk about it; focus on the investigation.'

'With what?'

'You know we have nothing.'

Even so, Tremayne knew they had to continue, careful to circumvent treading on governmental toes. 'On the face of it, I'd agree, but we can't let it stand.'

'How and why? He could have killed us, and how did he know the notebook wasn't in with the other evidence?'

'Assumed, or he'd been inside.'

'Or an inside job.'

Tremayne left the office and went upstairs. The superintendent was behind his desk, his assistant outside stating that the man didn't want to be disturbed. Tremayne took no notice and barged through the intervening door.

'We could have been killed,' Tremayne said. 'It was you, wasn't it?'

'You know what we're dealing with here, and they're not the boy scouts.'

'But why? When did you receive word that something was up?'

'When you were with Kempler. I'm not sure who they are, but I've got my suspicions, and they've been sniffing around for a week. I kept quiet for as long as I could, a tacit agreement between us, but in the end, the law's the law, even if it's an ass, and you know it.'

'I do, but Yarwood was scared out of her wits, pregnant as well. If anything had happened to her, then what?'

'You're sentimental towards the woman, and you know it. She's a serving police officer, trained to deal with difficult situations, and I can't have her or you crying wolf because your day didn't work out the way you expected. Accept retirement and put her on extended sick leave if it's too much. I'll authorise both, and she's the future; you're not.'

'What is this? My retirement and a generous offer to her, conditional on the enquiry stopping here?'

The superintendent paused and looked at a piece of paper on his desk. 'Yes, orders from above, drop it, put it in the too-hard basket. Whatever you've unearthed, it's lethal; others will investigate Montfield's death.'

'Or consign it to the bin.'

'Not the bin, not with these people. Those responsible, assuming they're not ours, will never see a court of law, but justice will be meted out, this year or next.'

Tremayne had to concede, aware that it wasn't two people frightened that night, but three, and that retirement was not a request from the superintendent but an order given by others.

'A week, give us a week, Yarwood and me, let us work over who we've got. It could be someone else, nothing to do with notebooks and weapon location or guidance or whatever it is.'

'I can't use my discretion here, only follow a directive, but yes, they'll go for that. Nothing personal, no emotion either. In an instance, they'll kill you and Yarwood, the same with me. It's a hornet's nest you've stirred. I hope you're prepared to get stung.'

'One week, and off the record, you had no option,' Tremayne said as he walked out of the superintendent's office.

***

Time heals, the fear lessens. After two days, mainly in the office, Tremayne and Clare returned to the usual banter, the sarcastic quips, the long hours. Phone interviews had been conducted with some but not with others. Marjorie Potts had been friendly, inviting the two over, but Clare could see the woman fixated on her inspector. Simon Potts was polite on phoning but offered nothing more.

Tremayne felt it was a needle in a haystack approach. The notebook was the crux of the investigation, and dredging through other avenues was a pointless exercise until eliminated.

On one occasion, he had contacted Kempster and received a terse response and a reminder that interference by the police in matters relating to state security came with consequences that nobody wanted. Even so, Tremayne had been adamant. In the end, Maureen Baxter had picked up the phone. She confided that her work was progressing and that the woman and the gun were sometimes in the facility, sometimes not. And she wasn't about to jeopardise a promising career by talking out of turn, even if she sympathised, and finally, she preferred the inspector and his sergeant over the other two.

'Did you get that?' Kempster had said after the woman passed the phone back.

'Loud and clear,' Tremayne replied.

'And understood, I hope. I don't want to escalate, and you know the consequences, the same as I do.'

'A bullet in a dark alley.'

'Or under the roof of an ancient building.'

'Proof?'

'Goodbye, Inspector Tremayne, and don't try to bait me. I can read newspapers the same as you, and I knew the person years ago. Officially, I know nothing;

unofficially, I know nothing, and that's on the record or off, but I won't answer your future calls, not unless it's critical.'

'Scared?'

'Who wouldn't be,' Kempler confided. 'For now, it's goodbye, and I hope we never cross paths again.'

Tremayne hung up, sure that Kempler knew more, but he wasn't speaking, not that he blamed him. He realised in that instance that it was his sergeant who was in the most tenuous position.

'Yarwood, the superintendent's offer of extended sick leave. I reckon you should take it, forget this enquiry.'

'I can't. That would be running away from the battle, cowardice in the face of the enemy.'

'The enemy lurks within, and you don't fight a battle you can't win, nor do you jeopardise your unborn child. No murder is worth that.'

Reluctantly, and with pressure from Tremayne and the superintendent, Clare accepted, and two days later, she was out of the office and at her home with Clive. For three days, she tidied up, put this over there, rearranged the furniture, called in a decorator to paint the baby's bedroom, and finally got around to buying a cot and anything else that came to mind.

Clive thought it was too much, but he had been an absentee father before, and now he was there, and he was having to deal with mood swings, morning sickness and a wife who was keeping herself busy for no reason.

'You'd be better at the police station,' he said at the end of the second week.

'It's complicated,' Clare said. 'You'd not understand.'

'Try me.'

They sat in the covered patio at the rear of the house, warm from a weak sun heating the glass roof. She explained the murder enquiry, the interest of two menacing people, one who carried a concealed weapon, and the reality that she and Tremayne were treading a fine line and that one slip and they were dead.

Clive, not intimately acquainted with such people, knew the reality existed. 'Jacob Montfield, harmless and eccentric, that important?'

'He was everything people thought of him, but he had a brilliant mind,' Clare said.

'Even so, you can't sit around the house indefinitely. Work with Tremayne, stay in the house, keep a low profile.'

'It could still be dangerous.'

'More so for Tremayne, and I'll take precautions, use my influence, keep a record of what's going on, ensure it's hidden from these people.'

'You can't do that, not with these people. They might be government, but they act like the Mafia. Nobody, not even you, understand the power they wield.'

'We live in England; we can't be intimidated by goons and hoodlums.'

Tremayne came over to the house and listened while Clive outlined the situation. Clive then left the two alone.

'It's risky,' Tremayne said.

'So is doing nothing. And who were these two? Were they on our side, and who would know, certainly not Kempler? It could be a setup, a plan to divert us while they make a fortune selling Montfield's work to the highest bidder.'

Tremayne thought that Clare's evaluation of the situation was flawed and that the woman and the gun were English, not because he had proof, but instinct told him they were. However, being in Homicide on his own, following up on dead-end leads, not having Yarwood to bounce ideas off had become a grind, worse than retirement.

'Very well, feed me what you've got, do your research here and see where this heads to.'

As the two spoke, Clive was upstairs in his study. He had a favour to call in.

Chapter 20

Due to her discretion and clandestine affair, Maureen Baxter was the one person Gustav Kempler could trust to maintain confidentiality.

For him, it was a relaxation from the monotony of a tiresome marriage, an overbearing wife and delinquent teenagers. His wife was all for socialising and had collected a group of uninteresting people around her. Of the two children of the marriage, the elder, a daughter of eighteen, spent most nights with her boyfriend. For the son, two years younger, his first tattoo, his third knife, in and out of police stations on several occasions. The magistrate had slapped him with a five-hundred-pound fine for possession of a banned substance and had placed him on probation for a year.

Maureen's reasons were more basic. The clever child of parents who had loathed each other, she was determined to live life on her terms, detached from the encumbrances that society demanded. For her, a long-term commitment to another person was anathema. An affair with her boss came with a degree of excitement, a modicum of pleasure in that her lover was twenty years older than her and didn't have the stamina, and it ensured that the best projects came her way.

'Maureen, what do we have?' Kempler asked as they lay together in his office that night.

'A complete rethink on rocket guidance and location; the possibilities are endless.'

'Cheaper, simpler, more expensive?'

'More accurate,' Maureen said.

'How much is it worth on the open market?'

'Does that concern us?'

'It should. Our government will use it, onward sell it to the highest bidders as long as they are our friends.'

'You mean to everybody.'

'Have you ever contemplated what we have?' Kempler asked.

'Technically, yes; financially, no, and neither should you.'

'I know, but it makes you think, doesn't it?'

'Not me, it doesn't. You know who those two are, what they could do?'

'The two police officers,' Kempler joked.

'Not them, the others. Don't get yourself killed.'

'I won't,' he said and put it out of his mind as he refocussed on the more immediate pleasure at his side.

***

Clive spent two days in London and returned with important information for Clare. Firstly, the two goons they met had received instruction to back off and not threaten. Secondly, what Montfield had was valuable and could have got the man killed, and thirdly, and most importantly, she was not to subject herself to excessive stress, not in her condition.

When she asked who he had seen and what had occurred, she received a hug, and, 'A friend, someone from my college days, big in government.'

'Nameless?' Clare asked.

'For now, but remember Montfield's death. If it wasn't someone local, then that person would be dangerous, professional, not answerable to anyone in this country.'

'The goons, him and her?'

'They're ours. You're safe with them, not with others. No chancing it, okay?'

'Okay, and thanks.'

Clare returned to the police station, light duties enforced by the superintendent and demanded by Tremayne. Her work was interrogative, not frontline, no knocking on suspects' doors, unless it was the harmless home-grown variety. She didn't see how she could comply with such an order.

Tremayne, aware that his sergeant's husband had connections from the boarding school he had attended, the sons of gentlemen, politicians, business people, spies, felt some relief that the woman and the gun were now on their side.

In the police station, they sat with Tremayne and Clare in the conference room.

'You can call me Dorothy,' the woman said. 'As for him, Eustace.' She nodded over in the direction of the gun.

Clare didn't like the look of either but encouraged by her husband's assurances, she did not feel the need to hold back her disapproval.

'Can we trust you?' she asked.

The gun looked over at Dorothy.

'You can,' Dorothy said. 'You were an unknown quantity before, not checked out by us.'

'And who exactly is us?' Tremayne asked.

'Government,' a terse one-word reply.

'MI5, MI6?'

'Does it matter?'

'I like to know who we're working with.'

'So do we. Both of you have been checked, deemed acceptable and that your confidence can be relied on.'

'Ground rules,' Clare said. 'This is a police investigation, a murder in Salisbury.'

'Then we work in tandem, a free exchange of information. If Montfield's death was local, then fine, but it doesn't explain the bulletproof vest, does it?'

'Something that's always concerned Inspector Tremayne. For now, she'd work with the two goons, and at least the four were talking, apart from Eustace, his contribution no more than grunting acknowledgement, short sentences, answering when spoken to.

Clare thought the man was probably not too bright but dependable, highly professional and ready to use the gun if needed. Surprisingly, she felt safer with him than with the woman, in that Dorothy was smart, deviously smart, and lying would be easy to her.

'Then,' Tremayne said, 'seeing that it's a free exchange of information, we'll let you lead off. Exactly what is in that notebook?'

Dorothy cleared her throat, cast a glance at Eustace and then fixated on Tremayne. 'Technically, I can't explain it. Security of the realm is my concern. Will you accept that?'

'I will,' Tremayne said. After all, he had run it past another person, someone much more intelligent than him, before showing it to Kempler, and that person hadn't been able to make sense of it, although Maureen Baxter had.

'It is, as we all know, a set of algorithms for weapon guidance and tracking. Allow me some latitude on this, as I'm not technical; write an email, send a text message, write a report, but not much more. Mild dyscalculia.'

'What's that?' Tremayne asked.

'Dyslexic, but with numbers,' Clare said.

'Exactly,' Dorothy said. 'Jacob Montfield didn't suffer from the condition. Whereas the man might have preferred the life of the homeless, his mind was still active, and in that notebook, as explained to me, a dramatic improvement on the science. However, as far as our government is concerned—'

'MI5,' Clare interjected.

Dorothy continued, sighed at the interruption. 'As far as *our* government is concerned, yours and mine, it's weapons that concern us. The arms race continues regardless of a world at peace, apart from the occasional skirmish and belligerent hermit states. And with the move into space, courtesy of ambitious entrepreneurs, whose interests might or might not be benign, the possibility of weapons in space remains a concern.'

'Why was Montfield so interested?' Tremayne asked.

'You knew the man. You tell me.'

'Idealistic, an enquiring mind, a genius undiminished by the murder of a colleague, estrangement from his sister.'

'You've answered the question. The man didn't concern himself with what his work would be used for, only with the problem, the chance to stretch his mind. Eccentric? Was he, or have I answered the question already?'

'You have, and yes, pleasant if you met him, but eccentric. Such an ability, something we would all have appreciated, yet wasted out on the street.'

'And getting himself killed,' the gun said.

'Tell us about yourself,' Clare said to Eustace.

'Not relevant,' the reply.

'Tell her,' Dorothy said. 'It's important she knows the sort of person who could have killed Montfield.'

'Sergeant Yarwood,' Eustace said. He had moved forward on his seat and placed the gun on the desk, pointing the barrel at the centre of the table, 'you've asked, I'll tell you. I follow orders. Here, in this room, I am rendered harmless. My function is to look after Dorothy, observe, and act on her command or that of others.'

'If she told you to kill?'

'If she told me to shoot, I would do so without emotion.'

'You'd consider it your duty.'

'I am trained to obey. Whether the order is wrong or not is not my concern, and if you would construe it as murder, I would not.'

'Thanks, Eustace, that's enough,' Dorothy said. 'Sergeant, you asked, now you know. He works for us; those who could have killed Montfield might work for another. Cold, emotionless, impassive about who and where and when. If, as we suspect, such a person killed Jacob Montfield, then you should be glad that Eustace is here.'

'I will be watching, so will some of my colleagues. Anything suspicious, and we will act, protect you and your inspector,' Eustace said.

'I'm not certain we need protecting,' Tremayne said.

'You do,' Dorothy said. 'Eustace will kill without compunction, so will they. Your desire to be involved and your sergeant's husband pulling in favours are to your detriment. Even so, I still believe there is time for the two of you to pull back. Once we've concluded, assuming we find nothing, then the police can resume their investigation.'

'We can't do that.'

'No, I suppose not. You're a man that doesn't back off, but this time, please do.'

'We won't, regardless.'

Clare could see the Tremayne trait, resolute, incapable of standing back, intending to pursue the murder investigation. She wondered if, this time, he was wrong and if Clive's involvement was advantageous. She feared for her child and husband, but primarily for her inspector.

***

In the days that followed, Eustace, who had taken up residence at a small hotel close to the city centre, could be seen around the city. Tremayne had run into him on several occasions, the first time close to the Poultry Cross where Montfield had died, the second time in a pub.

They had clear instructions from Dorothy at that meeting at the police station: 'Don't acknowledge each other, don't look or smile or nod.'

Clare queried why he needed to stay in the city, as those who might have killed Montfield wouldn't have waited any longer than necessary.

'You don't know that, no more than we do. Besides, there's the notebook to consider, and news tends to travel. Eustace is trained to look for the obscure, for persons of concern. He also has a portfolio of possible assassins, their subtle differences.'

'We could do that,' Tremayne had protested.

'You could, but you're visible, too well-known. Eustace is not, and he blends in.'

A phone call four days after the meeting; Clare answered.

'Dorothy here, we need you to conduct some checks for us,' she said.

Clare thought to say, aware that Tremayne would have, that they weren't the juniors, but did not. The woman on the phone was bombastic by nature, authoritarian by discipline, shrewd in her ability to maintain her position with whichever government organisation she worked for. Clare had to admit to a sneaking admiration for her, aware that both women worked in organisations that were outwardly equal opportunity, but inwardly the boys' club and male chauvinism.

'On what and whom?' Clare said.

Outside the police station, the rain was heavy, and Tremayne was out on foot patrol, trying to understand what Eustace was up to, to see if the man had skills he could adopt. Clare knew the most he would gain would be the flu and a couple of days in bed.

'Jerry Maloney.'

'A colleague of Inspector Tremayne from years back.'

'We know his history, time spent overseas, what he got up to.'

'Security for dubious personages.'

'That's what he told you?'

'He was open, told us he had almost died, had killed. Is there more?'

'There is, but in part, he's been honest. What did you think of him?'

'Personable, but the inspector doesn't remember him with fondness, although the two men were polite, met up with their wives for a night out.'

'Maloney's got a few secrets hidden from view. Security is correct but not always defensive. He took action to secure those he was protecting.'

'Such as?'

'Midnight raids, dragging someone out from their bed, giving them the third degree.'

'Murder?'

'Not sure. Others might have dealt with the more unsavoury, but persons disappeared, never found again.'

'You think that Maloney could be the killer?'

'We think he's capable, not confident that he is. So far, Eustace has only run up a bill for his accommodation and drinks at the pub.'

'All expenses included?'

'Not all, but the pub's a good place for loose tongues. It seems Maloney made an effort to be visible the night that Montfield died, at the pub and then with you two. As if he did it on purpose.'

'We assumed he'd interrupted the killer before he had a chance to rifle through the trolley and that the notebook was the reason for the man's death.'

'Which means somebody knew of its contents, whether in this country or overseas. This brings in another component, something you've probably thought about. How did others know of the notebook? Montfield wasn't communicative, apparently not interested in money or fame, although professional recognition might have been important.'

Clare did not say, but it was an avenue of enquiry that hadn't been fully explored, namely, who else knew about the notebook. Sure, his writing in the book was known, as he would often sit in the city and write in it, but the significance of it, who would have known that, or could someone engaging him in idle conversation or looking over his shoulder have figured it out.

Chapter 21

Clare picked up Tremayne from the market square in the city centre, explained why, and drove them out to the research establishment. The reception, this time, was friendlier than the last.

'Inspector Tremayne, Sergeant Yarwood, pleased to see you both,' Kempler beamed.

'A few questions,' Clare said, 'although others might have asked them already.'

'It doesn't matter, after all, this is a joint exercise, and I'm to offer you every assistance.'

Tremayne took the cup of tea offered, took one sip, and put it down. 'Dr Baxter, your colleague, understood the notebook's significance. Who else would have?'

'She understood the complexity of it, not sure on initial examination what it would do.'

'She knew it was something to do with weapons,' Tremayne reminded him.

'Montfield had worked here, as had Derek Sutherland. It was an educated guess, right as it turned out.'

'If she had seen the notebook, for instance, looking over Montfield's shoulder in the city, would she have understood?'

'If she had known who he was, maybe. But she didn't, just a schoolgirl when Montfield worked here.'

'So,' Clare said, 'someone other than Montfield knew of the notebook's contents before his death.'

'Certainly not me, and if I had looked over his shoulder, I wouldn't have understood. I can't say I have a lot of time for people of talent who turn their back on society. There are enough people out there who would have given a fortune for what God had gifted him.'

'Friends of Montfield or Sutherland, any still here?'

'Not certain that Montfield would have had friends, but Sutherland would have. I take it that you want to see them,' Kempler said.

A woman in her fifties came into the office.

'This is Dr Alice Frampton, our longest-serving researcher,' Kempler said. 'A colleague of both men.'

As tall as Clare, the woman was slim and upright. She shook hands with Tremayne and Clare. A firm handshake, Clare noted, an impressive woman.

'How can I help?' the doctor said as she took a seat.

'Can I ask you first, what was your reaction when you heard of Jacob Montfield's death?' Clare asked.

'A tragic loss.'

'Nothing more?'

'Jacob was brilliant, barely agreeable most of the time, treated me as the hired help when he worked here. I didn't like him, admired him, though.'

'And when he left, took up vagrancy, trudging around Salisbury?'

'I thought little of it, although sometimes I'd see him. I never spoke.'

'Out of disgust?'

'His behaviour towards me had been unacceptable and chauvinistic; I returned kind for kind. As researchers, we worked in isolation, although towards a common goal. That was possible, nothing more with the man. My position improved when he left and Derek failed to return.'

'Friend of Derek Sutherland?'

'I never understood their friendship, although on reflection it was for Derek, admiration for a searing intellect, and Jacob, friendship. Jacob was a serious man, solitary, but he seemed to hit it off with Derek.'

'What else, their friendship outside of here?'

'I knew about Derek and Jacob's sister, and he was incorrigible. In today's politically correct culture, he would have been guilty of sexual harassment in the workplace.'

'It was back then,' Clare said.

'Okay, I'll grant that it was. Derek was suggestive, but that was it. If you told him to stop, he would. And besides, Derek was married and with Jacob's sister at the same time. Jacob couldn't have been a prude, not with his sister. I asked him once what he reckoned and received a gruff "Mind your own business".'

'What did you think about it?'

'Jacob was right; it wasn't my business. No harm done to me, not to the sister, and Derek's wife was a player.'

'Explain that term,' Tremayne said.

'Liberal with her favours.'

'Yet again, not your concern.'

'I might have had an opinion, but I wasn't about to express it to them or you,' Alice Frampton said.

Clare thought the woman to be defensive.

'Let's come back to when the two men worked here,' Tremayne said, focussing back on the relevant, not the speculative, nor what was right or wrong.

'Jacob was the ideas, the instigator; Derek was the person who took Jacob's ideas, set up working models and tested them.'

'Where were you when this was happening?'

'Working with Derek most of the time. He was a clever man, dedicated, and when there was a job to do, he was all business, no time for merriment or teasing or chatting up.'

'He chatted you up?'

'Yes.'

'Did you respond?'

'Yes.'

'A conquest?'

'I'm an independent woman. Derek came without complications. You're not here to discuss me but to find out about Jacob.'

'We are. What we know is that Jacob's sister, Deidre, was ignorant of Derek's marriage and that when she found out, she reacted badly.'

'You can't blame her. Did she kill him?'

'Either her or Jacob. We can't be sure, and Jacob's death concerns us. He had a notebook, and it could be crucial.'

'I don't see how I can help. I didn't get to check out its contents.'

Kempler shuffled in his chair; Clare noticed.

'Would you have been capable of understanding it?'

'I believe so.'

'Did you know of this notebook before we brought it here?' Tremayne asked.

'No.'

'If you had?'

'If I had known of its importance, I would have tried to persuade him to let me see it. I don't see it's that important, not in the long term.'

'Why?' Kempler asked.

'Maureen knows its worth, so do you. I don't.'

'I think this is important,' Tremayne said. 'Why is Dr Frampton not involved with Montfield's notebook when the young lady is?'

'I believe that is an internal matter and not integral to your investigation,' Kempler said.

'That is for us to decide,' Clare said.

'I am led to believe that your involvement is subject to others and that you are cognisant of the Official Secrets Act. I am not obliged to answer your questions.'

'Five-minute break,' Tremayne said.

'Unlike you to back off,' Clare said as the two stood outside, Tremayne with a cigarette in his mouth, Clare holding a cup of coffee.

'How are you? No issues?' he asked.

'I'm fine for now, glad to be out of the office. You've not answered my question.'

Tremayne rested the cigarette on a low wall nearby and took out his phone. 'We've got an issue,' he said when his call was answered. He explained the situation, received a reply.

'Push,' Tremayne said to Clare once he had resumed smoking his cigarette.

'The mysterious Dorothy on the phone?'

'Yes. I need her and the gung-ho vigilante across this, as well.'

'You don't trust them?'

'Not for a minute, but your husband has helped, and I'm not without contacts.'

'Maybe it's you who is the mysterious one. What did Dorothy say, assuming that's her name?'

'It's not, but that's not important. Everyone's under suspicion, Kempler and his lover, Maureen Baxter, although I imagine you realised that. Also, Dr Frampton is under suspicion. Kempler has his concerns about her, and Dorothy's people are investigating. Let's see what else we can find out.'

Inside, Kempler sat behind his desk, Dr Frampton stood leaning up against a bookshelf on the other side of the room, and the meat in the sandwich, Maureen Baxter, sat on the chair next to Clare's, looking down at her iPhone.

'I've spoken to Dorothy,' Tremayne said, enjoying every moment. 'She's given us carte blanche on this, so no more of the Official Secrets Act. It's the truth we want, and we're all adults here.'

'I understand,' Kempler said. 'She's contacted me, instructed me to give you every assistance.'

Neither police officer took the man at face value. Kempler was, they had decided, a political animal who would play it to his advantage, and the truth was a dispensable commodity.

'Dr Frampton is the senior scientist here, is that correct?'

'Correct.'

'The most experienced?'

'Correct.'

'Then why wasn't she given the notebook?'

'Maureen was available. I deemed her adequate for the task.'

'Your take on this, Dr Frampton,' Tremayne asked.

'She's capable, a protégé of mine.'

'So technically, there was no reason not to give it to her.'

'No reason.'

'Yet you took umbrage.'

'I did. I wasn't here on the day, but I could have worked with Maureen, a joint effort.'

'Dr Kempler, your response?'

'Maureen was capable, and Dr Frampton was occupied on other research. I decided on the best utilisation of resources.'

'Not because you understood the complexity of the notebook and you're having an affair with the woman,' Clare said.

'That's not fair,' Maureen Baxter said. 'My relationship with Dr Kempler is not important.'

'Did you know?' Tremayne looked over at Frampton.

'Yes, I knew. Didn't care, not until Gustav sidelined me.'

'Let me make this clear; neither myself nor my sergeant is concerned with who sleeps with who unless it impedes the truth. Dr Kempler, I put it to you that you used your position to benefit Maureen. Professionally, you shouldn't have, but it's an imperfect world; it happens all the time.'

'She's still an excellent scientist, a true professional, and how was I to know that the notebook was so important,' Kempler said.

'If you weren't, someone was. How about you, Dr Frampton?'

'I didn't.'

'Maureen, you're a sociable person. You must have seen Montfield in Salisbury, spoken to him.'

'I had seen him on numerous occasions, spoken to him a dozen times.'

'About what and why?'

'I knew who he was, seen records of his work here, understood most, but not all. Although I never told him who I was and what I knew about him.'

'When was the last time you spoke to him?'

'Two days before he died. I was in the city, looking to buy clothes. He was there with his trolley outside the Guildhall. He knew me by sight, so I went and sat down by him, chatted to him for twenty minutes, maybe twenty-five.'

'What did you talk about?'

'He was a smart man. We talked about philosophy, books we had both read, that sort of thing.'

'Not about your work or his?'

'No. I wanted to, but I wasn't sure how to bring up the subject. He had a reputation here as difficult, even though it was long ago. I suppose I was hoping one day, once I'd gained his trust, to be honest with him.'

'Your involvement with Dr Kempler?'

'That's private.'

'In a murder enquiry, nothing is. Do you believe he assisted you in giving you the notebook?'

'Yes, I do. Dr Kempler knew of Jacob's brilliance, and he thought I would be the best person to check it.'

'Are you more competent than Dr Frampton?'

'No, she is an exceptional scientist. My affair doesn't concern her, nor should it concern you.'

'It doesn't, not unless it impacts our enquiries.'

'It doesn't; I believe that's been said.'

'Dr Frampton, any further comment?'

'Maureen's right. I wasn't concerned about her and Dr Kempler, only with my exclusion from working with her.'

'You asked him?'

'I did.'

'His response?'

'He said I was not security cleared.'

'Are you aware that you are under investigation for a possible breach of the Official Secrets Act?'

'I am.'

'Do you want to expand?'

'A misunderstanding.'

'I believe that Dr Frampton is correct in not answering that question,' Kempler said. 'Her case is subject to internal review, and she will argue her case. It is not a police matter, nor is it relevant.'

Clare looked over at Maureen, her face close to her phone's screen, an unusual activity for a serious-minded individual entrusted with the primary evidence in a murder investigation.

'Anything interesting?' Clare asked.

The woman looked up slowly and showed the phone to Clare. 'We're conducting a simulated test, not idly wasting time. This is Jacob's notebook cycling through.'

'Which you knew about?'

'I did, not that I saw it. Jacob, for whatever reason, felt comfortable in my presence, and he would talk, sometimes rambling, sometimes coherent, always interesting. He mentioned that his mind was active, and he jotted down ideas from time to time. I had no idea they were so well advanced.'

'Or complete?' Clare added.

'Apart from the missing page. Did you think that would stop us?'

'You had the notebook soon after, reluctantly by us, jeopardising a police investigation.'

'Progress invariably comes with casualties.'

'Dr Frampton, did you know of this notebook before it came into our possession?' Tremayne asked.

'I don't make a habit of talking with the homeless. No, I did not.'

'Dr Kempler?'

'Maureen told me about it, but neither of us thought much about it.'

'Too busy screwing,' Frampton said.

'You're embittered,' Clare said.

'Angry, embittered, contemptuous of the two of them. This used to be a great place to work. Jacob Montfield, brilliant and eccentric; Derek, charming and dedicated; and then me and a few others. True work for the betterment of this country, but now it's politics and self-aggrandising individuals, more interested in what they can get out of it for themselves, stealing Jacob's work if they can.'

'Is this what you believe? That the two in this room are in league, and they would have taken credit.'

'I do.'

'If you had had the notebook?'

'I would have acknowledged the man, although it would have been me who would have reaped the benefit, to sit in Kempler's chair.'

'Long-running feud,' Kempler said. 'She's jealous of my position, thinks she could do it better.'

'Could she?' Clare asked.

'Dr Frampton is direct, sometimes indiscreet, calls a spade a spade. On occasions, I have to butter up people I don't like, stroke their egos, pander to their vanities.'

'A correct summation, Dr Frampton?'

'It never used to be like that.'

'Dr Frampton is right,' Kempler said. 'Once, we were autonomous, given a generous budget and minimal interference, but that's the past, not the present. I'm sure the police force is just the same.'

'It is,' Tremayne said. 'I'm with Dr Frampton, more effective back then, but now, barely kick an offender up the backside, otherwise a disciplinary.'

'It seems, Inspector, that you and I are relics of a bygone age,' Dr Frampton said.

'We are, not much you and I can do about it, either.'

Chapter 22

Clare was to remain in Salisbury; Tremayne was to head north of the border, to Scotland.

Clare coordinated with her CCTV investigation officer in Salisbury to confirm Maureen Baxter's meeting with Montfield two days before his death. She had given the time as close to 2 p.m., sufficiently vague to cause delays in finding the two together, precise enough to provide a reference. She had confirmed a park bench twenty yards from the Guildhall where they had met. Two constables were dispatched with photos, their instructions to question people in the street, to confirm the veracity of the woman's story, to attempt to see if anyone could shed further light on what the two had discussed or if Montfield had ferreted in his trolley, or if they had seen a notebook.

Tremayne's focus was his drinking pal from years past, Jerry Maloney.

Dorothy's information, thought to be accurate by Tremayne, was that Maloney had taken a proactive approach to political opposition by removing the threat in advance. Several people had vanished in the weeks leading up to a sham election, a show of democracy for the country and world, and Dorothy reckoned Maloney was responsible.

Jerry was adamant on the phone that Tremayne should stay with him and Christine at their small hotel. Tremayne held firm and told him his visit was official and that it would be unprofessional and prejudicial if he accepted their hospitality. He knew that Jerry understood, but Christine didn't, and he had booked into a hotel nearby.

***

Salisbury wasn't London, there wasn't a camera on every other lamppost or traffic light, but even so, there were sufficient. The two constables returned on the second day of walking around the city; the first was a washout due to torrential rain and unseasonal cold. The weather had been better on the second day, and there had been a modicum of success.

'A lady on her way to work, afternoon shift at a hotel, she saw Montfield, saw a woman sitting with him. I showed the photos, and she was certain,' the first constable said. The second constable was a slow-moving male in his twenties, whereas the first, a pleasant female, was full of beans. Clare liked her, barely tolerated the man.

'An elderly couple, afternoon showing at the Odeon, *Star Wars*, part ten or eleven, although why that would have interested them, who knows. Anyway,' the slow-moving constable said, 'they're long-term residents of the city, saw Montfield as local colour, reckoned eccentrics were good for the image.'

'A homeless man wheeling his way around the city isn't eccentric,' Clare said.

'Agreed, but they knew Montfield from before, knew who he was, knew he was intelligent even if half-crazy.'

'Point taken. What else?'

'It was Montfield, not on the bench that we were told, but two over. I can show you the area on Google Street View. The woman, young, in her thirties, chubby, their words, not mine, dark shoulder-length hair. They were certain the picture I showed them was the same.'

'The notebook?'

'No mention of it,' the female constable said, the other nodding in agreement.

'Looks as though it's up to the CCTV cameras. What times?'

'Different times,' the male constable said. 'Mine was two forty-six in the afternoon.'

'Why so precise?'

'The couple were late for the movie, and it was a five-minute walk from where Montfield was to the cinema; I paced it out with them, their pace, not mine.'

'My time's not so precise,' the other constable said. 'Five minutes, either way, two thirty-five.'

'Close enough,' Clare said.

Jock was the best pair of eyes in the police station. When not busy, the self-professed nerd would be on his laptop playing games, but the man was diligent, the reason Clare entrusted him with the CCTV investigation. Close to where Montfield had been in the Guildhall square, the cameras were not that close to each other. Two cameras were sited at the corner of Blue Boar Row, a street that ran the length of the market square adjoining the Guildhall, and Queen Street, one pointing away from where Montfield sat, the other looking down Blue Boar Row. Also, there was a camera mounted high on the front of the Guildhall and another two in the market square below.

For once, Clare felt that luck was on their side.

Jock focussed, two screens in front of him, scanning from one to the other, adjusting the replays of the videos with scroll wheels. Clare thought he was too fast, but then, she had seen him playing video games, and they were rapid, intense, and to her, insanely dull. But Jock, single and contentedly so, loved them. He was in his forties and, when not involved in police work or his games, would only talk about the latest games on the market, the scores he had achieved, the difficulties encountered. And at the end of the day, he would take hold of his bicycle and pedal off home.

'Any luck?' Clare asked.

'Two twenty-eight, he walked down Blue Boar Row, I can see that.'

'Any sign of the woman?'

'Not yet. I'm trying to follow from the first sighting and up to the bench, but there's a blind spot. Ah, there he is, two thirty-six, must have stopped to look for food in a bin.'

'That would be Montfield, hardly gourmet.'

'He's sitting on the bench. I'll slow the video to fifty per cent; allow me to focus. If you don't mind, Sergeant.'

Clare understood the man needed to focus, and her talking or being present wasn't helpful. She walked away, determined not to disturb him again that day.

Tremayne was sitting in his office, which surprised Clare as she had expected him to depart for Scotland that morning. She walked in and took a seat.

'Promising?' Tremayne said.

'Jock has found Montfield on the video. Left him to it, for now. I thought you were off to see your pal, Jerry.'

'I've updated Dorothy on developments, and she's willing to let us run with the investigation.'

'Kind of her.'

'She knew the details of our visit to Kempler.'

'Eustace?'

'Kempler, covering his backside in case the proverbial hits the fan, which it may well do. If it's foreign involvement, it brings into consideration how you and I are to act.'

'Femmes fatales and spies, hardly our forte, not unless we include Marjorie Potts.'

'They don't kill, although Eustace and people like him do. He's bizarre, cold, unemotional, frightening.'

'He doesn't scare me,' Clare said.

'He should. I've met people like him before, and what Dorothy said is true, what he also said: he would kill without hesitation.'

'So would Jerry Maloney.'

Tremayne stood up, grabbed his coat off the coat stand in the rear corner of his small cramped office, threw a backpack over his left shoulder. 'You're in charge, back in a couple of days.'

'What time's your flight?'

'It's 12.30, Southampton to Edinburgh, direct. I've got a car organised at the other end.'

***

One hour stretched to two and then to three. In the end, tired of reports and going through the evidence collated so far, Clare went and sat with Jock, only to find him occupied with a video game.

'I thought you were busy,' she said, indignant that the man was slacking off.

'I am. I need the mental distraction, and I've got facial recognition software going through the videos. I have to run it in real-time, time consuming, but more accurate. Also, I've been online, found a couple of pictures of the woman, better than those that you gave me, although her passport photo wasn't much use.'

'Have you seen her with Montfield?'

'She's there, certain that it's her, but as for the notebook, not so easy. This might take all day, some of the night.'

'Can't be rushed?'

'That's it, Sergeant. Just one other thing, I tracked Montfield's movements down Fisherton Street, past the Poultry Cross. After the bench, he retraced his steps, back as far as the Poultry Cross.'

'The woman's important.'

'I'll run video enhancement on her and Montfield, see if I can zoom in, but it's not going to be easy, too far from the camera, designed for traffic control, not police investigations.'

'Anything else?' Clare asked. She was frustrated by the man's lack of progress, determined not to let it show.

'He wasn't on his own at the Poultry Cross.'

'The woman?'

'A man, although I can't give you much yet; later, after I've dealt with your initial request.'

'Thanks. It could be important.'

'Don't worry; I'll stay late. I'll send you an email when I've finished.'

'Whatever time, day or night.'

'Rest assured. I will.'

***

Jerry Maloney was a marked man; he was also a former colleague. Not to accept the man's offer that first night of a meal at the small hotel would not only have been impolite, it would also have tainted further discussions.

'You should have stayed here,' Christine said.

Tremayne had to agree. The Maloney's place was better than where he had checked in, and even though they had a dog of indeterminate breed, it was well-behaved and didn't hover around the dining table looking for food.

'Not a dog lover?' Jacob said.

'Indifferent,' Tremayne said. 'We had a dog the first time Jean and I married. It went with her, the right choice, and I've not felt the need since then. I even trained it to fetch my slippers, although it chewed more than it brought.'

'This is not social?' Christine asked.

'Unfortunately, no. If it were, I would have brought Jean, but Jerry's got some answering to do.'

'I didn't kill the man,' Jerry said.

Both men were drinking whisky, Jerry ahead on the count, but Tremayne not far behind, the reason he had organised a taxi for ten-thirty that night.

'That's not why I'm here,' Tremayne said. 'Besides, let's not ruin an enjoyable evening by talking shop.'

There was tension, Tremayne could sense it, and even though Christine had tried her best, the evening had not been the success it should have been. And then, just before ten, Jerry had fallen asleep,

'Sorry about that,' Christine said. 'He's struggled the last couple of years, a few medical problems. It gets to him.'

Tremayne understood as he had curtailed his smoking, his drinking, and he didn't bound over walls as he once had, nor did he walk as fast, his knees decidedly fragile, yet Jerry, who looked the fitter of the two, was not.

'Prostate trouble,' Christine said. 'He used to love it up here, out every weekend walking, either with me or a dog, but nowadays, he'll sit in front of the television from morning to dusk if I let him.'

'We're all getting old, can't be stopped, no matter how much we deny it.'

'Do you think Jerry killed that man?'

'I've no evidence.'

'But if he had? He did some wicked things in Africa, saw worse done.'

'He told you?'

'It affected him for a couple of years afterwards. Here, he wouldn't harm a fly, but where he had been, the people he had associated with, well, you know.'

The taxi drew up outside. Tremayne made his farewells, kissing Christine on the cheek and patting Jerry on the shoulder.

'See you tomorrow,' Tremayne said.

'Be gentle with him,' Christine said. 'He's not as strong as he seems.'

Tremayne wasn't sure if he was or not, but the man had questions to answer, and if what Dorothy had told him was true, then Jerry Maloney was not the person his wife believed him to be.

***

It was two in the morning when the phone rang. Clare had woken with a start, and even though she had said to Jock to contact her at any time, she hadn't expected he would.

'Two people as I told you. I've sent you an email with a couple of files. The first one was the woman, and she spent eighteen minutes with Montfield.'

'The notebook?' Clare asked. Clive was downstairs fetching a drink for her. He knew she wouldn't sleep again once she was awake.

'He showed it to her, not sure if he explained its contents. Why he did, I can't be sure, as there's no sound, and the images are indistinct, no chance of a lip reader to make any sense of it.'

'Friendly?'

'From what I could see.'

'Great. Can you spend the next week on this, go forward up until Montfield's death, go back five days from the Guildhall bench? See what else you can pick up, people he met, places he sat, bins he foraged in.'

'As long as I don't have to get to the station before ten this morning.'

'Take longer if you want, but as soon as possible.'

'There's more,' Jock said. 'It's in the email, or do you want me to tell you.'

'Tell, please.'

'I've identified the man; went through the case file you gave me.'

'Who is it?'

'Jerry Maloney.'

'Was he friendly, demonstrative, did you see the notebook?'

'Maloney didn't sit, but I'd say they were friendly. No arm-waving, no notebook, not with him, only with the first person.'

Clare got out of bed, forwarded the email to Tremayne, and Clive came in to the bedroom with a drink for her.

'Good news?' Clive asked.

'Confusing, cat among the pigeons. It'll keep Tremayne on his toes for a couple of days.'

The video rolled after Clare had clicked the link on the email. She watched for thirty minutes out of the thirty-eight that it ran for before switching it off, picking up her phone and dialling Tremayne.

The man, not pleased to be woken – Clare could tell that he had been drinking – spoke slowly, his speech slurred.

'Yarwood, here. Check your emails,' Clare said.

Slowly he regained consciousness, a couple of times cursing under his breath at his sergeant and Maloney, but in the end, after splashing water on his face, he focussed.

'Give me the short version,' Tremayne said.

'Montfield showed the notebook to Maureen.'

'She denied it; confront her with the evidence. Any more?'

'Jerry Maloney was in Salisbury two days before Montfield's death, met with him at the place where the man ultimately died. Friendly, or as much as can be ascertained from the video, but no notebook, not with Maloney. He's got some answering to do.'

'I met him and his wife last night. He got drunk and passed out, Christine making the apologies. The man's got problems, mental and medical.'

'Not the picture of health that you are,' Clare joked.

'Don't tell Jean. You know what she'll say.'

'I won't. All in the cause of the investigation, getting drunk, making a fool of yourself.'

'Too early for your sarcasm, Yarwood. Follow up with Maureen Baxter, push Kempler if you can, and as for Dr Alice Frampton, not sure what to make of her.'

'Careful with Maloney. He's a confessed killer, sadist if Dorothy's correct. You can't be sure how he'll react.'

'I will be carrying a weapon, just in case, Dorothy's recommendation and the superintendent okayed it.'

Clare didn't like the idea of a weapon. She knew that Tremayne would be reluctant to use it, although Maloney might not.

Chapter 23

Eight o'clock the following morning, Jerry was outside Tremayne's hotel. One of the two was bright, full of energy, raring to go; the other, a police inspector from down south, was not.

'Sorry about last night,' Jerry said. 'Made a fool of myself.'

'Christine said you're troubled, drink too much on occasions.'

'You know why. I told you.'

'Not the full story.'

'I did things, things I'm not proud of. It was my job, and believe me, it gets easier the more you do them.'

'Did you do them often?'

'Enough.'

'Do you want to talk about it?'

'No. I was erratic for a couple of years afterwards.'

'Why do it?'

'I signed on for the job, not naïve as to who I was protecting, nor what he was capable of. Rough justice overseas, and those that died would only have done the same.'

'It doesn't excuse you from guilt.'

'Nor should it, but it's the past. We've all done things we've regretted. Sure, you have.'

'I never killed someone.'

'Nor had I, but confronted with two options, you take the one of least resistance. Anyway, let's not dwell on the past. I've got a walk organised for us, not too difficult, a few miles, a couple of hills, a great view and a pub at the end.'

'My reason for this visit is not social,' Tremayne said.

'I know. You could have told me to return to Salisbury for further questioning. Why didn't you?'

The two men walked away from the hotel: Jerry kitted out for serious hiking, the dog following behind; Tremayne with a heavy coat and solid boots. Walking was not Tremayne's favourite pursuit, but the climate was bracing, and as Jerry had said, the views were excellent even in the village.

'I went to Singapore a few years ago,' Tremayne said. 'Hot as hell.'

'Never hot here, and if it warms up, you get the midges, bite like crazy.'

After what seemed an eternity, but Tremayne's watch said was thirty-two minutes, they rested. His legs ached, but he was still holding up, with no sign of cramp or excessive muscle fatigue.

'Great, isn't it?' Jerry said.

'Every day?'

'The dog needs exercising, so do I, not as far as I used to go. I don't want to get rusty, not like you.'

'Tell me about Africa,' Tremayne said. He was not ready to broach Jerry's meeting with Montfield and the fact that he had been in Salisbury two days earlier than he had mentioned at the time of the murder. And then there was Christine, who never mentioned it.

'If you must. Things weren't so good with Christine and me. The hotel was fine, making enough to pay the bills, not enough to keep me occupied, and I was an action man, not someone to make small talk with those staying. Anyway, we thought that time out would do us good, and I couldn't go back to the police, not after so many years. It wasn't money we needed, just a change.'

'Did you enjoy Africa? I thought they'd want proven ex-special forces, mercenaries.'

'I know, but they still went for me, put me through a vigorous physical, a couple of days of commando training. I was always fit and strong, and I got through. Compared to some of the other recruits, I was better than them. Ex-military, commando or the American equivalent didn't mean you were cut out for all the jobs they had, and they had plenty. Some could take orders, shoot a gun, protect this rogue or another, but they didn't see further than the end of a barrel. I'd had police training, the ability to observe, to see danger before it was standing in front of me.'

'Star candidate.'

'Not a star, but useful to head up security for the dictator. He had locals, some good, mostly bad, protecting him, a couple of Americans trying to organise them, but getting drunk more often than not, screwing anything in a skirt. They were worse than the locals, who were at least willing to try.'

'You took control?'

'Not at first. This dictator is suspicious of everyone, apart from his locals, family members, most of them. After a couple of months of working with the locals, trying to involve the Americans, although they weren't responsive, I'm there with my mark. He's making a speech announcing a new deal that will benefit the people and raise them from poverty; although I knew the truth, that wasn't my job or concern.

'I could see a man at the back of the crowd, three or four hundred people. Those at the front cheering, waving banners, and the rest, doing what they had to, looking excited. But there's this one man, and he's neither smiling nor cheering.'

'The dictator?'

'He's behind bulletproof glass, and I positioned three of the locals to move in closer to him, form a barrier.'

'The Americans?'

'It was their day off.'

'Screwing and drinking.'

'Exactly.'

'The man you killed?'

'Still alive, but seriously wounded.'

'Hospital?'

'That night, they worked him over, the locals.'

'You were there?'

'I was. In the end, he gave the name of a freedom fighter, the leader of another tribe.'

'Torture?'

'Either you can handle it, or you can't.'

'You could.'

'I had to, not that I liked it, but you become inured, the same as you do when confronted with a dead body.'

'But I never caused the body to be dead.'

'Politics and life in emerging countries is war, something people in the west don't realise. Emotionally you detach, and then you become complicit. The dictator trusted me after that, got rid of the Americans on the next plane, lucky they didn't get a severe beating on the way out.'

'You dealt with the freedom fighter.'

'Not that I'm proud of it now, and maybe the freedom fighter was a better person, but they're all tainted with the same brush. Tit for tat, revenge and violence is what they know.'

'As you did.'

'I did then, not now, and up here with this view and the dog, I can forget. In the hotel, I can't. Don't blame me, Tremayne. It's easy to be critical when not confronted with the reality.'

'Why were you in Salisbury two days before Montfield died, and why did Christine lie? Why did you contact the police?'

'It's not far, a couple of miles, easy walking, and we'll be at the pub.'

'You've not answered the question.'

'Who put you up to this?' Maloney said as the men continued walking.

'Nobody, it's a murder enquiry. We were looking at CCTV footage of Montfield, found you as well.'

'Christine didn't lie. She doesn't know that I was in Salisbury two days earlier, kept to myself, a low profile. The only person I spoke to was Montfield.'

'Why didn't she know? Why in Salisbury?'

'The questions are simpler than the answers, or one of them is.'

'We've got time.'

The dog took no notice and continued to walk ahead. Tremayne felt unexpectedly alert, the adrenalin rush of confronting a possible killer with no witnesses, no protection as the gun was back at his hotel, and down below, not far from where the two men were, a two-hundred-foot drop onto rocks.

'I grew up in the Salisbury area, went to school with Jacob. You know that.'

'Not your friendship with Montfield.'

'Not exactly a friendship. Once or twice, I helped him out of a scrape when someone was bullying him.'

'No one would stand up to you.'

'No one, strong even as a child.'

'Why did you lie?'

'I found Montfield dead, but if you had known about my earlier conversation with him, you would have made assumptions. I know my record in Africa and that I could either be blackmailed or blamed for the man's death.'

'Why? What's so important about you?'

'What did they tell you?'

'Who?'

'Whoever told you about my time in Africa. That's the reason you're here, isn't it? On their say-so.'

'I have received additional information about you from persons I don't necessarily trust. Persons I believe are acting in the national interest, but I can't be sure.'

'No one can, a law until themselves. I've had dealings with them.'

'In Africa?'

'Yes.'

'We've got two days. Let's make the best of it. I'm more inclined to trust you than them, but we both know that they can never be prosecuted for crimes committed, crimes to be committed. If you are guiltless, then you must level with me.'

'I am not guiltless, but that was in Africa. Here, in England, Montfield was looking to me for support.'

'The reason for the bulletproof vest?'

'Yes. It was me who organised it. We had been in contact for three months, hadn't met, not until the time you mentioned.'

'What was he frightened of?'

'The same people we are.'

'Who did you meet in Africa?'

'They don't come with a business card, and if they did, would it be their names and their position?'

'British?'

'Vested interest, the dictator had given the concession to mining in the country to a consortium of British firms, worth a fortune. The country was rich in minerals. The opposition was for nationalising, keeping the British out, making deals with the Chinese, lining their back pockets.'

'Did you know this when you went there?'

'To some extent, although not the skulduggery or how prevalent it was.'

'If you were cooperating with the British government, then why are they updating me?'

'They're conspiracy theorists, red in the bed, around every corner lurks the enemy, everyone they work with is a potential traitor.'

'Are you?'

'Not me. I resigned and came back to Scotland and Christine. What they believe I am doesn't matter, but they might need a scapegoat. I'll do as good as any.'

Tremayne had to agree that the walk was excellent, the air exhilarating, the views dramatic, yet he was troubled. By the time the two men reached the pub, he was exhausted, and the dog, after it had raw meat given by the pub, drunk water from a bowl, relieved itself outside, fell asleep on the pub floor.

'The problem is,' Tremayne said as he downed his beer, 'that I don't know if you are lying or they are, or it's all of you.'

'It's all. Your problem is deciding who's lying the least and if it's relevant to your murder enquiry.'

'How would you suggest I go about that?'

Two plates appeared on the table, steak and kidney pie for Tremayne; a steak for Maloney.

'I was helping Montfield. That's a start.'

'How did Montfield know you could help him? How did he get in contact with you?'

'I'm back in Scotland, and they are threatening to reveal what I did in Africa.'

'Even distort the truth if it suited them.'

'Believe me, you can't win with these people; no point trying. If they want Inspector Tremayne thrown to the wolves, they'll do it, and as for your sergeant and her husband, tell him to back off.'

'What do you know about him?'

'That he contacted someone senior and ensured protection for you and your sergeant. They're playing the two of you, the same as I was, the same as I am now.'

'We're talking in circles,' Tremayne said.

'Are we? They told me that Montfield needed a confidante, a person he would implicitly trust. They know everything about us, about my childhood, my friendship with Montfield.'

'Photos of your misbehaviour in Africa?'

'Everything.'

'You agreed?'

'No option. I contacted him, he did have a phone, renewed the acquaintance. Not sure he appreciated it, but he agreed to keep in touch.'

'But how?'

'What do you mean?'

'How did Montfield know they were watching him? Why was he afraid? Who had he been in contact with? And that last point's the most important. It can't have been those who put me onto you, or could it?'

'Conspiracy at every turn, someone watching your every move, play one off against the other, yes, they would. Do you think we're alone?'

'I haven't seen anyone,' Tremayne said.

'You won't, not trained to. I've had dealings with these people. There's an army of them out there, and I've seen a few suspicious characters in the last few months. How about them in the corner? Harmless?'

Tremayne could only see an elderly couple in their seventies.

'Are they?'

'Look at his phone, latest model, and her with expensive jewellery, clothing from the bargain basement.'

'Are you sure?'

'I'm not, but they knew about me in Africa, got me involved, slowly drew me in, only to spit me out. You never get away from these people, and Montfield's frightened, and then a week after I made contact with him, he phoned me for help. I organised a vest and told him we'd meet up as soon as possible. Who frightened him? That's a question worth pursuing, could lead you down a hole you don't want to go.'

Tremayne picked up his phone and called Clare. 'Jerry organised the vest, and that Montfield was frightened. He must have told someone about the notebook, either Maureen Baxter or Alice Frampton, long shot, Kempler. Play it low-key.'

'I'll meet with Dr Frampton first. She seems out on a limb, and Maureen and Kempler are playing footsy, sharing secrets over the pillow.'

'Competent, your sergeant,' Maloney said after the phone call ended.

'As good as they come. Back to where we were. You get a phone call from the goons?'

'Yes, not the current ones, but some others. Jacob's suspicious when I phone, almost hung up on me, but I remind him of our friendship, the times I helped him out, the bullet-proof vest.'

'When's this?'

'Three days before he died.'

'It still doesn't answer the question as to how the goons knew about the notebook. Someone's been talking, important we find that person and soon.'

'I'd agree, not sure I can help.'

'I'm not sure I can trust you, either,' Tremayne said. 'You've been there; you've sullied yourself, swum in the same muck as them.'

'You can't trust me. I'm compromised. Find your murderer and then back off, retire, go overseas, enjoy yourself, forget what a grubby world this is. As for Christine, we're trying to sell the hotel, come down South. It's a sensitive subject, certain we'll take a massive loss on it. I was in London meeting with hotel brokers, that's what she thought.'

Tremayne knew he might have just been fed lies and that Jerry Maloney wasn't outside the organisation that dealt in secrets and mayhem. He had protected evil men, endorsed torture and murder. He could be one of them.

Chapter 24

A police sergeant and a scientist sitting in a café seemed innocuous, but Clare knew it wasn't. The subsequent phone call from Tremayne, where he expanded on the people they were dealing with, had left her nervous.

'You've been hard done by,' Clare said. 'A fair statement?'

'I've been passed over for reasons other than competency,' Alice Frampton replied.

Clare could see a serious-minded individual, taciturn by nature, moderately ambitious, sidelined by a cheerful thirty-year-old woman with a sweet bedside manner.

'Kempler? A good director?'

'He's acceptable, ensures the budget and that we're paid a liveable wage.'

'His relationship with Maureen Baxter?'

'Unimportant. She's competent, and she'll do a good job with that notebook; take credit for it if she can.'

'Are you a person who doesn't make waves?'

'If by that you mean do I go with the flow, then yes. I do my job very well, to be honest, and then I go home to a small house and a couple of cats. Life is simple, and it suits me. However, I was upset the other day.'

'Out of character?'

'Yes.'

'Jacob Montfield?'

'Yes, I knew him when he worked at the establishment, but you know that.'

'Why did Jacob Montfield contact you?'

Clare had taken the lead from Tremayne. She was sure that Alice Frampton had informed others about Montfield's work.

'I was young and impressionable when I started working alongside him and Derek. Foolishly, I became infatuated with Jacob. Intellectual prowess is an aphrodisiac, and he had the first in excess. He knew how I felt, knew that he couldn't reciprocate, and it would have been fatal if he had.'

'The age difference?'

'The senior scientist and the junior dashed on the weight of public opinion, and it would have caused issues. No one would have taken me seriously after that, and I was, still am, a dedicated scientist.'

'Did that worry him?'

'He was sorry for me, not for himself. We used to spend time together, discussing research projects, places we'd been, philosophical discussions.'

'But no romance.'

'Mild, but it was me who made the play, and he'd respond the best he could, but he soon lost interest. Not his thing, not that I blame him. We're all different in our needs.'

'Had you maintained contact over the years?'

'Not when he went crazy and took to the street. I rarely went into Salisbury, drove to Southampton instead for shopping. I couldn't bear to see him like that.'

'He still contacted you when he needed help.'

'He could trust me; knew I would never tell anyone.'

'But you did.'

'It's complex.'

Clare caught the waitress's eye and ordered two more coffees, as well as a croissant for her and a small salad for the doctor.

'We've got time,' Clare said.

'He told me that he had come up with something special and that he needed me to help him publicise it.'

'How do you publicise what he had?'

'He wasn't interested in money, only that his genius be recognised.'

'You've not answered my question.'

'He could have released it in a technical publication, announced it at a seminar, but he wasn't capable of that, not any more. I work for the government, and they would have a claim on what I might present on his behalf, and he knew, as I did, that it would be directed towards weaponry and not where he and I would prefer.'

'I still don't understand why the man would want anything. After all, he'd been on the street for decades.'

'He was dying, and his work was to be his requiem. Who knows? I never understood him; nobody could. I asked him why me and why now, but he was vague, unable to answer.'

'What did you suggest? Did you meet him?'

'Not for some time, but then I met him at a hotel in the country.'

'With his trolley?'

'No. He had cleaned himself up, taken a bath, shaved. He wore a clean shirt, a pair of trousers, and he had a jacket.'

'How did he look to you?'

'As though he had had a rough life. His skin was rough, his hair grey, and he ambled. Even so, it was him.

We spent four days in the hotel, no romance. That was the past, and I didn't want him, impossible for him.'

'So, I'm led to believe that you and him, cosily tucked up in a hotel, did nothing other than talk.'

'Not only talk but to revel in each other's company. You might not understand, but we did. He explained what he had, how it could revolutionise, the impact it could have on humanity, good and bad, and he was determined.'

'So before Maureen Baxter got hold of it, you knew all about it?'

'I did, but I hadn't checked it. I was sure it would work, even so.'

'A week of cosy nothings, then what?'

'I involved Kempler.'

'Did Jacob know?'

'Yes. He had met the man a long time ago, and apart from Kempler's domestic arrangements, I respect him. I told Kempler that Jacob had something for the world and that we three needed to ensure that only good would come of it and that it would be Jacob who got the recognition.'

'Naïve?'

'Idealistic. Kempler promised to ensure that it would be for good.'

'But how? Weapons guidance and satellite tracking can be peaceful or not. How do you negate the bad?'

'It wasn't possible, and I knew that, so did Jacob, but I tried. I told Kempler that I would get what he needed, ensure that I dealt with it and be the custodian, with no financial gain. If it were so important to Jacob, he would have to go along with it.'

'Did he?'

'Seven days later, he was dead. I was wrong to trust Kempler, and it must have been him: realised he could take the credit and Maureen's expendable. I misjudged the man, as have others. It's Maureen who will suffer, a man she loved, who had loved in return; at least she had that.'

***

Tremayne contacted Dorothy. Not that he trusted her, nor anyone else, apart from Clare, who he now worried about.

The two met in London, the woman sitting behind a small desk in a nondescript office in a rundown part of the city.

'Who are you?' Tremayne said. 'Am I your dogsbody?'

'Tremayne, forces are at work, and they're not ours. Someone blabbed to us, which we'll accept, but also to others, which we don't like.'

'We, is that the royal "we"?'

'I mean the government. Montfield was an idealist, so is Alice Frampton. Kempler understands, and yes, he contacted us, told us what the situation was, how important it was to find out what Montfield had.'

'Why was he concerned?'

'Do you know how much it could be worth? A fortune. If he hadn't gone mad, who knows what he might have achieved.'

'You're not concerned that he might have committed murder, that he was murdered?'

'We would have covered up the first if we had known. The second concerns us, not that he died, but who passed the information to a third party. It wasn't

Frampton, too timid for that, nor Baxter. A clever woman, she couldn't find the notebook.'

'She spoke to him.'

'We know she did, talked around the subject, but walked away empty-handed.'

'Do you trust Kempler? And why this room?'

'I don't trust Kempler, but he's under tight control, knows that if he acts out of order, he'll be shipped out of the country, back to where those who don't like him will have a solution.'

'Are you saying he's one of yours?'

'One of them, basking in our protection.'

'But he's visible; they know where he is.'

'They do, but there's an agreement in place. Don't touch our man, and we won't touch yours. But the agreement could be broken, and he knows it. Although messing around with Maureen Baxter comes with complications.'

'Is she one of yours?'

'No.'

'Alice Frampton?'

'No.'

'Jerry Maloney?'

'He behaves himself, comes in handy sometimes. Convenient that he came from Salisbury, knew Montfield; not so convenient that he met you that night. We hadn't factored you in.'

'If you had?'

'You're expendable.'

'That's not an answer.'

'It's the best you'll get. This office, you asked. Tight, secure, nobody gets in or out without my approval, nor does information. If I level with you, it stays with you, not with your wife or your sergeant, not unless you run it past me.'

'Are you watching Maloney?'

'We are. You weren't alone with him in Scotland.'

'The old couple in the pub?'

'I don't keep tabs on the minor functionaries, but sounds probable.'

'Dorothy's not your name.'

'One of several I use. Tremayne, you've jumped into the deep end, and you swim with us, or you sink. What's it to be?'

'I want a murderer. What you get up to, whether it's for the betterment of this country or not, I don't care.'

'Very well. Someone wanted that notebook. We know we did, but who else, and how did they find out? The latter's not your concern.'

'That's not my area. I don't understand these sorts of people; you do. Who do you suspect?'

'Kempler had the contacts, but he wouldn't risk it. Maureen Baxter had him twisted around her little finger, and Frampton's got her nose out of joint. One of those three, I'd say, but we can't get any closer.'

'If it was one of them? An assassin's bullet?'

'Melodramatic. No, if it's one of them, feed bogus information through them to flush out the real culprits.'

'A sting?'

'Sort of. Dangle another carrot, wait to see who comes running.'

For now, Tremayne would go along with it, aware that the benefits remained, and they may still get their murderer. As long as Dorothy talked, the two of them were safe, and with Eustace and others lurking in the shadows, they were afforded some protection.

'This room?' Tremayne said.

'Secret, secure, somewhere we can talk with impunity. I've already told you that.'

'If it's so good, then answer some questions for me.'

'As much as I can.'

Tremayne leant back on the chair and heard it creak. 'You could afford better furniture,' he said.

'It's not a place for staying, purely somewhere to talk. Say what you have to, and then we leave.'

'Montfield contacted Frampton, who then spoke to Kempler out of necessity.'

'You know that already.'

'What do you know about Montfield's time at the establishment? You must have researched it, only logical. The people you work for don't play their hand, nor do they communicate with the police unless it's vital.'

'We never intended to, but Tremayne, you've got a reputation, a person who never gives up. Either we worked with you or scared you off, or else.'

'Do you kill that easily?'

'Regardless of what you might think, we're subject to as much red tape as the police force. Your life and your sergeant's life were never under threat. Your job could be. Out of the police, neither of you could do any more than shout in the wind, no one listening, no credibility.'

'You'd ruin our careers to protect a murderer?'

'If it's a local, we'll leave it alone; let you solve it. If the murderer is from another country, that becomes a matter for our people. We'll decide how to proceed.'

'Not you?'

'Not me. I'm of a similar rank to you, answerable to others. And about your question, would we ruin your careers? Yes, we would. Subtle innuendo, criticism of cases from the past, although we've not even started on that, and I don't think we need to. You've stumbled into something that none of us expected, and now we're all playing this out.'

'Who of the three do you trust?'

'Baxter.'

'One of yours?'

'Younger, idealistic, interested in promotion and the respect of her peers. Trusts in the system, distinct left-wing tendencies. Not a traitor, but could be vocal if she believes she's being sidelined.'

'She has been already.'

'Nose out of joint, that's all, Kempler will take the credit. Kempler was right in giving it to Baxter, not sure that Frampton would have acted wisely, and she wanted Montfield to have the recognition.'

'If it's so good, then nobody gets the recognition, am I correct?'

'We're surmising,' Dorothy said. She opened a small window to her rear. 'It'll let in some air, but not sound, in or out.'

'Kempler?'

'He can never be trusted. He grew up in former East Germany. Nothing firm against him, but we can't be sure. He might know persons back there, or to be more precise, he does, who were indoctrinated.'

'Yet he's the director.'

'Tremayne, let's be blunt. When you're conducting a murder enquiry, who do you trust? Do you fail to question someone because you know them to be innocent? Does everyone have a skeleton or two they'd rather not have revealed?'

'True, and the more obvious, the less likely to be the guilty party.'

'That's Kempler. Although we're certain he's not been affected, we can't be sure, not when exposed to the worst elements. And if he has, then it would have been in this country. No idea why he would be, as he has a good life in this country, a family, no financial troubles.'

'And Maureen Baxter.'

'Who do you suspect?' Dorothy asked.

'Derek Sutherland's widow, although it's been two decades since one of the Montfields killed him. Who knows what gestates, and her lifestyle has been unusual? Now she's saddled with another man who doesn't excite her.'

'She's getting older, feeling her age, no longer the fruit that's picked first at those parties she used to go to.'

'You've done your investigations?'

'Yes, not that we found much of interest, certainly no threats to the realm. Montfield's death showed a degree of skill. What about next door?'

'Marjorie, unlikely, not a woman to be that emotional, and even if she were, Montfield wouldn't have been the man for her.'

'Any man is for her, although she teases more than does, or didn't you realise that?'

'She made a play for me, embarrassing.'

Dorothy laughed. 'Sorry,' she said. 'Inspector Tremayne, I never saw you as bashful.'

'It wasn't funny at the time, but she's harmless. Her husband gives us concern. He's a disappointed man, stays away from the house for extended periods, acts affectionately with his wife, but not loving. She seems to think he's still incapable, but he's not.'

'Is he? Have you checked?'

'We've taken his word for it. Explain Eustace.'

'No James Bond.'

'Licensed to kill?'

'Emotional detachment, rare to find in an individual; ex-military, behind enemy lines, they make the best. Eustace has seen things that would disturb us. So has Jerry Maloney. Did you believe him? What did he tell you in Scotland?'

'That he had seen and done things that he regretted.'

'And that he feels shame for them.'

'Words along that line, yes.'

'Given what we know of him and what he had been involved in, it's unlikely that he's not been psychologically affected. He has been compromised and could have killed Montfield, although we don't know why. Any insights?'

'Montfield was frightened, contacted Maloney, unaware that he was in your pay. Or maybe it was the other way around; I can't be sure about that. At school together, Maloney helped Montfield out when he was bullied.'

'How did Montfield find him? The man had no access to technology.'

Tremayne thought Dorothy's statement unusual. If her research were complete, she would have known that Montfield had a smartphone, would have checked all his calls, and who he had surfed on the net, also a complete list of Maloney's calls.

Either Dorothy wasn't who she said she was, or she was not as open with him as she claimed to be. And why the room, when confidentiality could have been ensured by walking in Hyde Park. This was getting very strange, and he didn't like it.

He and Clare were in too deep, and the water was murky, and they could drown. He decided he would not indulge in further conversation with the woman. He had been open; she had not.

Chapter 25

He had been warned off once before, and Tremayne considered if now was the time to do so. Afraid as he had not been in the past, he drove to his sergeant's house. Any decision was dependent on her, in that any move forward had a degree of risk attached, and eyes were watching their every move.

Tremayne went through his visit to Scotland, the meeting in London, the concerns he held.

'It's impossible to know,' he said. Compared to the barren room in London, the house Clare shared with Clive was magnificent. He remembered when she had first entered his office at the police station, in her twenties, fresh and beautiful, yes, he could concede that she was and that he had disparaged her for her inexperience, believed that he worked best on his own, and he wasn't a babysitter. And then, over the years, a fondness between the two, almost father and daughter, the child he had never had, and now the reality they were courting physical harm, careers dashed, hers before it had got off the ground, dead.

Clare's husband, Clive, sat with them, an arm around his wife. 'You can't let these people intimidate you,' he said.

'I must,' Tremayne's response. 'I'm not even sure I know who they are.'

'My contact, someone I've known for a long time, said the two of you were safe.'

'Can you trust him implicitly? Anyone and everyone could be tainted. Jerry Maloney, decent as a police officer, has changed. He's admitted that much. And

Dorothy, who is she? What is she? The flunky or the leader? And Eustace, Clare's met him, a ruthless man. I want your wife out of it, to stay home and let me persevere.'

'Clare won't agree,' Clive said.

'We can't stop, not now. People are nervous; that much is obvious. If we keep up the heat, someone's going to crack,' Clare said.

'I don't advise this, and if I spoke to the superintendent, he'd agree,' Tremayne said. He could see it was a losing battle, and he needed her to work with him. Still, he knew that in that uninviting room in London, he had felt fear, that they were heading where no police officer should go, into the jaws of death, and nobody could offer protection.

'We continue, same as before, taking into account what we know, realising that a murderer lurks.'

'Here, you can say that, but out there, you can't. If Maloney knew of the threat to Montfield, did Montfield know of his background?'

'It's possible, but how? Montfield might have had a phone, able to research people on the internet, but it's not the same as a laptop, and why Maloney? The man was an acquaintance from years back, and then he's phoning up, doesn't make sense.'

'Unless Maloney was recommended, but by who and for what reason? Was Maloney meant to get the notebook, and was Montfield's death circumstantial, a snatch gone wrong, Montfield reverting to type, recalcitrant, not trusting the man who had advised the bulletproof vest, and if the vest, why leave it at that? Surely Maloney, if he had taken on the role of the man's protector, would have phoned you.'

'Maloney didn't know I was still in Salisbury.'

'My dear Inspector,' Clive said, 'everyone knows who you are, almost an institution in this city. You're easy enough to find on the station's website.'

'He knew you were in Salisbury; not certain it would have been you at the body,' Clare said.

Tremayne's concern was that it always returned to the notebook and the bulletproof vest. If the investigation was to continue, it needed a different approach. Even if he and his sergeant attempted to steer clear of Dorothy and her people, they would inevitably cross paths at some stage. He left the house more unsure than when he had arrived. He was exhausted when he got home to Jean, but he knew he wouldn't sleep much that night.

***

The superintendent sat high up in the building, a view out of the expansive window to a park, people strolling, jogging, throwing a ball for a disinterested dog, a couple of young lovers snatching a kiss. Tremayne wished he could have been down there with them; the possibility existed, he just had to say the word 'retirement' as he sat across from his senior, but he couldn't.

He had tossed and turned all night, weighing up the options, considering the possibilities, the evidence they had so far, the risks if they continued, and he knew it was 'they'. His sergeant was as determined as him, and she wouldn't back off.

'If, as you say, this is dangerous, why pursue it?' the superintendent said. 'Or I can assign it to another officer. Plenty would relish the challenge.'

'I'm telling, not backing off, but you need to know,' Tremayne said, taking offence at the superintendent's suggestion.

'Know, yes, but what do you expect me to do? If we're dealing with nefarious individuals whose names we can't be sure of, nor who they work for, there's not a lot I can do, or do you believe I can?'

'Is there a liaison office between them and us? Do we have one?'

'I believe so, Special Branch, terrorist activities, but is there free interchange, and how will that give protection?'

'It will help. I need contact with them, your agreement on that.'

'You've got it.'

'If there's enough money involved, anyone could be swayed.'

'Except you, Tremayne. You're possibly the most honest person in the country, and you're going up against the worst kind of scum. Are you prepared for the battle?'

'No. I'm not backing off, but we need as much protection as can be mustered.'

'Your sergeant with you on this?'

'Regrettably, she is.'

The superintendent mulled over the situation before speaking. 'I'll give you an additional week, and then I'm pulling out your sergeant. After that, Tremayne, you're on your own.'

'Agreed. I want her out anyway. This is not a straightforward murder investigation, and others could die.'

***

Derek Sutherland's remains had been cremated, a low-key ceremony to commemorate his passing, Gloria and her present husband in attendance, also a brother of the deceased. No one spoke other than greeting each other and saying farewell, a brief eulogy from Derek's brother. After the ceremony, they had a chance to socialise but did not.

Jacob Montfield – his only relative, Deidre – was cremated, Tremayne and Clare in attendance, as were Doctors Frampton and Kempler. Another person was present, although she did not speak, unusual for Marjorie Potts.

'I'm surprised to see you here,' Clare said after the ceremony. There was no eulogy, no viewing of the body, only a five-minute silence while everyone waited before an attendant ushered them into the next room.

'He was a good man,' Marjorie said. 'It seems so tragic. What about Deidre?'

'No ceremony, no remembrance, cremated last week.'

'Unusual.'

'A disappointed woman. There are no relatives that we know of. An empty house next to you for some time.'

'Tragic. On reflection, decent people, even if one of them killed Derek. Strange how there are crossroads in our lives; take the wrong exit, and you end up like them two, take the other, and you end up like me.'

'Did you?'

'The right road, yes, I like to think so. How about you?'

'I believe so, although encountering death, often violent, is not always easy.'

'Simon's left me, found himself a fancy woman. Supposedly she can do for him what the experts and I couldn't.'

'What's that?'

'Get past that mental block, although I'm not certain it was ever there. I reckon he'd lost interest in me, no disgrace in that, but he hadn't the nerve to tell me to my face. Men are like that, aren't they?'

'Some are.'

'Just one thing,' Marjorie said. 'Someone was in the house.'

'When?'

'Two nights ago. I didn't think much about it, though it might be you.'

'Why?'

'It was a woman, similar to you, tall, but I only saw a silhouette through the curtains.'

'It wasn't me. Did you see a car?'

'A Volvo, a man inside, not sure if he was with the woman. Honestly, I thought it was you, and I didn't overthink it.'

Clare took hold of Tremayne, who was chatting to Kempler and took him outside.

'Good conversation?' Clare asked as Tremayne lit up a cigarette.

'It could have been if you hadn't dragged me out.'

'Someone's been in the Montfields' house.'

'Who?'

'Marjorie Potts doesn't know, only that Simon's got himself another woman, left her. There was a woman in the house, tall, similar build to me, a Volvo on the street, a man inside.'

'And here today, the two of them, bidding farewell to Montfield. What do you reckon?'

'The third degree.'

'Now? Here? It would seem insensitive.'

'Let them leave, don't raise their suspicions,' Clare said. 'I'll stay with Marjorie, and you talk to the two of them, friendly, not interrogative.'

Back inside, Marjorie was helping herself to another sandwich, a waiter giving her another cup of tea. 'Surprising, isn't it?' she said as Clare joined her.

'What is?'

'Her over there, as tall as you. You don't reckon?'

'Marjorie, drink your tea and come with me.'

'I'm not under arrest. Simon taking off has been enough for me; a prison cell, I don't relish.'

'It might be a medal, certainly not a cell.'

Outside the room, Clare took hold of Marjorie's arm. 'I want you to see something,' she said. 'And after that, I want you to go home and say nothing more to anyone here. Is that agreed?'

'I was going to stay with my sister for a few days. I've got a bag in the car.'

'Over there, the third car from the left, next to a Jaguar. Can you see it?'

'Not from this distance, not without my glasses.'

Marjorie opened her handbag, took out a pair of glasses and put them on. 'For driving only,' she said. 'The car next to the Jaguar, it could be. It's a Volvo. The only reason I know is that Simon used to drive one.'

'Thanks. Now, please leave, don't talk to anyone, don't look at anyone.'

'Do you think?'

'I don't think anything, nor do you. You've been a great help, sorry about Simon.'

'Why do men do that, pretend and then find other women?'

'One of life's mysteries. Why was Jacob so unusual? It takes all sorts to make a world.'

'Yes, I suppose you're right,' Marjorie said.

***

Doctors Frampton and Kempler were formally requested to present themselves at the police station at nine in the morning the next day. Tremayne thought they would comply and that there was no need for heavy-arm tactics or a police vehicle to pick them up.

His faith in their inherent decency was rewarded when they presented themselves ten minutes before the allotted time, having arrived in different cars, Kempler in the Volvo, Frampton in a Jaguar.

'We'll need to conduct separate interviews. Dr Frampton, you first,' Tremayne said.

'Why here? Why not in my office?' Kempler said. He appeared frazzled, whereas Frampton looked calm.

Tremayne went through the formalities in the interview room before laying the facts out. 'Two nights ago, someone entered the Montfields' house. Was it you?'

'I need a lawyer,' Alice Frampton replied.

'We're not here to charge you with trespass, only to solve a murder. Unless you have grave reservations, I would suggest that you answer.'

'Yes, it was.'

'Fine,' Tremayne said. 'For what reason?'

'Jacob's formula, it's not complete, even with the page your sergeant removed.'

'Did you believe you would find the missing part in his house?'

'No. I thought it was a long shot, but Kempler was adamant we should look.'

'Without any idea where to look and aware that Jacob rarely entered the house?'

'I had an idea.'

'Kempler's involvement?'

'He's proactive, and I trust him.'

'Even though he favoured Maureen Baxter?'

'Even then. She's not important. The missing formula is.'

'How can you be certain it's missing? Did you know that it was complete?'

'Jacob told me. You know he was in communication with me. I trusted him.'

'From your past involvement with the man?'

'Yes.'

'An error or missing?' Clare asked.

'It may have been intentional by Jacob. Maureen did great work, programmed in the algorithm, everything worked perfectly, and then errors appeared. It could be a bug in the system or intentional.'

'What do you think?'

'I think that Jacob was cautious, aware that the missing piece of the puzzle was the glue that held it together. We can't solve it. Nobody could, not without massive computing power and time.'

'What would this have looked like?' Tremayne asked.

'If Jacob used a laptop, which he didn't, a USB stick, otherwise a slip of paper, a few lines of code, an algorithm, nothing more.'

'And you thought burglary was warranted.'

'We did.'

'Where's Maureen while you're in the house?'

'I've no idea, nor do I care. It was late, maybe at home, tucked up in bed.'

'Not with Kempler.'

'She's his floozy, nothing more.'

'Did you find what you wanted, and how did you know where to look?'

'Derek told me a long time ago of a secret place where Jacob kept some of his more radical ideas, not for any particular reason, but he thought it odd.'

'Sutherland's bedding Deidre, passing asides on to you. Why?'

'Men talk.'

'You were involved with Derek. Was it the same time as he was with Deidre?'

'It would have upset her, but not me. Derek didn't overthink Jacob's hiding place, only told me in conversation. You know how it is.'

Clare and Tremayne weren't sure they did, but the piece of paper was important.

'Did Maureen know that you were breaking into the house and that her lover was waiting outside for you? Did you find what you were looking for?'

'We didn't tell her. Kempler doesn't trust her. And no, I didn't.'

'Why doesn't he trust her?'

'Ask him.'

***

'Because I've given her the push, that's why,' Kempler said after Tremayne had dealt with the formalities, outlined the case against him and Dr Frampton, omitting certain parts of her testimony, not wanting to give the man everything on a plate. He needed to sweat first.

'Why?' Clare asked.

'Maureen's an office romance, but she wanted to get serious, and I don't need or want that.'

'A woman on the side, is that it?'

'Nothing wrong as long as no one's harmed.'

'Maureen is, though.'

'Is she? She's young, attractive, and there are plenty of men for her.'

'Then why you?' Tremayne asked.

'I could be flippant and talk about my charm.'

'You'd be wasting your time. We know you were outside Montfield's house while Frampton was inside. Don't deny it.'

'I won't. Our intentions were honourable.'

'If they were, you would have phoned us up, asked for permission to enter. No reason for us to stop you.'

'Honourable with a proviso.'

'Money, fame, am I close?'

'Close enough. You asked about Maureen.'

'What about her?'

'She's ambitious, but with her, it's obsessive. I was one way for her to get ahead, and Montfield's work, when she got hold of it, not aware of this when I gave it to her, allowed her to make the quantum leap.'

'How?'

'I was told she wasn't to be trusted, and they were monitoring her phone calls and emails.'

'Yours, as well.'

'I know, so does Dr Frampton. They know everything.'

Tremayne saw three smart people playing off each other, equally guilty of a crime or a misdemeanour, similarly capable of covering it up or diverting attention away from themselves and at another, and for now, the other was Maureen, either the jilted lover or the villain.

'How did you know that there was a problem with Montfield's formula?'

'Maureen picked it up, passed it on to Alice Frampton, who went through it with her, confirmed and then informed me.'

'Who else knows of the formula?'

'It seems just about everybody.'

'Your superiors?'

'No.'

'Why?'

'OSA.'

Tremayne knew bluster when he heard it. 'Three-letter acronym and we're meant to swallow that. Your superiors are cleared, the same as you.'

'Not for this, they aren't.'

'And if they aren't, that means someone is pulling the strings, attempting to gain the advantage. You want the credit, so does Maureen, but she wants wealth as well. Enough to sell to the highest bidder?'

'I think so.'

'Even if they're not English, a foreign power, a foreign company?'

'Not sure about a foreign power, smacks of espionage. Not sure she's into that, but who knows. Enough money, and we're all tempted, even me.'

'Dorothy, whatever her name is, believes you're suspicious.'

'To her, everyone is a counter-revolutionary, communist, deviant, terrorist or any other conjugation you can come up with. It's in her job description. I grew up under those bastards in the former Democratic

Republic of Germany. I know what they are. I might be many things, but a traitor to this country, I'm not.'

'I believe him,' Clare said. 'Too much to lose if he's working for them.'

'Thank you, Sergeant, perceptive. Dr Frampton's a patriot, concerned for Montfield's legacy, concerned for hers.'

'What is the way forward if you don't have the missing piece of paper, and can you be certain that Montfield had resolved all the issues? After all, he didn't have your facility to check.'

'He told Maureen he had.'

'Did he know who she was?'

'Unlikely, but she made friends with him, don't know how. He showed her the notebook, said it was his life's work, and he wanted the world to know.'

'Too glib, too easy from you, Kempler.'

'What do you mean?'

'Just this, there is no piece of paper, and the formula is correct. Frampton was in that house for something else. What was it?'

'It was only the missing piece of paper.'

'If she was, as you say, where's this hiding place? How did Sutherland know? And why tell Frampton? Sure, the two of them were cosy, but he was interested in getting his leg over, not discussing work.'

'Maybe that's what turns her on, not that I'd know.'

'You don't? I thought you and Sutherland were both tarred with the same brush, and there is poor old Jacob Montfield, the gooseberry in the corner, the man that made both of you look like dullards. Maureen would have gone for him if he had been interested.'

'Inspector, being facetious and crude is unnecessary,' Kempler said. 'I can't show you the formula in operation, warts and all, but Frampton can show you the hiding place.'

Chapter 26

Clare turned the key. It was three-thirty in the afternoon, and outside, a group of locals had gathered. Four vehicles, two marked and a police van had drawn the curious and the plain bored.

The Montfield house was in darkness, and there was a musty smell. Tremayne found the fuse box and put on the electricity. One of Jim Hughes's CSIs dusted the front door and took photos. After a few minutes, those assembled moved upstairs, with the CSI in the lead. Four others followed: Tremayne in the front, then Gustav Kempler, followed by Alice Frampton. Clare kept to the rear, observing the two in front of her.

At the first-floor landing, the CSI paused. 'Which room?' she said.

'Off to the right,' Alice Frampton said. 'Jacob's old bedroom. Deidre had the one at the front.'

'Nobody's to touch anything, only point or tell me. That's important. I'll check the doorknob first. Anywhere else I should check?'

'In the wardrobe, to the rear, down low, where the wood is pulling back from the corner,' Frampton said.

Only the CSI, Frampton and Clare entered. Tremayne stayed with Kempler, watching him like a hawk.

'I can see it,' the CSI said. 'Pulling it back now.'

'You got this far, Dr Frampton?'

'Not in the dark, not with a torch other than my phone. I thought I could feel it, but I couldn't open it, assumed it wasn't true or it wasn't there.'

'Got it,' the CSI said as she opened an evidence bag and slipped in a piece of paper. 'Is that what you were looking for?'

'Can I see it?' Frampton said excitedly.

'It's evidence for now,' Clare said. 'It'll be some days before we can release a copy, and even that is conditional.'

'On what?'

'On us finding a murderer.'

'You don't trust us?'

'Breaking and entering, a possible fortune, and as for espionage – how could we?'

***

The following day, Tremayne sat in his office, a smugness that they were in the home stretch, and soon he'd have Montfield's murderer.

Clare was coming in at midday after an appointment with the gynaecologist, an almost certain request for her to take it easy, something she was determined to do in a couple of days. She could feel the momentum building, the crescendo when the metaphorical cannons boom. Clive was also pressuring her, conscious that as long as she stayed working with Tremayne, she wouldn't slacken.

The last of the research establishment's three, Maureen Baxter, arrived at the station at one thirty in the afternoon; it was her turn in the hot seat.

She had brought a young lawyer, identified as her boyfriend. Clare had shrugged after shaking his hand, and he had looked away. Maureen made eye contact and smiled. Not up to Gloria's standing in matters of the flesh, but it was clear that the young woman regarded virtue as a disposable commodity.

'Is it alright for Bob to sit in?' Maureen asked.

'Okay by us,' Clare said, 'as long as he doesn't mind the unedited version.'

'If you mean my sleeping with Kempler, that's over, and besides, we have an open relationship.'

To Clare, Bob looked a sensible young man, not given to open relationships, but she was there with Tremayne to solve a murder, not to offer an opinion.

'You acknowledge that you were in a relationship with Gustav Kempler,' Tremayne said.

'I do,' Maureen replied. 'It was casual and non-committal.'

'He said you wanted to take it to the next level, the reason he cooled the relationship,' Clare said.

'He lied.'

'That doesn't concern you?'

'No. Why should it? What else did he tell you about me? That I'm ambitious, scheming, and I won't let anything or anyone get in my way?'

'Substantially correct. What part is true?'

'All of it. I'm a bitch, no apologies for it.'

'Bob?'

'Casual. He knows he's onto a good thing, and I'm portrayed as the whore, but I'm not. I'm honest if you ask, trustworthy if I want, a bitch if I have to be.'

'Usually, we have to coax this out of people, but you've been upfront with us,' Tremayne said. 'What else is there?'

'I liked Jacob Montfield, eccentric, knowledgeable, and a great conversationalist. Kempler is decent and honourable, and yes, I expected favours from him, and Alice Frampton's not to be trusted.'

'She said she was your mentor.'

'She was, and she's clever, more than me, but she doesn't have the drive. We all lie, even me, but here, the four of us, I'll give you the truth. I haven't committed any crime, nor do I intend to, and yes, the formula is worth a fortune, with or without the missing part.'

'We've found it.'

'Great, makes the original more valuable, but what I have is substantially correct, and with time and enough resources, it could have been fixed. Kempler and Frampton knew that, although why they were in Montfield's house, I don't know.'

'You don't communicate with them.'

'Professionally, I do, and with Gustav, conversation didn't figure that much.'

'The scientific equivalent to the casting couch?'

'No shame, not from me. Maximisation of assets. Besides, what do you want from me? Bob, you can speak if you want.'

'Maureen's innocent of any crime,' Bob meekly said.

'He's a better lay than a lawyer,' Maureen said.

Clare thought her comment humorous.

'No charges are pending, none are anticipated,' Tremayne said. 'Your *client*,' he accentuated, 'has nothing to answer for. She is helping us with our enquiries, and she is one of the last people to talk to Jacob Montfield.'

'I knew about the notebook, understand what it meant, but I never approached him because of it,' Maureen said. 'I got to know who he was. I thought we should meet. I didn't expect to like him, but I did. And then after a few times talking to him, he's starting to talk about his research, what he was in another life.'

'Do you know why he was homeless?'

'I do now, but no, I didn't, not when we used to speak. I assumed he was the archetypal mad scientist.'

'When you found out the truth?'

'I didn't give much thought to it.'

'Would it have affected your friendship?'

'Unlikely. I like who I like, not the baggage they come with, and I'm not easily shocked.'

'After your last conversation with Montfield, he met another person, a man. Did you know this?'

'No.'

'That person is known to us, a former police officer.'

'Is this relevant?'

'To us, it is. To you, probably not.'

'Then focus on what is.'

'Very well. Gustav Kempler knew communism as a youth; Dr Frampton has worked at the research establishment since before Montfield and Sutherland. That one action determines her credibility, and Kempler is open and honest about his love of this country. It appears that your allegiance and personal relationships bend with the wind.'

'They do, but selling the formula to the highest bidder doesn't strike me as a good career move. The formula is now government property, covered by the highest security rating. To sell it in England or overseas would be espionage, and that comes with a hefty prison sentence, something that doesn't appeal. I'll take the credit, become the acknowledged expert, find another Kempler, another Bob to make up the difference. Works for me.'

Either it was all bluff, or the woman was unique. Yet, Clare thought, the story just spun required forethought, the ability to make fiction out to be fact.

Whatever it was, there was no reason to believe she had killed Jacob Montfield.

***

Dorothy's visit to Homicide concerned Tremayne. Previously secretive, the woman was open, agreeable and willing to speak. Clare had never warmed to her, and she did not now. Attempting to butter up Tremayne wasn't going to work; Clare knew that much, yet Dorothy persisted.

'For the good of the country, patriotic, a great way to end a career,' Dorothy said, all in the one sentence.

Tremayne didn't need platitudes, insincerely given, nor did he want to be reminded that his career was coming to an end. Informed as the woman might be, she had misinterpreted what he should have longed for but didn't.

'Which means you want something,' Tremayne said.

The two were in his office, the door ajar. Clare was able to catch snippets of the conversation and the occasional glance through the glass divider from Tremayne. She wasn't sure if he needed rescuing or expressing exasperation. Either way, she'd leave them alone for the present, see what came out of it.

'The situation has changed. We've been told to back off.'

'Which means?'

'I don't know, and that's the truth.'

'Dorothy, truth and you don't hold up. Your career is based on deception and half-truths. Why should I believe you now?'

'You shouldn't, but you have to.'

'Why?'

'The formula's important. The three, Kempler, Dr Frampton and Maureen Baxter, are exonerated.'

'Exonerated of what? I don't have them down for any crime.'

'Nor do we, not now. Not after you grilled them.'

'That was confidential.'

'Inspector, nothing's confidential. We know everything, our job to do so. Maureen Baxter's got her problems, Alice Frampton's fussy, and Kempler wants to stay in this country, not interested in a Gulag or whatever they have these days.'

'They still exist,' Tremayne said.

'Maybe they do, but the three are vital.'

'Is the government sharing the formula, selling it to the highest bidder? Another casualty of technology shipped overseas?'

'It could be. I don't know for sure, but the USA is what I'd reckon, and Baxter and Frampton can go with it, but Kempler's staying where he is.'

'What was he before he came to England?'

'He worked for us undercover. Didn't do much, ran a few errands.'

'If one of them is guilty of murder?'

'Filed somewhere, not sure that satisfies. Let me remind you that you signed the Official Secrets Act, and if you reveal any of what I'm telling you now or if you attempt to arrest any of the three, then my organisation will be forced to act.'

'Not a friendly visit, but a threat.'

'It's friendly, Inspector, for now. Back off, bury the investigation. That's not a request.'

Tremayne understood the severity of the situation where unknown persons had ultimate power over life and death. He couldn't resist, but he could delay.

'Seven days to wrap the case. If it's one of the three, you can deal with it. If it's not, that person is mine.'

'Five, make no waves, keep away from the three mentioned. I wish you well, hope you succeed.'

'I will,' Tremayne said.

He didn't like the situation, but he had no option but to concede.

Clare wasn't excited either, but her pregnancy concerned her more than murder. Her focus was life, not death.

With carte blanche, as long as Homicide kept away from the research establishment, Tremayne and Clare took stock of what they had.

Even though the relationship between the three at the establishment seemed unusual and hard to understand, it had to be accepted at face value.

'Notebook aside,' Clare said, 'what do we have? There's a love triangle with Marjorie, Deidre and Derek, as well as Marjorie, Simon Potts and Jacob if we're to believe that, and then there's Gloria. No idea how many love triangles she's involved in now or back then.

'Not too many now. And aren't you forgetting Jacob, Derek and Alice Frampton? By her admission, she carried a flame for Jacob, getting it off with Derek, and then you've got Maureen Baxter and Kempler, possibly Frampton in between.'

'Process of elimination,' Tremayne said. 'Are we clear on the bulletproof vest?'

'How can we be? It's only Jerry Maloney's word, and how come Montfield and him make contact after four decades? Nobody remembers back that far, yet Jacob contacts him, Jerry advises, assuming that's the order, and then he's in Salisbury two days before his wife, and she doesn't know.'

On a board in Homicide, photos of all those interviewed at the top; below them a spider's web of interconnecting bits of information: what was certain, what wasn't, and what was open to debate. Although Clare thought that others were involved, Tremayne still had concerns that the notebook and the bulletproof vest were coincidental, red herrings leading them off in another direction.

'Explain,' Tremayne said.

'I can't,' Clare said.

'Do we have proof of the relationship between Montfield and Maloney? Did they go to the same school?'

'I checked. Maloney was in the year below Montfield, but Maloney was big for his age, played for the school rugby team, captain for a year. Did you know he was local?'

'Not sure we spoke much about it, but back then, he and I had different interests.'

'A dubious past of debauchery.'

'That's about it. I never liked him much, not enough to keep in contact when he disappeared up north, and since then, he has had a chequered career. Mine's been boring by comparison.'

'Yours has been better, but it doesn't explain Montfield and Maloney,' Clare said.

'It can't, and how can we prove it? And does Maloney have any involvement with Baxter and Frampton? What about Dorothy? And if Montfield was frightened, who talked?'

The constraints tested their patience, and neither of them enjoyed the situation.

'Maybe we should back off. If there are killers out there, and Clive's admitted his contact might not be as solid as he once thought.'

'A realisation that such people don't play by the book?'

'Something like that, and his contact is being told to hold back.'

'He told Clive that?'

'Not in as many words, but he said for us to be careful, heading into dark places, things that go bump in the night or vanish.'

'CCTV at the time of Montfield's death?' Tremayne said.

'Nothing conclusive. The inebriated locals, Jerry walking to the pub two hours before finding Montfield dead.'

'Two hours? He was drunk when he discovered the body. Enough time?'

'It might not have been the only pub he went to.'

'It was according to him, but let's focus on Montfield. We know the approximate time of death from when Maloney discovered him. He could have killed him, walked away or stayed there and then phoned the police.'

'Easiest way to divert focus, and if he had found out you were still in Salisbury, idle conversation in the pub, it might have caused him to rethink how to kill Montfield,' Clare said.

'Or if he should.'

'That makes no sense. He couldn't have known it would be you in attendance at the murder scene.'

'No, but he had my name as a contact, probably thought it might give him credibility as he was ex-police and he knew me. Who knows how the man thinks, and he's changed from when I first knew him, a killer now, torturer probably, his perception of right and wrong distorted.'

Clare called a time-out. Focussing on the notebook was not productive, and they had worked it to exhaustion. It was a fresh take they needed. 'We revisit the primary suspects,' she said.

Tremayne concurred, glad of the chance to get out of the police station.

Their first port of call was the Montfield house. Soon after entering, there was a knock at the door.

'Hi, thought it was you two,' Marjorie Potts said.

'It's off limits unless you're kitted up,' Tremayne said.

'What do you want?' Clare asked, not pleased to see the woman.

'Neighbourly, lonely if I'm honest.'

'Simon?'

'He came here a couple of days ago, begged me to take him back, and when I wouldn't, he grabbed some clothes and left.'

Clare's translation was that the man had visited, told his wife that it was all over, grabbed his clothes and gone off.

Tremayne went out to Clare's car. He removed gloves and boot protectors from the car boot. 'Here, put these on,' he said.

The two were now three, and Tremayne showed Marjorie where Derek Sutherland had died; she touched the adjoining wall to her house. 'Never heard a thing,' she said.

It wasn't true, as Marjorie had admitted in the past that sound travelled between the two houses and that Derek and Deidre's lovemaking had been heard in the

Potts' residence. There was a clear view to the end of the garden from the kitchen.

'Don't touch,' Clare said as Marjorie wanted to touch things, not out of curiosity, but because it was a natural reaction. 'This is still a crime scene.'

'Sorry, I used to come in here a long time ago. It's not changed much. Deidre wasn't much of a housekeeper, none of those touches that make it a home.'

'It wasn't, not after Derek died and Jacob took off; more a mausoleum.'

'Not before, but why am I here? You didn't invite me in to be sociable,' Marjorie queried.

'A fresh perspective,' Tremayne said. 'We have a solid motive as to why Jacob died, but there's the possibility that it might not be the one that got him killed.'

'I don't understand.'

'You don't need to, but for now, we'll go through this house slowly, discussing what we see, what you remember. You said you used to come into the house.'

'Over twenty years ago, but not often. Deidre was always standoffish.'

'She had Jacob.'

'That's not what I meant. Besides, he wasn't talkative; esoteric, self-absorbed, weird.'

'Yet some people liked him.'

'I did, so did Simon. Jacob was harmless, but obliging, help if he could, but he was clumsy, clueless with the practical.'

'We'll grant you that,' Clare said.

In the hallway, there was no conversation, and as they climbed the stairs, a creaking of the wooden steps.

'Eerie, as though we're walking through a graveyard at night,' Marjorie said.

It was, Clare thought, similar to that night in Avon Hill when the crowd came for her and Tremayne.

The bathroom appeared normal, a toothbrush in a jar, the faint odour of sewage, a dripping tap.

There were three bedrooms. The first was little more than a large closet. Inside, a few boxes, a stack of newspapers and a sewing machine covered in dust.

The second bedroom, previously Jacob's, and where the piece of paper had been found, was morbid; his bed in the centre of the room, a table to one side, a wardrobe on the wall opposite the window, a small dressing table.

Marjorie, previously wanting to talk, had become quiet.

'Are you alright?' Clare asked.

'Sad, I suppose. It makes you reflect on how our lives have turned out, for better or worse.'

'Yours?'

'I miss Simon. He was a good man, even if he had problems.'

'We all have problems. Deal with them in different ways.'

'But your life is so good, a child on the way, a successful husband, well-respected, a beautiful house.'

'Now, it is, but I've experienced the rough, and I don't get on with my mother.'

'Even so.'

Clare knew the woman was right, her life was good, and a house that had experienced violent death and sadness wasn't a place she wanted to be. She put a hand to her eyes and realised she was crying.

'Sorry,' she said as she went downstairs and out into the back garden.

'What's up with her?' Tremayne asked Marjorie.

'Emotional. This house, what do you feel?'

Tremayne should have said that he felt nothing but didn't. 'Tragic, I would agree,' he said instead.

Chapter 27

Outside, in the fresh air, Clare chastised herself for her silliness. The house wasn't any different to others she had been in, and after years in Homicide, a wave of sadness shouldn't engulf her.

She phoned Clive; he answered on the second ring.

'What is it?' he asked.

'Nothing, I just wanted to hear your voice.' It was more than that, she knew: the need for reassurance, to talk to someone she loved, who loved in return, to think of happiness and the baby. She was overly emotional, and she knew why.

'Are you with Tremayne?'

'We're at Jacob Montfield's house, trying to figure out what we've missed.'

'You will, busy for now, love you,' Clive said before hanging up.

Tremayne and Marjorie remained in the house, the woman surprisingly subdued.

'We should go outside,' Tremayne said as the two walked into Deidre's bedroom. Compared to her brother's, it had the feminine touch, a pink blanket on the bed, a stuffed toy on a chair, a dressing table with ointment bottles.

'This is where Derek worked his magic,' Marjorie said. It was an attempt to lighten the mood, which Tremayne didn't need, and she wasn't responsive to.

'You heard?'

'Hard to avoid, and the bed used to bang against the dividing wall, not that I worried about it, never mentioned it to her, too embarrassed if I had.'

Tremayne looked out the window, Clare down below pacing out the length of the garden, crouching down, standing up, waving to him to come down.

'Yarwood wants us,' he said.

The three stood in the rear garden, Marjorie standing to one side as Clare and Tremayne conversed.

'It came to me,' she said.

'The pacing up and down?'

'Precisely. The night Derek Sutherland died, what did Marjorie say?'

'She didn't hear anything, or else she wasn't in her house. I can't remember; I need to check my notes.'

'There are inconsistencies here. Remember the fence?' Clare said.

'I can't miss it. We're standing next to it.'

'It was in the wrong place, an error with the boundary, enough to cause conflict.'

'I remember that much.'

'I just saw it. Follow me.'

'What about her next door?'

'Don't worry,' Clare said. 'It might do some good for her to see.'

Clare walked to where Sutherland had been buried, crouched down, as much as her condition would allow. 'Your knees up to it?' she said.

'If you can, Yarwood.'

Clare moved to one side as Tremayne steadied himself on her.

'Now, look to where the fence is and next door. What can you see?'

'A fence.'

'I suggest we get one of Hughes's CSIs down here, a theodolite.'

'Why? I don't get it.'

'If I'm right, and the fence was not where it is now, but on the previous boundary, then Marjorie would have been able to see over the fence from the far corner of the bedroom on the left. She had a clear view of the burial.'

'But she wasn't here, and it was late at night.'

'According to her. All supposition is based on Deirdre's word, and now I believe Marjorie might know more.'

'No need for the CSI before we challenge the woman.'

'We need him or her to prove my theory.'

'Very well, you contact Hughes, get someone over here today. In the meantime, the police station, do this by the book.'

Tremayne walked back to Marjorie. 'We'll need you to come to the police station,' he said.

'If I must. Is it that important?'

'I believe it is, new evidence, propitious that Yarwood was in the garden.'

'Can we do it here?'

'No. We can drive you there, bring you back.'

***

In the interview room, Marjorie sat.

'Mrs Potts, Marjorie, we're checking, but it appears that if we take into account the boundary issue and the fence previously in a different position, you could have seen over the fence and to where Derek Sutherland was buried.'

'Even if I could have, what does that mean?'

'It means that you could have observed, become involved, taken advantage.'

'But why? I couldn't condone murder, could I?'

'You're a kind, generous-hearted woman,' Clare said. 'A friend in need, you might have wanted to help. You said that you liked Deidre. You knew that the man she loved was a philanderer and that she was only one in a long line of women.'

'Generous, giving, kind, I would agree. But murder is murder, not a frivolous roll in the hay, and yes, I knew Derek for what he was.'

'You knew it was going to end badly for Deirdre?'

'She was going to experience the heartache, but we've all suffered from that. She'd get over it, might find another man, but might not.'

'Why not?'

'She wasn't gregarious or naturally sociable, a plain woman. No disrespecting her, but the competition is fierce, and she wasn't a frontrunner. She knew that, confided in me that she didn't know what he saw in her.'

'What was it that he did?'

'Jacob.'

'That sounds cruel,' Clare said.

'You asked the question, and I'm not about to lie in a police station.'

'Can you elaborate?' Tremayne asked.

Marjorie took a sip of a coffee and focussed on Clare. 'You understand, don't you?'

'I'm not sure I do,' Clare replied.

'Very well, let me spell it out. Derek's married; Jacob knows that. He's also got a lonely sister.'

'Are you saying that Jacob set it up, the same as your husband did with Jacob?'

'I am. Jacob was devoted to his sister, as she was to him. He can see that she needs to experience life and figures that Derek's the best person for her. Derek was Jacob's work colleague, the two men implicitly trusted each other, and Derek realises that it's a good idea to cement their relationship further, and he's agreeable. Soon, Derek's next door, once or twice a week.'

'Did Deidre know the truth?'

'She suspected, and at first, she goes along with it, but then she gets serious, imagines him and her, happy family, married, all the rest of the Mills and Boon novels.'

'Callous?' Clare said.

'Not at all. I'm a sucker for romance, I had my heart broken a few times when I was younger, but I've experienced life; she hadn't. Soon, she's getting agitated, and Derek, not wanting to destroy his relationship with Jacob, is playing along. But he's not so good with conflict, and she knows it. And then, one day he's over here, and we make love, not immediately, but he needed a willing ear, saw me as the best option.'

'And then you're over with Deidre spilling the beans, belittling her?'

'No, I kept quiet, but then, these things tend to come out.'

'How?'

'It was my fault, not intentionally. She's over here, a Wednesday afternoon ritual, the two of us. I give her a glass of wine, take one for myself. She talks about Jacob; I talk about Simon, although I'm careful with the truth. I knew she'd not understand our relationship.

'Did you?'

'With Simon? No, I never could. The psychoanalyst said it was a known condition, but he finally got the therapy he needed, a tart in Southampton, twelve years younger than him. Anyway, I'm digressing. She gets around to Derek, how much she loves him. I can see that it's not healthy and that if she's going to be heartbroken, she'd better get prepared, and with me, I could let her down gracefully, rather than him blurting it out in the throes of passion or afterwards.'

'How did she take it?'

'She thought I was joking at first, and then she got angry, and after that, she's out of the door.'

'You can't blame her,' Clare said.

'Not at all, but it couldn't continue. It would affect her badly, and she was a fragile woman.'

'The day Derek died, you said you weren't here.'

'I did, but I didn't want to be involved, not sure how I would have explained what had happened.'

'You heard the ruckus next door?'

'Yes.'

'Who killed Sutherland?'

'Deidre, I know that.'

'And then you helped to clear up?'

'I had to. Jacob was out of his mind, deranged, and Deidre was inconsolable. I was the catalyst, and it wasn't murder, not strictly, more a violent affray.'

'You were afraid that you'd be an accomplice.'

'No, it never entered my mind. I took control, not from an upstairs window, and Deidre couldn't help Jacob to dig the hole, but I could.'

'Where was Deidre?'

'Sleeping tablets, upstairs in her room. I was worried she'd wake up, scream the place down.'

'Where did the tablets come from?'

'Mine, prescription, insomniac, suffered from the condition since young. I knew the dose, gave it to her, almost forced her to drink it, but I had to protect the two of them.'

'Why the shed in the wrong place?'

'Not sure. It might have been Deidre, or Jacob paid the supplier to erect it, didn't tip them, or they didn't care. Anyway, Simon dealt with the issue.'

'Does he know?'

'I never told him, best if he doesn't find out.'

'He will now. After all, you've committed a crime, concealing a body, aware that a murder had been committed.'

'After so many years?'

'That depends, but it was a long time ago,' Tremayne said.

***

Dorothy made her presence known in the station again. A bleak overcast morning, the threat of rain, it seemed to sum up her presence.

Clare was out of the office, personal issues to deal with, and Tremayne was idling in his office, leaning back on his chair, his hands behind his head.

'We've cleared the three of them, but you know that already,' she said, disturbing Tremayne's train of thought.

'Just going through the case so far. We've got a few more days left.'

'You have. Kempler checks out, loyal citizen that he is.'

'Is he?'

'For now.'

'Double agent, triple?'

'Who knows, not your concern.'

'You trust me too much?'

'I don't,' Dorothy said as she settled back on the chair opposite. 'Smoking allowed in here?'

'Not anymore. There's a place outside, not the best, but it's where I go.'

'Lead on.'

Outside, the rain had just started, a persistent drizzle, and it was cold. Tremayne shrugged, raised his collar and lit up. Dorothy drew out a packet of cigarettes from her handbag, placed a cigarette in her mouth and accepted a light from Tremayne.

'We're alike,' she said.

'I don't see it.'

'Two people uncorrupted by the system, aiming to stay with it, aware that we won't.'

'Are you, Dorothy? You could be stringing me along, trying empathy, aiming to stop our investigation.'

'My orders are precisely that.'

'Is that why you're here today?'

'Officially, yes, but off the record, I want you to succeed. Not only because it was murder, but for Montfield.'

'Why Montfield?'

'Another decent man, but brilliant, and the person who killed such genius needs to be brought to trial or else…'

'Are you saying that if we find the person, you'll dispose of them?'

'Not if they're civilians, as long as secrets are kept.'

'Risky to let it go to trial. You never know what might fall out.'

'Find the person, charge them, make the case tight. We won't interfere, not yet.'

In the car, not fifteen yards from where they stood, Tremayne espied Clare getting out of her car. She looked over at him, noticed the sideways nod of the head, left the two with their cigarettes.

'You'll not see me again after today,' Dorothy said.

'Eustace?'

'Nor him. We're pulling back. We have Montfield's work, and Maureen Baxter's done a great job with it, some assistance from Frampton. Both know what's in it for them if they keep quiet.'

'Kempler?'

'He's in England at our favour. One word out of line, not that he'll do it, and we'll ship him back to where he came from.'

'East Germany's not communist anymore.'

'Does it matter?'

Tremayne knew it didn't. Those who would have preached communism and run agents, dealt in official secrets, would still be there, banging another drum, but with the same tune.

Chapter 28

Clare sat with Jock, the CCTV investigation officer. He had been feeding updates whenever he could, and for days he had focussed on Maureen Baxter's movements, which he thought to be the most important. For Jacob Montfield, Clare had suggested the five days up to when he had sat in the Poultry Cross. Jerry Maloney, who had been in Salisbury for four days prior, whereas he had told them none at the murder scene, had adjusted it to two days on further questioning, and now there was proof that was a lie.

'Montfield maintained a regular route, down Fisherton Street, along Blue Boar Row, down Minster, sometimes down to Harnham, but only on two of the days,' Jock said. 'Otherwise, he was slow-moving, easy to pick out, although not all the camera lenses are clear. Lack of maintenance or the council hasn't got the budget.'

Clare took the criticism of the council with relief: somebody who didn't know who her husband was.

'Budget aside,' Clare said. 'What else? Do you have an interactive plot of the three?'

'On the screen.'

They moved over to a large screen that dropped down from overhead. Montfield was green, Maureen was red and Maloney was blue. The three lines started at the five days and moved forward, one minute every hour.

'Too slow,' Clare said, 'or is there a reason?'

'Clarity, but I'll move forward to four days, which is when Maloney appears. Clare found it difficult to focus on the blurring lights, a flashing screen, jerking lines, but the man alongside her seemed to have no problems.

'Is that him?'

'It is. Looks as though he came out of a house up Castle Road, could be where he was staying.' Blue was the focus, and he was heading down the road to the centre of the city, while Montfield was heading at almost ninety degrees to him, down Fisherton Street.

At 10.28 a.m., the two lines intersected.

'Do you have a camera there?' Clare asked.

'Not clear, and it's distant. Even so, I'll show you, bottom right of the screen.'

'I can't make sense of it. Are they talking?'

'You need training, but no, just walking past each other or shuffling in Montfield's case. But it's clear enough, Montfield and Maloney. You said he wasn't supposed to be in Salisbury?'

'That's what he said, and why be visible and then lie to us? He must know we'd find out eventually.'

'Can't answer that. I'll forward to two days before; only Montfield on day three.'

'Where does Red enter?'

'She's in a car, parks it in the market square, pays the fee and then heads over to Montfield. He's sitting on the bench of interest, but remember this is not the actual day he died, but two days previous.'

'They're talking.'

'He's demonstrating something, pleased to have the company, nothing out of the usual.'

'She's moving,' Clare said.

'Twenty-four minutes with Montfield, and she's off to the shops. Maloney appears in another ten, not with him, but with her.'

'They meet?'

'On the corner of New Canal and High Street. Red and Blue bought a couple of coffees walked into

Cathedral Close and up past your house. No doubt they didn't consider you back then.'

'I thought you didn't know.'

'I did, a bit of a socialist, but you're alright, so's he.'

'Thanks. It's sometimes tiring, being reminded of my better half when I'm trying to solve a murder.'

'No doubt. Anyway, they walk around for thirty-six minutes, out of camera range for twenty-eight, before they reappear in New Canal. He walks her to her car, they shake hands, and he wanders off back up Castle Road, and she drives off, no idea to where, difficult to follow.'

'The fact that they're acquaintances is important. Well done. Is there any more?'

'The final day, Montfield's in the centre. Maureen, or Red as I know her, meets with the man, but we know this already. I can't see a notebook, only him remonstrating, explaining something to her. Not much help here, and then she's off, and over to the right, Maloney. He's watching the two of them, not approaching. Once she's gone, he's over to Montfield, stops for a moment, puts some money in a cup, or maybe it's a mug, not important anyway.

'Then he's off again, and Montfield's moving, albeit slowly. Something's happened, not sure what, and I can't make it out, only assume.'

'Assume is fine, something to check later.'

'Red and Blue meet, the same modus operandi, two coffees and a stroll. He's got his head down, a peaked cap.'

'Any sign of friendship?'

'Not that I can see. Important?'

'It's all-important; the fact that they're together is critical. It brings the two together and gives us more questions to ask. What about later?'

'The light's not so good, and definition is difficult. Montfield, I can pick out because of his trolley. As for Red, she's there, one hour before Montfield died.'

'With Blue?'

'I can't tell you that with the same degree of certainty. There are street lights, lit shop windows, car headlights, a lot of glare, but I picked up her parked car, so she's around. Whether she met with Maloney, I can't tell you that.'

'Did she meet with Montfield?'

'Yet again, no luck there. This is the best I can do.'

'Montfield, one hour before his death and up to it, any possibility?'

'Grab a drink before we continue. I've got two cameras nearby, and I reckon we run them in real time. It won't make for easy viewing, but it's more precise.'

Clare took the opportunity to pop across the road to McDonald's. She was sure that he'd appreciate less-than-healthy food.

She was right.

'Great, just what I was going to buy on the way home,' he said.

The video rolled, full screen this time; no need for a map. The focus wasn't good, and the view was blocked each time a car went by. In the first scene, Montfield sat quietly, his trolley to one side, a book in his hand.

'Can you zoom in?' Clare asked.

'Two hundred per cent, no more, or you'll not see anything; besides, it's a paperback, not what you're looking for.'

'Move on.'

At twelve minutes, Blue appeared, heading to the pub, not acknowledging Montfield. Eleven more minutes, a couple walked by, took no notice of the man and his trolley, engrossed in their love, not in the homeless. Clare found it tiring, appreciative that her colleague was still able to focus.

'Have you watched this before?' Clare asked.

'Double speed, just to do some cursory work. You saw Blue at twelve minutes. Did you see him at sixteen?'

'No.'

'That's because you're looking too closely. Let's your eyes roam, focus away from the road and the pavement.'

'That's where he'd be.'

'Agreed, but look at reflections in shop windows, not so easy, but you can see around corners sometimes.'

Jock restarted the video fifteen minutes before Montfield's death. The video slowed to half-speed.

'There, in the jeweller's window, can you see it?'

'I can, but what's he doing?'

'Looking at Montfield, checking his watch, using his phone.'

'But who's he calling?'

'No sound, I'm afraid. You might be able to check.'

Clare made a phone call to Tremayne. He would follow through, see if they could get a track on the call as the time was accurate, as was the location, and the number, assuming it to be the same that Tremayne had, was known.

Clare followed Jock's advice, adopting a lazy eye approach to the video.

'There, back a few seconds,' Clare said. And there it was, what she had been looking for, a missing woman.

She phoned Tremayne, told him what they had and that she would watch the rest of the video, one frame at a time if she had to, and she'd see him in the office the following morning at six.

The video rolled forward, no further sighting of the two, not until Maloney staggered out of the pub and over to where Montfield was dead. He hadn't killed the man, not then.

It wasn't good enough, Clare decided. 'Back up ten minutes. Run the video as slow as you can.'

'You'll barely make out any detail.'

'Don't worry, just do it. If you can pick up Maloney, you can find the murderer.'

'I can't get us inside the Poultry Cross, only on the roads nearby.'

'Look for reflections; that's important.'

The video rolled, Clare focussed, saw a detail she had glanced at before. At nine minutes before the end, she shouted, 'Stop there, back a couple, give me a copy.'

She had told Tremayne 6 a.m., but she was so excited, she was sure she wouldn't sleep that night, but she needed rest, as did the baby.

***

Six o'clock and both were in the office. Outside, a cloudless sky, as if the weather had acquired the optimistic spirit of the two in Homicide.

'We've got Maureen Baxter and Maloney at the crime scene,' Clare said.

'What do you want? After all, it's your show,' Tremayne, who felt fresher and more alert than he had for the last week, said.

'Maloney's not guilty of a crime, not that I can see, although he has questions to answer.'

'Either here or in Scotland?'

'Here would be preferable. Will he come?'

'One way to find out, and besides, he's got nowhere to hide,' Tremayne said.

It was early, too early to wake people from their slumber, but Tremayne wasn't waiting.

A voice at the other end, that of Christine. 'What is it? Don't you know what time it is?'

Tremayne thought it an inappropriate response, given that the Maloney home was also a hotel, and customers could phone at any time. Even so, it wasn't his concern.

'You want Jerry, I assume.'

'I do. It's important. Make sure he's awake, and he might need a cup of tea.'

For five minutes, then ten, Tremayne waited, his phone on speaker. At last, a response.

'Heavy night last night,' Jerry said. 'Drank more than I should. Besides, why so early? Are you coming up here again?'

'No, you're coming to Salisbury. Take a flight to Southampton, and I'll see you're picked up.'

'What for? I've got plans for today.'

'Either you get yourself on the early flight out of Edinburgh, or I'll have you taken into custody. Is that plain enough?'

'It is, but why? What have I done? You can at least let me know that.'

Clare spoke. 'Mr Maloney, I've just spent a couple of exhausting days watching CCTV footage of Salisbury.'

'So?'

'You were in Salisbury the day of Montfield's murder.'

'Correct.'

'And then two days before.'

'I was.'

'Jerry,' Tremayne spoke. 'We've got footage of you in Salisbury two days before that. You never told us. Does Christine know?'

'She doesn't, and besides, I'm not proud of what I did.'

'And what's that? Is Christine with you?'

'No, I can hear her downstairs.'

'Why were you in Salisbury four days before.'

'An old girlfriend. No idea how she got my number, but I thought I'd go, rekindle the flame.'

'Four days?' Clare reiterated.

'I've just told you the reason.'

'Okay, leave it at that,' Tremayne said as he ended the call.

'Why?' Clare asked. 'Why let him off the hook?'

'I haven't. He's got friends, secretive friends, and he'll use them to slap the Official Secrets Act on us, and then he's off scot-free, as is Maureen Baxter. There's another way to get him here.'

'Threaten to tell Christine?'

'He's not refused, so no need to caution and have him clapped in irons. And if I did make it official, involve the Scottish Police, it would backfire. We'd soon have the infamous Dorothy breathing over us, threatening us with fire and damnation.'

'The time is now before we reveal what we have.'

'It is, although we could scare him a little.'

Tremayne phoned Scotland; an angry man answered the phone.

'Tremayne, you're making waves, and Christine's suspicious. What's so important?'

'Clarification as to your movements, that's all. No doubt it's harmless, but your constant lying is jarring. Get to Salisbury, answer a few questions, back in Scotland before nightfall.'

'And if I don't?'

'My sergeant's a prude, might phone Christine, have a little chat about your romantic interludes in Salisbury and Africa, and one word to Dorothy, mention that you've been talking, and who knows? They've protected you from the excesses you committed in Africa, see you as a worthwhile asset, but they could drop you in an instant if they believe you to be indiscreet, willing to cut a deal with the police.'

'You're talking in riddles.'

Tremayne knew he was willing to take a risk, to try to strike a raw nerve. If what he knew of the secret service was half true, and Dorothy had admitted that it was, Jerry was a disposable asset.

'Okay, first flight, 8 a.m., make sure there's an unmarked car to pick me up, and you're paying for the flight.'

'I'll be there. Yarwood's busy in the office.'

'You, driving?' Clare said with astonishment.

'Time for you to start taking it easy.'

She felt a flush in her face and warmth for her inspector. It was one of the few times when he let his guard down and showed the affection he held for her.

***

It was 11.25 a.m., and Jerry Maloney sat in one of the interview rooms at the police station. In another,

Maureen Baxter. Each was unaware of the presence of the other.

When Clare had arrived at the research establishment earlier to collect Maureen Baxter, the woman had made two phone calls, one to the incompetent lawyer boyfriend and another to an unknown person, although Clare assumed it was Dorothy.

In both rooms at the station, there was a video screen. Maloney sat quietly as the video rolled, edited to show the crucial times and images. In another room, Maureen sat, a phone in her hand, idly scrolling through it, making the occasional call, but otherwise not complaining.

Clare stopped the video and explained what they were looking at and why it was interesting. Maloney said nothing, a sure sign to Tremayne that he had had time to make phone calls, send emails, receive instructions on how to act. As if someone else had forewarned of the video, a mole inside the police station.

Even so, it made little difference, and for now, the interviews would continue.

'You can see yourself there, four days from the murder. Anything to say?' Clare asked.

'No,' Maloney, usually verbose, remarkably silent now.

'Your path is crossing Maureen Baxter's. You meet, acknowledge each other, shake hands,' Clare went through the highlights one by one.

Maloney said nothing other than to ask for another cup of coffee.

At the end of the showing, Tremayne spoke. 'Jerry, this girlfriend? Not true?'

'No reason to lie.'

'That's not an answer.'

'You're getting too close, treading on toes, risking too much,' Maloney said. 'I suggest, no, not a strong enough word, that you and your sergeant back off.'

'Or else?' Clare said.

'You're dealing with forces you don't understand. You're amateurs with this.'

'Let me put it to you, Jerry,' Tremayne said. 'You and Maureen Baxter were working together. She spent time with Montfield, knew he had a notebook, and that the man wasn't going to hand it over until certain assurances were made. She also knew they never would be.'

'Maureen's not that astute, purely a determined woman. She's not idealistic, not like Frampton or Montfield, and Kempler's a stooge, only interested in protecting himself.'

'You admit that you know these people?'

'I know Maureen, purely as a functionary, and no, I didn't have a girlfriend, but I had a task to complete.'

'Which was?'

'I'm not at liberty to divulge, way above your need to know.'

'It's murder, Jerry. We have every right.'

'No wonder you only made inspector if that's what you believe.'

Chapter 29

Dorothy arrived at the station at 1.05 p.m. Enough time for Tremayne and Clare to show the video to Maureen, for her to admit essentially the same as Maloney that they were attempting to find out where the notebook was, for her to become Montfield's friend, for him to deal with its retrieval.

'Tremayne, I told you to back off,' Dorothy said. 'What you don't know won't hurt you or your sergeant.'

'I'm interested in the murderer, not Maureen or Maloney. They're innocent of the crime but not of intent. Am I right?'

'It was a bodged retrieval, complicated by unforeseen circumstances.'

'Why Maloney?'

'We know what he's capable of; he's in our control, and he did know Montfield. Serendipity in that Montfield did know him and that it was Frampton who spoke to Kempler.'

'You collect flawed people?'

'We maintain a record of useful people, and if we hadn't had Maloney, our approach would have been different.'

'The result would have been the same.'

'It might have, who knows.'

'Maureen Baxter?'

'Ambitious and easily melded to our will.'

'You'll reward her?'

'We will use her again if we can, or maybe we won't.'

'You're remarkably open,' Tremayne said.

'Am I? I don't think so. I'm only telling you what you've figured out already, and you won't talk.'

'No, no reason to, not now.'

'Not ever. If one word ever leaks, we know where to find you and your sergeant, but I don't want to go there.'

'Maureen and Maloney, the night Montfield died?'

'What do you reckon?'

'Maureen was to grab the notebook; she knew where it was. Maloney was to help if needed and deal with the witness later. Did Maureen know Maloney's final part that night?'

'She didn't. She knew to give the notebook to Eustace, who was hiding nearby.'

'And then to get away, not to look back?'

'We didn't want her there.'

'When Maloney dealt with the witness.'

'Only someone else beat him to it, and then he's compromised, decides to find the body.'

'He planned to kill Montfield; it's still a crime,' Tremayne said, but with little conviction.

'Is it? Maloney can have his idyll in Scotland. And you can have a murderer. Fair exchange, don't you think?'

Tremayne had to agree.

***

The person was known; the reason was not. Whereas a trial would accept the evidence, a blurred image of the person, there would be a dispute, an attempt by the defence to debate if CCTV was admissible, if the timing on the video was correct, even if it was showing Montfield and the person of concern.

What Homicide needed, and the reason the key players were assembled, was to go through what Tremayne and Clare had, to show the video, create conflict, and cement a motive and a statement of guilt. It was not going to be easy.

The conference room at the police station, the recording equipment in the centre of the table, video cameras mounted up high in two of the four corners, a microphone strategically placed in front of all present.

Tremayne sat at the front to the right, not wanting to obscure the screen. Clare sat further back on the left side of the table, diagonally opposite from Tremayne, in an excellent position to observe the reactions of the other four.

Next to Clare, and one seat closer to the screen, sat Marjorie Potts, constantly looking at her husband, who was one down from Tremayne. The seating positions ensured less compliance between husband and wife, although that wasn't seen as a problem with the Potts.

To Marjorie's left, Jim Hardcastle, the current husband of Gloria Sutherland, sat one down from Simon Potts.

'One of you is a murderer,' Tremayne said.

'Are we safe?' Marjorie said flippantly.

There was nervousness in the room. Tremayne thought it was a good sign.

'If you know the murderer, why this charade?' Jim Hardcastle said.

'Murder needs a motive,' Tremayne said. 'Individually, three of you have reasons, strong enough to kill, most people do, but only one of you is guilty. We need to wrap up this enquiry, and visiting each of you individually, asking questions, receiving non-truths in return, is too slow and non-productive, better things to do with our time.'

'Non-truths, what does that mean?' Simon Potts said.

'It's not strictly lying, but an attempt to minimise the impact, to throw us off the scent. It may be that you and the others here are not conscious of it.'

'Let's get on with this,' Marjorie said. Clare could tell that she spoke purely to make her presence known, not to be left out of the meeting – or was it a diversionary tactic?

'Yarwood, if you would?' Tremayne said. 'Unfortunately, Mrs Potts, the truth must be revealed.'

'I told you in confidence not to tell my husband.'

'It can't be avoided, not in this room.'

'What is this? A witch hunt, trial by innuendo? My wife's guilty of nothing,' Simon Potts remonstrated.

Clare continued. 'Derek Sutherland died over twenty years ago. Of that, two in this room had proof back then: Gloria Hardcastle because she saw the murder; Marjorie Potts because she was complicit in covering up the crime, assisting in the man's burial.'

'Is this true?' Simon Potts said.

'Yes,' Marjorie's replied.

'If we may,' Tremayne said. 'Both women have committed a crime. Whether and if they are charged, it is not the reason we've assembled here.'

'Jacob Montfield?'

'Yes, his death. We know where he died. We know how and when, although the motive confuses us. We do know of the man's brilliance and that since then, unhinged from the trauma, he's plied his way around Salisbury, substantially homeless, bothering no one, pushing a supermarket trolley.

'Also, he had a sexual relationship with Marjorie Potts, with her husband Simon's approval.'

'Why rake old coals?' Simon Potts said. 'I wasn't happy about it; not much I could do.'

'For the others in this room,' Clare said, 'Mr Potts was in a car accident which left him compromised.'

'Unable to get an erection, why don't you spell it out, shout it out of the window.'

'Mr Potts, this is official. Getting upset about the truth isn't worth it when others here also have embarrassing and personal details they would prefer not to be revealed,' Tremayne said.

'Such as?'

'Derek and Gloria Sutherland, as she was back then, indulged in an open marriage.'

'Enjoyed,' Gloria corrected.

'Jim Hardcastle was one of the other men.'

'He was.'

'Did you meet him other than at group events?' Clare asked.

'Sometimes, not often.'

'Your marriage with Derek was shaky.'

'I've told you this before. Maybe he preferred Deidre Montfield, or there could have been another. He slept with Marjorie, but she wasn't his type; Deidre was.'

'You've already indicated that he wasn't serious about her, and the letters we've found would indicate a cooling of his ardour. Or have we misread the situation?'

'I wouldn't know. Even I could see the advantage in a normal relationship, one man, one woman. I wasn't wired that way, nor was Derek, but even so.'

'Even so, Derek is enjoying the idea, and you are feeling left out. Not something you appreciate, is it? I put it to you,' Tremayne focussed on the woman, 'that you are not a good person. You saw Derek murdered, and then two days later, you're knocking on the Montfield front door, acting humble pie, not scratching out Deidre's eye, aware of the probable trauma she was going through. All the makings of a sociopath, caring for nobody but self.'

'You can't talk to my wife in that manner,' Jim Hardcastle said. 'She's not committed a crime, and she's not a murderer.'

'Isn't she? Are you so sure? Haven't you sometimes wondered when you're alone with her what she might be capable of? Or if she could be trusted? Has she been unfaithful, strayed from the nest, or is she the devoted wife? Which is it? Only you can answer it.'

'I knew Derek was dead,' Hardcastle said, his voice quiet.

'How?' Tremayne was quick to react. Maintain the pressure, see who cracks, talks out of turn, makes a mistake. He was enjoying himself.

Clare thought her boss was pushing too hard. They were after a murderer, and he was fishing for more.

'Gloria kept a box under the bed, life's mementoes,' Jim Hardcastle continued. 'I knew about it, never looked, and then one day, a few years after he was last seen, she's there, a photo in her hand, crying.'

'Sociopaths don't usually cry,' Tremayne said.

'She was. It was Derek in her hand, and she was talking to herself, saying sorry that he was dead. No mention of how or where, nor if it was violent.'

'What did you do?'

'I made myself scarce, left her there, and then she was back to her usual self later that day. We're all allowed downtime, even me, even you, Inspector. A few regrets, no doubt.'

'I didn't kill anyone. One of you did. Who's going to confess, who's going to give us evidence?'

'Are you saying that one's a murderer and another is an accomplice?' Simon Potts said.

'I'm not, but it's a possibility. Your wife's involvement makes no sense. Why is she covering up a murder when it's nothing to do with her? Deidre and Jacob were neighbours, not true friends or relatives.'

'It seemed the right thing to do,' Marjorie said.

'Accomplice to a murder? I don't think so. You're smart enough to know that's a lengthy prison sentence.'

'I didn't think.'

'Not good enough,' Clare said. 'Inspector Tremayne's right; neighbourly doesn't cut it with us. You're hiding something, and we need it and now.'

'Okay, okay, Simon was away, and Jacob used to come around occasionally. I got used to him, and I could hear the commotion. And then, I was around there, and Deidre's inconsolable and Jacob's not rational.'

'Was love that important?'

'Not love, but in the heat of the moment, confronted with the reality, what could I do? I couldn't walk away, phone the police, or yes, I could have, but I wasn't thinking straight. I've got two people in trouble, and my mind was confused, shocked, disbelief, stupidity on my part. I made the wrong decision, and then, once I've helped move the body, I'm frightened, know that Simon won't stand by me, but Jacob might.'

'I would have,' Simon Potts said.

'You wouldn't. I loved you, but you're a weak man, hiding away during the week, not willing to deal with what was psychosomatic. A man would have faced it head-on, taken pills, hypnosis, surgery if it would have helped, but you wouldn't, kept going on about how it was unnatural.'

'It was, still is.'

'And then a cheap tart supplies the cure. You could have popped next door, stood in for Derek.'

'Which brings us to a critical juncture,' Tremayne said. 'By her admission, Gloria saw her husband die, and Marjorie heard it. The question is, why didn't the two women meet, or did they? Gloria, you first.'

'I didn't stay around, made myself scarce. I was frightened, in shock, not sure what to do. Should I have stayed? I should have, but I didn't, no more guilty than Marjorie. We both erred. I left soon after, sat in my car for hours, cried, laughed, went stupid, no idea how I got home or how I survived for the next few days. I thought it was a bad dream, and I was convinced by talking to Deidre, calm as could be.

'Until?' Clare said.

'Slowly, it dawned on me, and then I started looking for his car, found it eventually, checked with his work, went around his usual haunts, spoke to some of the women in our group, but nothing.'

'And that was it?'

'I've told you this before. Time moves on, one week becomes a month and then a year, and then I'm with Jim. I didn't forget, just ceased to think about it.'

'Marjorie,' Tremayne said, 'your recollection?'

'I was upset, who wouldn't be, and then I've got my husband there at the weekend, complaining, and I knew Deidre was in trouble, and Jacob's gone wrong, in the garden, up and down, up and down, shouting at the top of his voice in the house. I took to the bottle, drunk more often than not, and then one day, Jacob was not there. I saw him go, shuffling slowly, an old coat, old trousers, a pair of trainers on his feet.'

'Deidre?'

'She was in the house. I knocked on the door, and she let me in.'

'What did she say?'

'Jacob told her that he might be back or not. She was calm, bags under her eyes, her clothes dirty, and she hadn't eaten for days. I fed her, cleaned her up, put her in bed, gave her two of my sleeping pills. A regular Florence Nightingale, tending to the ill, and she was, I knew that, but I couldn't call the doctor, not then, not after what had happened. She would be bound to talk, to tell all that had happened, and the house was a mess. For two weeks, I busied myself, took out the carpet in the sitting room, painted the walls.'

'Deidre?'

'Asleep or watching, but most times a vacant look on her.'

'When did she become the street harridan?'

'Once the house was clean, and after I had gone back to my place, she started to come around, unhinged, not as bad as Jacob, but a screw loose. I'd done what I could, and as with Gloria, life moves on, albeit different than before, but it does. Time heals, forget most of the time, and then twenty years have passed, and Jacob's dead. No idea why.'

'Then let me tell you why,' Tremayne said. 'Jacob had a secret, a notebook he carried. He used to write in it, to jot things down, items of importance related to his research in the past. He wanted recognition, not for financial gain but his self-satisfaction.

'He contacted someone he trusted who showed it to another, whose trust was conditional. Jacob became a marked man, and once aware that his life was in jeopardy, someone came to his assistance, not knowing that person was compromised.

'Jacob's in trouble. He knows it, but he's determined. He continues with his life, takes to wearing a bulletproof vest, and realises that he needs to go public. The last part is surmised but assumed.

'People want that notebook, some good, some bad, some only interested in personal gain, others for money. Jacob's going to die, regardless, but he's murdered by someone else before others do it.

'The guilty person here did not have to kill him, as he was due to die at the hand of another, and all for this notebook.'

'You're still talking in riddles,' Simon Potts said.

'I'm telling you all as much as I can. Yarwood, play the video, the last part.'

The lights dimmed in the room; the video played.

'You'll see two people, a man and a woman. They're not important,' Clare said.

'Were they the murderers?' Jim Hardcastle asked.

'No.'

'I'll pause the video. The shopping trolley is easier to see than Jacob if you all study the Poultry Cross. He's alive here. Across the road, the man and woman are watching. To the rear of one of the support columns, a hand, can everyone see it?'

'It's unclear. I can't make out the detail,' Simon Potts said.

'Okay, here's a single frame image,' Clare said. 'Clearer now.'

'It can't be.'

'It is.'

'The ring on the finger is unmistakable. It was you, Marjorie, who killed Jacob Montfield. Why?' Tremayne said.

Marjorie Potts broke down, her husband beside her, consoling her. She blurted out, 'It was Jacob, a week earlier at the shed. He told me what he had to do, to reveal what he had in his notebook and that he would admit to the murder of Derek Sutherland. I realised that if he were sane, my part in the deception would be revealed. I couldn't allow it.'

'Yarwood, the next image.'

On the screen, a lone figure in a doorway, that of Gloria Hardcastle.

'We had to, don't you see,' Gloria said. 'Marjorie contacted me; we had no option. We had both failed to report a murder, and we would have gone to prison. We had seen Derek die, or I had, and Marjorie had been there afterwards, and yes, she had seen me.'

'If you had waited another twenty minutes, you wouldn't have had to kill him,' Tremayne said. 'You will be both charged. You do understand?'

'Yes,' the two women answered in unison. The husbands were silent, a look of astonishment on Simon Potts' face, a scowl on Jim Hardcastle's.

Tremayne, on reflection, had to consider that their trials would bring focus on the other two hiding out of sight. He would not be surprised if the women never stood before a judge and jury.

He and his sergeant had done their duty and solved the murder. They would spend another few days dealing with the paperwork, and then he would take a month's break.

The two women were led away, their husbands walking out of the police station together, to a pub to drown their sorrows and those of their women.

The End.

ALSO BY THE AUTHOR

DI Tremayne Thriller Series

Death Unholy – A DI Tremayne Thriller – Book 1

All that remained were the man's two legs and a chair full of greasy and fetid ash. Little did DI Keith Tremayne know that it was the beginning of a journey into the murky world of paganism and its ancient rituals. And it was going to get very dangerous.

'Do you believe in spontaneous human combustion?' Detective Inspector Keith Tremayne asked.

'Not me. I've read about it. Who hasn't?' Sergeant Clare Yarwood answered.

'I haven't,' Tremayne replied, which did not surprise his young sergeant. In the months they had been working together, she had come to realise that he was a man who had little interest in the world. When he had a cigarette in his mouth, a beer in his hand, and a murder to solve he was about the happiest she ever saw him, but even then, he was not one of life's most sociable people. And as for reading? The occasional police report, an early-morning newspaper, turned first to the racing results.

Death and the Assassin's Blade – A DI Tremayne Thriller – Book 2

It was meant to be high drama, not murder, but someone's switched the daggers. The man's death took place in plain view of two serving police officers.

He was not meant to die; the daggers were only theatrical props, plastic and harmless. A summer's night, a production of Julius Caesar amongst the ruins of an Anglo-Saxon fort. Detective Inspector Tremayne is there with his sergeant, Clare Yarwood. In the assassination scene, Caesar collapses to the ground. Brutus defends his actions; Mark Antony rebukes him.

They're a disparate group, the amateur actors. One's an estate agent, another an accountant. And then there is the teenage school student, the gay man, the funeral director. And what about the women? They could be involved.

They've each got a secret, but which of those on the stage wanted Gordon Mason, the actor who had portrayed Caesar, dead?

Death and the Lucky Man – A DI Tremayne Thriller – Book 3

Sixty-eight million pounds and dead. Hardly the outcome expected for the luckiest man in England the day his lottery ticket was drawn out of the barrel. But then, Alan Winters' rags-to-riches story had never been conventional, and some had benefited, but others hadn't.

Death at Coombe Farm – A DI Tremayne Thriller – Book 4

A warring family. A disputed inheritance. A recipe for death.

If it hadn't been for the circumstances, Detective Inspector Keith Tremayne would have said the view was outstanding. Up high, overlooking the farmhouse in the valley below, the panoramic vista of Salisbury Plain stretching out beyond. The only problem was a body near where he stood with his sergeant, Clare Yarwood, and it wasn't a pleasant sight.

Death by a Dead Man's Hand – A DI Tremayne Thriller – Book 5

A flawed heist of forty gold bars from a security van late at night. One of the perpetrators is killed by his brother as they argue over what they have stolen.

Eighteen years later, the murderer, released after serving his sentence for his brother's murder, waits in a church for a man purporting to be the brother he killed. And then he is killed.

The threads stretch back a long way, and now more people are dying in the search for the missing gold bars.

Detective Inspector Tremayne, his health causing him concern, and Sergeant Clare Yarwood, still seeking romance, are pushed to the limit solving the murder, attempting to prevent more.

Death in the Village – A DI Tremayne Thriller – Book 6

Nobody liked Gloria Wiggins, a woman who regarded anyone who did not acquiesce to her jaundiced view of the world with disdain. James Baxter, the previous vicar, had been one of those, and her scurrilous outburst in the church one Sunday had hastened his death.

And now, years later, the woman was dead, hanging from a beam in her garage. Detective Inspector Tremayne and Sergeant Clare Yarwood had seen the body, interviewed the woman's acquaintances, and those who had hated her.

Burial Mound – A DI Tremayne Thriller – Book 7

A Bronze-Age burial mound close to Stonehenge. An archaeological excavation. What they were looking for was an ancient body and historical artefacts. They found the ancient body, but then they found another that's only been there for years, not centuries. And then the police became interested.

It's another case for Detective Inspector Tremayne and Sergeant Yarwood. The more recent body was the brother of the mayor of Salisbury.

Everything seems to point to the victim's brother, the mayor, the upright and serious-minded Clive Grantley. Tremayne's sure that it's him, but Clare Yarwood's not so sure.

But is her belief based on evidence or personal hope?

The Body in the Ditch – A DI Tremayne Thriller – Book 8

A group of children play. Not far away, in the ditch on the other side of the farmyard, lies the body of a troubled young woman.

The nearby village hides as many secrets as the community at the farm, a disparate group of people looking for an alternative to their previous torturous lives. Their leader, idealistic and benevolent, espouses love and kindness, and clearly, somebody's not following his dictate.

An old woman's death seems unrelated to the first, but is it? Is it part of the tangled web that connects the farm to the village?

Detective Inspector Tremayne and Sergeant Clare Yarwood soon discover that the village is anything but charming and picturesque. It's an incestuous hotbed of intrigue and wrongdoing. And what of the farm and those who live there. None of them can be ruled out, not yet.

The Horse's Mouth – A DI Tremayne Thriller – Book 9

A day at the races for Detective Inspector Tremayne, idyllic at the outset, soon changes. A horse is dead, the owner's daughter is found murdered, and Tremayne's there when the body is discovered.

The question is, was Tremayne set up, in the wrong place at the right time? He's the cast-iron alibi for one of the suspects, and he knows that one murder can lead to two, and more often than not to three.

The dead woman had a chequered history, though not as much as her father, and then a man commits suicide. Is he the murderer, or was his death the unfortunate consequence of a tragic love affair? And who was in the stable with the woman just before she died? More than one person could have killed her, and all of them have secrets they would rather not be known.

Tremayne's health is troubling him. Is what they are saying correct, that it is time for him to retire, to take it easy and put his feet up? But that's not his style, and he'll not give up on solving the murder.

DCI Isaac Cook Thriller Series

Murder is a Tricky Business – A DCI Cook Thriller – Book 1

A television actress is missing, and DCI Isaac Cook, the Senior Investigation Officer of the Murder Investigation Team at Challis Street Police Station in London, is searching for her.

Why has he been taken away from more important crimes to search for the woman? It's not the first time she's gone missing, so why does everyone assume she's been murdered?

There's a secret; that much is certain, but who knows it? The missing woman? The executive producer? His eavesdropping assistant? Or the actor who portrayed her fictional brother in the TV soap opera?

Murder House – A DCI Cook Thriller – Book 2

A corpse in the fireplace of an old house. It's been there for thirty years, but who is it?

It's murder, but who is the victim and what connection does the body have to the house's previous owners. What is the motive? And why is the body in a fireplace? It was bound to be discovered eventually but was that what the murderer wanted? The main suspects are all old and dying or already dead.

Isaac Cook and his team have their work cut out, trying to put the pieces together. Those who know are not talking because of an old-fashioned belief that a family's dirty laundry should not be aired in public and never to a policeman – even if that means the murderer is never brought to justice!

Murder is Only a Number – A DCI Cook Thriller – Book 3

Before she left, she carved a number in blood on his chest. But why the number 2 if this was her first murder?

The woman prowls the streets of London. Her targets are men who have wronged her. Or have they? And why is she keeping count?

DCI Cook and his team finally know who she is, but not before she's murdered four men. The whole team are looking for her, but the woman keeps disappearing in plain sight. The pressure's on to stop her, but she's always one step ahead.

And this time, DCS Goddard can't protect his protégé, Isaac Cook, from the wrath of the new commissioner at the Met.

Murder in Little Venice – A DCI Cook Thriller – Book 4

A dismembered corpse floats in the canal in Little Venice, an upmarket tourist haven in London. Its identity is unknown, but what is its significance?

DCI Isaac Cook is baffled about why it's there. Is it gang-related, or is it something more?

Whatever the reason, it's clearly a warning, and Isaac and his team are sure it's not the last body that they'll have to deal with.

Murder is the Only Option – A DCI Cook Thriller – Book 5

A man thought to be long dead returns to exact revenge against those who had blighted his life. His only concern is to protect his wife and daughter. He will stop at nothing to achieve his aim.

'Big Greg, I never expected to see you around here at this time of night.'

'I've told you enough times.'

'I've no idea what you're talking about,' Robertson replied. He looked up at the man, only to see a metal pole coming down at him. Robertson fell down, cracking his head against a concrete kerb.

Two vagrants, no more than twenty feet away, did not stir and did not even look in the direction of the noise. If they had, they would have seen a dead body, another man walking away.

Murder in Notting Hill – A DCI Cook Thriller – Book 6

One murderer, two bodies, two locations, and the murders have been committed within an hour of each other.

They're separated by a couple of miles, and neither woman has anything in common with the other. One is young and wealthy, the daughter of a famous man; the other is poor, hardworking and unknown.

Isaac Cook and his team at Challis Street Police Station are baffled about why they've been killed. There must be a connection, but what is it?

Murder in Room 346 – A DCI Cook Thriller – Book 7

'Coitus interruptus, that's what it is,' Detective Chief Inspector Isaac Cook said. In a downmarket hotel in Bayswater, on the bed lay the naked bodies of a man and a woman.

'Bullet in the head's not the way to go,' Larry Hill, Isaac Cook's detective inspector, said. He had not expected such a flippant comment from his senior, not when they were standing near to two people who had, apparently in the final throes of passion, succumbed to what appeared to be a professional assassination.

'You know this will be all over the media within the hour,' Isaac said.

'James Holden, moral crusader, a proponent of the sanctity of the marital bed, man and wife. It's bound to be.'

Murder of a Silent Man – A DCI Cook Thriller – Book 8

A murdered recluse. A property empire. A disinherited family. All the ingredients for murder.

No one gave much credence to the man when he was alive. In fact, most people never knew who he was, although those who had lived in the area for many years recognised the tired-looking and shabbily-dressed man as he shuffled along, regular as clockwork on a Thursday afternoon at seven in the evening to the local off-licence.

It was always the same: a bottle of whisky, premium brand, and a packet of cigarettes. He paid his money over the counter, took hold of his plastic bag containing his purchases, and then walked back down the road with the same rhythmic shuffle.

Murder has no Guilt – A DCI Cook Thriller – Book 9

No one knows who the target was or why, but there are eight dead. The men seem the most likely perpetrators, or could have it been one of the two women, the attractive Gillian Dickenson, or even the celebrity-obsessed Sal Maynard?

There's a gang war brewing, and if there are deaths, it doesn't matter to them as long as it's not their death. But to Detective Chief Inspector Isaac Cook, it's his area of London, and it does matter.

It's dirty and unpredictable. Initially, the West Indian gangs held sway, but a more vicious Romanian gangster had usurped them. And now he's being marginalised by the Russians. And the leader of the most vicious Russian mafia organisation is in London, and he's got money and influence, the ear of those in power.

Murder in Hyde Park – A DCI Cook Thriller – Book 10

An early-morning jogger is murdered in Hyde Park. It's in the centre of London, but no one saw him enter the park, no one saw him die.

He carries no identification, only a water-logged phone. As the pieces unravel, it's clear that the dead man had a history of deception.

Is the murderer one of those that loved him? Or was it someone with a vengeance?

It's proving difficult for DCI Isaac Cook and his team at Challis Street Homicide to find the guilty person – not that they'll cease to search for the truth, not even after one suspect confesses.

Six Years Too Late – A DCI Cook Thriller – Book 11

Always the same questions for Detective Chief Inspector Isaac Cook — Why was Marcus Matthews in that room? And why did he share a bottle of wine with his killer?

It wasn't as if Matthews had amounted to much, apart from the fact that he was the son-in-law of a notorious gangster, the father of the man's grandchildren.

Yet the one thing Hamish McIntyre, feared in London for his violence, rated above anything else, was his family, especially Samantha, his daughter. However, he had never cared for Marcus, her husband.

And then Marcus disappeared, only for his body to be found six years later by a couple of young boys who decide that exploring an abandoned house is preferable to school.

Grave Passion – A DCI Cook Thriller – Book 12

Two young lovers out for a night of romance. A shortcut through the cemetery. They witnessed a murder, but there was no struggle, only a knife through the heart.

It has all the hallmarks of an assassination, but who is the woman? And why was she beside a grave at night? Did she know the person who killed her?

Soon after, other deaths, seemingly unconnected, but tied to the family of one of the young lovers.

It's a case for Detective Chief Inspector Cook and his team, and they're baffled on this one.

The Slaying of Joe Foster – A DCI Cook Thriller – Book 13

No one challenged Joe Foster in life, not if they valued theirs. And then, the gangster is slain and his criminal empire up for grabs.

A power vacuum; the Foster family is fighting for control, the other gangs in the area aiming to poach the trade in illegal drugs, to carve up the empire that the father had created.

It has all the makings of a war on the streets, something nobody wants, not even the other gangs.

Terry Foster, the eldest son of Joe, the man who should take control, doesn't have his father's temperament or wisdom. His solution is slash and burn, and it's not going to work. People are going to get hurt, and some of them will die.

The Hero's Fall – A DCI Cook Thriller – Book 14

Angus Simmons had it made. A successful television program, a beautiful girlfriend, admired by many for his mountaineering exploits.

And then he fell while climbing a skyscraper in London. Initially, it was thought he had lost his grip, but that wasn't the man: a meticulous planner, his risks measured, and it wasn't a difficult climb, not for him.

It was only afterwards on examination that they found the mark of a bullet on his body. It then became a murder, and that was when Detective Chief Inspector Isaac Cook and his Homicide team at Challis Street Police Station became interested.

The Vicar's Confession – A DCI Cook Thriller – Book 15

The Reverend Charles Hepworth, good Samaritan, a friend of the downtrodden, almost a saint to those who know him, up until the day he walks into the police station, straight up to Detective Chief Inspector Isaac Cook's desk in Homicide. 'I killed the man,' he says as he places a blood-soaked knife on the desk.

The dead man, Andreas Maybury, was not a man to mourn, but why would a self-professed pacifist commit such a heinous crime. The reasons aren't clear, and then Hepworth's killed in a prison cell, and everyone's ducking for cover.

Murder Without Reason – A DCI Cook Thriller – Book 16

DCI Cook faces his greatest challenge. The Islamic State is waging war in England, and they are winning.

Not only does Isaac Cook have to contend with finding the perpetrators, but he is also being forced to commit actions contrary to his mandate as a police officer.

And then there is Anne Argento, the prime minister's deputy. The prime minister has shown himself to be a pacifist and is not up to the task. She needs to take his job if the country is to fight back against the Islamists.

Vane and Martin have provided the solution. Will DCI Cook and Anne Argento be willing to follow it through? Are they able to act for the good of England, knowing that a criminal and murderous action is about to take place? Do they have an option?

Steve Case Thriller Series

The Haberman Virus – Book 1

A remote and isolated village in the Hindu Kush Mountain range in North Eastern Afghanistan is wiped out by a virus unlike any seen before.

A mysterious visitor clad in a spacesuit checks his handiwork, a female American doctor succumbs to the disease, and the woman sent to trap the person responsible falls in love with him – the man who would cause the deaths of millions.

Hostage of Islam – Book 2

Three are to die at the Mission in Nigeria: the pastor and his wife in a blazing chapel; another gunned down while trying to defend them from the Islamist fighters.

Kate McDonald, an American, grieving over her boyfriend's death and Helen Campbell, whose life had been troubled by drugs and prostitution, are taken by the attackers.

Kate is sold to a slave trader who intends to sell her virginity to an Arab Prince. Helen, to ensure their survival, gives herself to the murderer of her friends.

Prelude to War – Book 3

Russia and America face each other across the northern border of Afghanistan. World War 3 is about to break out and no one is backing off.

And all because a team of academics in New York postulated how to extract the vast untapped mineral wealth of Afghanistan.

Steve Case is in the middle of it, and his position is looking very precarious. Will the Taliban find him before the Americans get him out? Or is he doomed, as is the rest of the world?

Standalone Novels

Malika's Revenge

Malika, a drug-addicted prostitute, waits in a smugglers' village for the next Afghan tribesman or Tajik gangster to pay her price, a few scraps of heroin.

Yusup Baroyev, a drug lord, enjoys a lifestyle many would envy. An Afghan warlord sees the resurgence of the Taliban. A Russian white-collar criminal portrays himself as a good and honest citizen in Moscow.

All of them are linked to an audacious plan to increase the quantity of heroin shipped out of Afghanistan and into Russia and ultimately the West.

Some will succeed, some will die, some will be rescued from their plight and others will rue the day they became involved.

Verrall's Nightmare

Jacob Montfield, regarded as a homeless eccentric by the majority, a nuisance by a few, had pushed a supermarket trolley around the city for years.

However, one person regards him as a liability.

Eccentric was correct, a nuisance, for sure, mad, plenty thought that, but few knew the truth, that Montfield is a brilliant man, once a research scientist. And even less knew that detailed within a notebook hidden deep in the trolley, there is a new approach to the guidance of weapons and satellites—a radical improvement on the previous and it's worth a lot to some, power to others, accolades to another.

And for that, one cold night, he died at the hand of another.

Inspector Tremayne and Sergeant Clare Yarwood are on the case, but so are others, and soon they're warned off. Only Tremayne doesn't listen, not when he's got his teeth into the investigation, and his sergeant, equally resolute, won't either. It's not only their careers on the line, but their lives.

ABOUT THE AUTHOR

Phillip Strang was born in England in the late forties. He was an avid reader of science fiction in his teenage years: Isaac Asimov, Frank Herbert, the masters of the genre. Still an avid reader, the author now mainly reads thrillers.

In his early twenties, the author, with a degree in electronics engineering and a desire to see the world, left England for Sydney, Australia. Now, forty years later, he still resides in Australia, although many intervening years were spent in a myriad of countries, some calm and safe, others no more than war zones.

Printed in Great Britain
by Amazon

12421681R00192